The North End of Sapelo

The author warns readers that this book is steeped with actual events intertwined with fictional bits to enhance reader pleasure. It has been said ,that every great story has its toes buried playfully in the sands of truth. However, the author also files a disclaimer that it is the sole responsibility of the reader to sift through those facts...and the fiction.

The North End of Sapelo

Be not forgetful to entertain strangers: for thereby some have entertained angels unaware. (Hebrews 13, verse 2)

Chapter 1- Drool

Ten-year-old Rock rolled over in his bed; barely cracking one eye open in dispute of the appearance from the early Florida sun. It was Saturday...his day...to do with as he pleased and usually, he was pleased when he used the opportunity to sleep late. Unfortunately, this wasn't going to be one of those days as his mind raced with thoughts of going on an adventure...something every ten-year-old boy wanted to do. Once the initial flurry of excitement settled, he simply could not go back to sleep. He reached up to an odd uncomfortable feeling on his neck. *Ohhh!* He was forced to remember what had happened during the night.

The day before, once he had arrived home from school, he noticed a Siamese cat rustling around up next to an orange tree in his front yard. He skipped over to introduce himself to the furry little friend, twitching a branch from the orange tree...cackling each time the cat made a jump at some unseen prey. They bonded quickly with Rock feeding the feline a can of tuna and entertaining it for the rest of the daylight. He was surprised when his mom not only noticed...but approved of the quick friendship, thinking it was a good thing with his father still over in Vietnam. Once nightfall arrived, little Rock managed to sneak the sleek cat into the house but also into his bedroom without his mom finding out, allowing the pet to sleep up on his pillow. That was the heartwarming story-book portion of their relationship.

Rock flashed his attention back to the now, rubbing his neck, his memory shifting to the part of his night when his sleep had been interrupted...and violently so. Apparently, during the wee morning hours, he had either rolled over onto the cat or it had just plain gone crazy...but the furry critter chomped down with an apex predator style bite on the little boy's neck.

Rock was nothing if not tough, but the behavior of the cat woke him furiously. He remembered flinging the cat against the wall to defend himself. The cat landed on its feet hissing at him as if to mock the little boy...and that response would just not do at all for Rock. He jumped up out of his bed and chased the cat from one wall to the next, snatched the feline by the back of the neck...marched him to the front of the house and flung him out of the slim slatted glass door, swearing he would never trust an animal again.

Still rubbing his neck, he retained the clouded image of the cat growling back at him as it hit the ground outside. Still , by the events of the night, the boy decided it was time to relieve the strain on his bladder. He lowered his feet over the top of the bed to the floor and shuffled his way awkwardly toward the bathroom, finished his business then stumbled to the kitchen for a bowl of Cap'n Crunch. This was his usual routine for a Saturday morning. About the time he shoved a big ole spoon full into his mouth, his mom made her first appearance around the corner. "What are you planning for today, son?" she asked., "Oh...while I am thinking about it, did you happen to hear all that ruckus last night? It woke me up and I was a little scared to go look to see what it was." He didn't answer, simply continued chomping his cereal and oblivious to the fact he was on the verge of receiving a scolding for not chewing with his mouth closed. She didn't wait for his reply. "You do realize the Murphy's down the road want you to come over and play with their son! Would you mind doing that?" Rock, not overly talkative in the morning, shook his thickly haired head to affirm he heard her.

The son, Jeremiah, was a lot of fun to play with. He only lived a block away, but every time Rock went to his house...Jeremiah's mom spoiled the heck out of him, always encouraging him to come back and she always treated him well. Rock's mom had shared that Jeremiah had something called "Cerebral-Palsy." Rock didn't know exactly what it was and certainly could not pronounce such a big phrase, so he just called his friend "retarded" like the rest of the boys in the neighborhood. It was also a word that he had heard Mr. Strickland, his sweet old neighbor from across the street, use from time to time to describe the little boy, as did the Beckham brothers, who lived down the road a bit. He had to admit that it occurred to him they might have called him that after hearing Rock say the word.

Once Rock finished his cereal, he ran to his room, pulled on a pair of old jeans and a fresh white t-shirt before dashing out of the front door without saying as much as a word to his mom. He heard her yell after him seconds after he slammed it behind him, but he didn't look back. He just bounded down the road towards Jeremiah's house as his mom made her way to their front door, hollering a sharp criticism about his lack of finesse. "Love you…!" He shot his response back to her this time, knowing it would soothe her objections…it always did.

Once he arrived at the large brick ranch style home, he banged on the door inside the garage. Seconds later, Mrs. Murphy swung the door open, adding her usual squeal at the young boy. "Rock Razie…it is such a delight to see you this morning. Come on in here!" He bounded up the three brick steps, noticing her husband was sipping from a cup of coffee while reading the morning paper at the breakfast table. "How are you, boy? Can we get you anything…some cereal…toast? Honey, fix this boy some oatmeal!" Rock plopped down in a chair next to him, shaking his head to indicate he was not particularly hungry. "Well…how about some orange juice then…buddy?" Rock thought for a second before deciding to appease them both for a moment. "Sure…where's Jeremiah?" As she reached into the icebox, Mrs. Murphy responded, "He is in the den, Rock…I have to be the one to warn you...he is very excited today...we told him you might be coming over to play!" Rock got up and bolted towards the den.

He heard his handicapped friend before he ever saw him with his awkward garbled moans of delight, muffled from behind the couch as he entered the room. Rock jumped in front of the couch to play hide and seek, before Jeremiah could lay eyes on him, making little puffing noises...playing with Jeremiah's senses as the crippled boy clumsily crawled his way over to the edge of the couch. When he did, Rock leapt over the furniture to grab him. Jeremiah produced yowling sounds of glee. Rock chuckled. Jeremiah mock scolded him with twisted jaw muscles that prevented the sweet disabled kid from resonating even one clear syllable...but it didn't matter. It didn't matter to Rock if all of Jeremiah's words ran together and made no sense at all, and even though Rock realized he was being scolded by his handicapped little friend, he could see the sheer joy in his eyes that he was tickled that his play-pal had finally arrived. It made Rock feel good deep inside...to know the boy was happy and that he could somehow be a part of that.

"Oh yeah! Well...what are you going to do about it, big boy?" He challenged his friend who crawled on all fours back to his side of the couch. Rock noticed the Murphy's had a big new television set...and this one was in color too. He had never seen a color television before. His jaw dropped as Jeremiah reached up with a lame twisted hand to push him from the couch causing him to land flat on his rear on the carpet, as he continued to intently watch the magnificent television. Jeremiah inched his way up beside him to help him admire the television. "Man...that is nice!" Rock said.

"Awhhhh...wehhaaaaa....waaa....." Jeremiah replied. Rock looked over to his buddy...confident his friend had uttered a smart mouthed response in his very own special language. "Oh yeah?" Rock wrapped his arm around Jeremiah's head and began to give him a gentle "noogie", as the boy squealed yet again. Rock released his friend, then scurried around the couch on hands and knees of his own. The handicapped boy gave chase to catch him and they continued their cat and mouse play for several minutes. Then Rock circled around and jumped on his less fortunate friends back. Jeremiah was slightly bigger and older than Rock, slightly taller...but had never learned to walk and though he couldn't speak at all...somehow...from time to time...Rock knew exactly what he was saying...as if they had developed their own version of a shared language.

Unexpectedly, Jeremiah reached out grabbing Rock with one of his abnormally strong hands, twisting his wrist before slamming him strongly to the floor. Rock played along, allowing Jeremiah the illusion of having the upper hand. He worked his way on top of Rock...pinning his shoulders down solidly to the floor. Rock couldn't help but laugh at his friend as he preened from on top of him as if he had 'DONE" something. Like he had climbed some impossible mountain. That is when Rock saw it though...clear as day and as if in slow motion it developed as he watched at the corner of Jeremiah's mouth, noticing a gleaming line of spit making its way from the joyful crease in the corner. Rock's eyes suddenly widened with anxiety as he looked at the thin line of slobber. At this moment...it was the only thing that Rock could see. It inched its way further and further toward Rock's face. The hardened ten-year-old tried desperately to get out from under his friend...he struggled mightily because apparently what God had taken away in the form of speech for Jeremiah, he had added in strength. Rock could not budge. The silver, almost glowing stream of saliva made its way directly towards his face. He tried to turn his head, but Jeremiah's hands limited his motion, causing panic to set in as Rock realized the long line of drool was merely inches away. He freaked completely out and began to yell at the top of his lung capacity, but the drool dropped squarely into his cheek bouncing off and landing directly on Rock's tongue.

In that moment, Rock became the disabled one. Because as much as he loved to play with Jeremiah, never in his wildest dreams did he imagine that he could ever be in this situation. Some energy from deep inside, welled up from his physiology, probably produced from a large burst of adrenalin. He launched his friend Jeremiah clear over the couch to the other side on the carpet. Rock jumped up and ran into the Murphy's kitchen, opened the door and bolted down the road, screaming all the way...."AHHHHHHHHHH!!!!!!!!!!!" Once he got to his own house, he ran through his door, slamming it hard behind him as he rushed to the bathroom spitting, choking and gagging. He rotated the sink faucet knob to flush water into his mouth...anything to get the drool out but it just wasn't good enough. The thought of Jeremiah drooling in his mouth continued to play of his mind's eye, over and over. "Ahhhhhhhhhh!" He yelled yet again. His mother ran into the bathroom...prepared to fetch up her mischievous adolescent and rush him to the emergency room for yet another reason and set of stitches to fix some sort of gash...or cut...or other adventure he had been involved. She examined him intensely while he continued his screaming. She was somewhat relieved when she saw no obvious signs of blood. Grabbing him by the shoulders, she turned him to her. "What are you screaming about? Are you hurt somewhere I can't see?" Rock's eyes were wide with terror. "Mom!" He yelled at her. "I think I just caught RETARDATION. Jeremiah drooled in my mouth...I am retarded now!" Her shoulders slumped once she realized her heightened state of alertness was unwarranted, and the anxiety immediately drained from her body. "That is what you were yelling about?" Rock looked at her, confused by her lack of concern. "Mom...I am telling you that I have caught...RETARDATION!" She walked away relieved...but disgusted, shaking her head.

Chapter 2- Be a clown

"If you gentlemen would be as kind as to follow me?" The waiter suggested, prompting Rock and Jewell to oblige. Jewell, dressed in his company clothing, brown suit, white shirt, brown thin tie with red crusted cross tiepin, that made him feel special escorting his big friend. His new boss, Capone, had offered him the privilege of being Rock's primary guard for the week. It was an honor considering Jewell had just finished his Knights Protego training. They had planned to meet Paul and Capone for an update concerning their good friend Harry Moorer, who had gone missing several months earlier back at headquarters in Ft. Knox where he had been handling the financial affairs of the Knights Protego'.

The two friends took their chairs as the waiter handed them each a menu. Rock handed his immediately back to the waiter with an explanation. "Thank you but I know exactly what I would like to order." The waiter was slightly taken aback. "Okay, very well, then can I get your drink order first?" Rock thought for a second. "How about a large glass of milk?" Jewell did the same. The waiter looked to Jewell expecting him to return his menu as well. Jewell pondered for a second. "If you don't mind, I might need another minute or two." The waiter started to walk away when Rock stopped him. "You can go ahead and bring me a slice of that fantastically famous Coconut Cream Pie!" The waiter nodded his way. "A fine choice." He then turned toward the kitchen, having to avoid running into a large man dressed in a garish clown costume. "Watch what the hell you are doing, you buffoon!" The clown barked rudely before plopping down at the table just adjacent to the two friends.

He was accompanied by another clown, this one thin and dressed in sad face and it was obvious the two circus performers were on break from a performance in downtown Atlanta, probably the convention center nearby. Rock remembered seeing billboards indicating the circus was in town, but it hadn't been important, when he was deciding to come for a piece of his favorite pie. The small outdoor cafe located in Olympic village made some of the best he had ever tasted.

The rotund and rude clown bellowed, "Hey...can we get some service over here for Christ sake?" While his thin friend sat quietly.

Rock exploring the uncouth Clown's face, couldn't help but be agitated by the rudeness the man exhibited, but decided to ignore him, thinking perhaps the man was just grumpy from having worked one to many performances for the day...or week...or month. Plus, Rock suspected, part of his own annoyance revolved around the lack of any news about Harry.

"Could I get some bread-sticks over here?" The clown yelled at another waiter who just happened to be walking past in front of him. Jewell shuffled in his seat uncomfortably, feeling pressure to do something to calm the clown himself. Rock didn't realize it, but he was looking directly at the clown with an unemotional stare. Out of the corner of his eyes, he caught a married couple and their five-year-old son sitting at the table to the right of the pair of clowns, wincing each time his loud mouth complained about something. "Hey, buddy! Could you bring me a damn menu?" Crudely shouted the clown, which prompted Rock's waiter to scurry to the front of the restaurant and retrieved a pair for the unnecessarily harsh customer. Rock whispered to Jewell, clearly agitated. "I have to admit; this guy is starting to get under my skin a little." Jewell stood protectively and whispered back. "Would you like me to handle this?" Rock shook his head. "No, maybe he will settle down once he gets some food in his belly." Jewell eased back into his seat as the waiter brought the menus to the two painted men. Moments later another employee brought out Rock's glass of milk. The clown chastised the waiter for not asking them for their drink order. Rock dragged his hand over his face in frustration, partially to distract himself from the disrespectful attitude of the circus character. "I want a Bloody Mary and a diet soda," barked the loud clown.

Rock's eyes caught a glimpse of the small child at the next table, realizing that the kid was absolutely scared of the clown. He leaned over and whispered to Jewell. "That's not right. This guy is supposed to represent fun, joy and whimsy...he is supposed to delight young kids, yet his bullying attitude is offending everyone in this restaurant." Jewell pursed his lips while Rock simmered. "Hey asshole! Still don't have any bread-sticks over here!" The rotund clown yelled out to any waiter that walked by him, while his companion seemed to ignore his behavior. "Excuse me, could you perhaps tone it down in front of the kid?" Jewell directed his comment to the fat clown, knowing Rock well enough to understand how irritating the man had become. "Mind your own business, you scar-faced punk ass Mexican!" He yelled back at Jewell. Rock put his hand on Jewell's arm to prevent him from doing something rash, knowing all too well his Bronx-raised friend was sensitive about the inch-long scar that traveled from cheek to chin.

Rock had just about had enough of this clown, not necessarily because of all the rudeness, he had experienced rudeness many times in his life. In Rock's mind the Clown was an aberration by failing to represent what a clown should be all about. He should be jolly and goofy, perhaps a little bit of a klutz, but this clown for whatever reason had decided to become a bane, rather than a delight. "He isn't representing the true nature of the costume that he is wearing, is he?" Rock churned inside. The waiter broke his tension momentarily by delivering the coconut cream pie, then took Jewell's order, before proceeding to the clowns table. "I want some tomato bisque soup and a buffalo chicken wrap." The clown requested. "Umm...sir, we don't have tomato bisque today, we do have a nice broccoli cheddar though." The clown exploded on him. "I don't want damn broccoli cheddar. I want Tomato Bisque...you had it yesterday tell the cook get off his lazy ass and make some now." The waiter scurried away for assistance.

The other occupied tables murmured underneath the loudness of the circus entertainer. Rock was beside himself and Jewell knew it. Rarely did the big man allow anything to really get under his skin, but his friend knew that the big man was not at all happy because he wasn't talking. That was never a good sign. Again, Jewell stood to politely handle the clown; but Rock quickly pulled him back to his seat again.

A few moments later the cafe manager came to the clowns table as he took a huge gulp from his Bloody Mary. "Sir, I apologize but we do not have any Tomato soup today, if I could offer a nice bowl of chowder or perhaps a bowl of our Broccoli Cheddar?" The clown spit out the contents of the Bloody Mary in his mouth, directly toward the restaurant manager, causing him to step back a few steps in order to prevent being sprayed with the red cocktail. The entire cafe vibrated with tension. Rock stared at the clown intently. The clown noticed and decided to engage him. "What are you looking at you freakin retard?" The clown then turned slightly to avoid Rock's menacing deep brown eyes. The descendant of the Messiah inhaled to calm himself, then calmly stood as if he were leaving the cafe or perhaps visiting the restroom. Jewell made a move to follow but Rock once again halted his little friend from rising. Still standing, he retrieved his fork and took a quick bite of his creme pie, moaning at how good it was. He then snorted like a bull and picked up the remainder of the pie, walked over toward the rude clown who was looking off toward the kitchen mumbling obscenities. His sad clown companion stared at Rock as he approached. The rude clown noticed his thin companion staring at something behind him. When he turned his face to see what was going on Rock smacked the coconut cream pie fully in the clown's fat painted face.

The entire establishment became eerily silent as the pie dripped from the clown's nose. He sat with stunned disbelief, time seemingly moving in slow motion as his red nose abruptly detached, plopping into his Bloody Mary, while Rock loomed stoically above him. As quickly as it had gotten quiet, the noise level zoomed through the entire restaurant when it burst into laughter at the rude clown's ridiculous situation. Justice had been served. Even the fat clown's friend, the sad slim clown seemed to smile and enjoy the sudden turn of events, while the rude clown began to tremble with anger. Rock turned toward Jewell. "Now, that...is the true nature of a clown." At that moment, the embarrassed clown reached for the steak knife on the table and jumped towards Rock's back. He was immediately redirected when a bean bag struck him in the face. He fell straight to the ground beside his table and whimpered as he pivoted on his shoulder running in circles while he fanned his cheek where the bean bag had struck him, attempting to rid himself of the sting. Even this thrilled the customers of the café as the laughter elevated, yet again.

Jewell immediately placed himself protectively at his big friend's side, noticing six men dressed similarly to himself, separating themselves from the crowd. Rock noticed Capone, the leader of this branch of the

Knights Protego', standing at the café entrance with a large shotgun looking device which had fired the bean bag. Standing behind Capone, he noticed his mentor, the two-thousand-year-old Apostle Paul. Rock glanced back one last time to the clown rubbing his face where the bean bag had struck. The manager and waiter rushed to help the clown only to be gruffly shoved away as the snickering sad clown companion knelt to help his friend get up from the floor and leave the restaurant.

Paul walked over to where Rock stood and positioned himself with arms crossed. "I have to admit. I did not see that coming." Jewell looked nervously to his new boss, Capone, worried he would be provided feedback that he had failed in protecting his bigger friend. Capone looked back at him with a look of appreciation. "You performed well, young man. I was wondering if you had the restraint to not make a huge scene here." Jewell smiled, but looked back confused at the scene Capone had created firing the odd weapon. "If you would be so kind, will you retrieve my bean bag?" Capone asked. Jewell darted off to do just that.
The remaining Knights Protego' blended themselves back into the crowd, while Paul directed Rock, Capone and Jewell to the closest table. The appreciative waiter appeared with another piece of complimentary pie, just before Jewell strutted up with the bean bag and both glasses of milk at the new table.

"Paul, can you give me any sort of update on the search?" Rock was still agitated about absence of any news concerning the location of his Jewish friend. Paul scratched his ear and calmly sat next to Rock, wearing a conservative khaki colored suit. "Unfortunately, there isn't a great deal to report. We are tracking a few leads, but nothing substantial at this point. I am here to offer you an opportunity to dig into a totally different issue, if you would be so kind?"

Paul could see the irritation on Rock's face, obviously aggravated but showing signs of being curious for whatever else Paul could offer to distract him. "I would like for you to talk to a man located outside of Reno, Nevada." Jewell raised his eyebrows and immediately began to dig around on his smart phone. "Hey...Burning Man is this week." Jewell smiled, through the cheek to chin scar he had earned last he was in that area of the country. Paul sat quietly as if to let his words soak. Rock looked to Jewell's face, then Paul, then Capone. "Wait...what?" The big man suddenly realized that ever since he had learned of his heritage the year before at the famous Burning Man festival, he had not been alone to think for more than a half-dozen times and he was pretty sure there were Protego' lurking in the background even then. "Alone?" He blurted like a child. Paul snickered. "No, I am pretty sure you realize those days are over for you. Capone and Jewell and perhaps a few other hand-chosen associates will travel with you to meet a man who goes by the name 'Gogondo'. He is an Apache medicine man. I have good reason to believe he may be able to

assist us in uncovering information as to the whereabouts for Mr.
Moorer." Jewell scrunched his nose. "A doctor?" Paul turned to the ex-
stripper. "Not exactly my friend. Gogondo is an elder of the Apache
tribe based in Arizona and each year, he establishes a sweat lodge at
Burning Man to help those in need of life journey advice or guidance.
My sources indicate that he is quite effective uncovering hidden
secrets with some rather unusual and ancient techniques." Jewell
jumped at the opportunity to have some fun. "Great, I will call Randall,
Scooter and Clark and..." Capone glared at Jewell, shushing him with a
nonverbal warning. "Slow down my young energetic recruit. This is not
a vacation...you will be on guard for this trip."

Rock looked to Capone. "That doesn't mean our friends can't join,
does it?" The grizzled warrior knight responded matter of factly. "Your
friends, along with Lt. Cruz and several others have earned their own
vacation and if I remember correctly are all camping or in route to an
Island off the Georgia coast named Sapelo, where your friend Clark
appears to think that Blackbeard's treasure might be located! He
intends to find it." Capone rolled his eyes and looked back to Jewell.
"Besides, you volunteered for this watch with Rock." Paul provided
more details for Jewell. "Capone..." He glanced playfully at the
inexperienced KP. "and the rest . your crew here will be plenty of
protection I believe."
Rock cleared his throat. "Is that it? How will I find this Gogondo?" Paul
smiled. "You talk to people...you ask around, you take these tickets for

entrance to the festival..." He handed Capone a book of ten or so tickets. "Then you search till you find him. There is no easy way." Rock didn't stop. "How will I know when I have found him?" Paul got up to leave his freshly informed student. "Oh...you will not miss him. He is quite the character." Capone directed Rock to follow him as they parted ways with Paul.

Chapter 3- Squirrel peril

Randall swatted away a cloud of gnats, his muscles weary from loading equipment onto the ferry, prompting him to take a brief break to battle the confounded insects. Scooter, being his usual Scooter self, used his usual skepticism to ask. "So, the old man signed off on this little adventure?" Clark answered his question as he hauled supplies up the boats ramp. "Yep, Paul thought it would do us good to get away from our training." Lt. Cruz with the four other Knights Protego finished loading the remaining items. Randall quizzed. "Why didn't Rock want to come?" Cruz provided an answer, as he took his turn at swatting gnats. "Paul gave him a small task to keep his mind off your friend, Harry. If you guys haven't noticed he seems to be pre-occupied at our lack of success finding him. Capone assigned Jewell to join him."

The group had traveled from Atlanta to the coast of Georgia, where they purchased the necessary items to go camping on Sapelo Island, located between Savannah and Brunswick. Clark had planned with one of the descendants of slaves that had inherited the island, to camp in Hog Hammock, the only village on the island. Sapelo was only accessible by private boat or DNR ferry but even then, permission must be given from one of the Gullah culture inhabitants just to board the ferry. Hog Hammock being the home place of the slaves who worked on the sea island cotton, rice and sugar cane plantations, were deeded their portion of the island by the late tobacco tycoon, RJ Reynolds, who once had owned a plantation on the south end of the island and donated much of his property to the University of Georgia. The group of men were cleared to take this mini-vacation by their leaders, The Apostle Paul and Agent Capone, after having completed the initial phases of training to become Knights Protego.

Scooter took his turn at resting and associated waving at the pesky insects. "How did you find this place?" Clark answered. "Ahh...I was surfing the internet, looking for some type of adventure and found this island. I was looking for Blackbeard Island which is adjacent to Sapelo on the other side. There are rumors that the old pirate, Blackbeard, buried some of his treasure on the island named after him, so I decided it might be fun to come look for the lost treasure. Supposedly it is buried somewhere, just over the channel from Sapelo." Lt. Cruz added. "Capone sent us to ensure you didn't get into any trouble. Your friend Jewell, was not at all interested in camping at a Georgia barrier island."

Thirty minutes later, after a trip across the channel separating Sapelo from the Georgia coast, the ferry swung around to tie up to the Marsh Landing where most of the island inhabitants made their way to and from the mainland. Cruz followed Clark as they met up with their sponsor, Montel Barkley, the local story teller and one of the leaders of the Sapelo Island folk. Montel had pre-arranged for the group to rent a van from a Hog Hammock woman who went by the name of Dorothy. Randall and Scooter joined the three men as they discussed details of their weekend. Randall interrupted them to ask, "Anything specific we need to know about the Island?" Montel responded, "Well, we don't have no police presence, there is only one paved road that goes down to Reynolds Mansion, the rest are just dirt roads. Lucille Beatty runs a kitchen and if you let her know a day ahead of time, she will get up and go to town early to collect supplies to cook for you tomorrow. Oh…and…don't be going up to the north end of the island." Randall, Scooter and Clark each looked at each other. "Why is that?" Clark asked. Montel looked down at the ground as if he were hiding something. "I would just warn you to not go past Duck Pond road. There ain't nothing past that to see." The three friends looked at each other curiously as Montel walked back to his own van. The group of men then loaded up their rented van before hopping in to follow their host to a clearing near the rear of his home where a makeshift campground stood. The Knights Protego unloaded their van and launched into a flurry of work, pitching their tents, collecting firewood and setting out their camping chairs. Randall brought out the cooler full of beer as they sat around while Scooter took charge of creating a fire.

Randall, slurping on an ice-cold beer, offered Lt. Cruz a sip, which he declined, then asked. "So, what is there to see on the island?" Clark popped the top of his own beer. "Well…obviously, we should go see RJ Reynolds mansion. I believe Jimmy Carter had some sort of diplomatic summit here once upon a lifetime ago. Montel tells me that event is the sole reason they have the one single paved road, the government put it in to make the ride from the dock a little smoother for the dignitaries. There is a light house somewhere around the mansion and I believe looking at the map there is something called the Chocolate Mansion on the west side of the island, toward the north. There is something called a shell ring located a little more north than that." Scooter looked disapprovingly at Clark. "Our host just warned us about going to the north end of the island." Clark looked up at him slyly. "And your point is?" Randall challenged Scooter. "You have to admit when he warned us not to go to the north end, the very first thing you thought was what?" Scooter tossed another log onto the large fire. "Well...you have me there. Just thought I would point it out again."

Lt. Cruz and the other four KP, were forced to move their chairs back ten steps from the fire that raged in front of them. "Good lord Scooter!" Clark complained, "Are you attempting to make a fire they can see from the moon?" Scooter stepped back to look at the pile of wood, realizing he should sit down and let it burn before adding more fuel. Randall directed a question to Clark. "What are our eating plans?" Clark replied to the entire group. "Tomorrow if we are going to eat anything, we either have to catch it or kill it!" He glanced over to the bundle of fishing rods leaned up next to the make-shift bathhouse. "Everyone clear on that?" Lt. Cruz rolled his eyes and looked to his other KP members. "We don't have a problem with that, it has been a long while since we were in this position, but two hundred years ago, we didn't have coolers or packaged ham, soda's and the such." Randall took his turn with the roll of his eyes, wondering how long they would keep reminding the newbies that while the three friends may all be in their forties, the youngest man of the other Knights was over two-hundred years old.

Scooter warned Clark. "Just so you know, if we find ourselves riding around tonight, I was reading that they have a population of brahma bulls roaming the streets. We probably should be careful." Randall and Clark prepared a huge pot of beans for the group and after they ate their fill, the friends coerced a few of the older KP into downing a few beers with them as they made plans to ride around and see what the island had to offer in the deep of night. All eight loaded into the van with the map of the island and ventured out to see the Reynolds mansion. As they turned down the paved road to travel the mile distance, they marveled at the vast number of whitetail deer present. They were everywhere. Randall drove, while Clark had to half sit in Scooters lap in the front seat for them all to fit into the van. Two minutes later they arrived at the considerably illuminated mansion. Clark rolled his window down, leaning half out to look at a group of five deer standing on the mansion lawn, unafraid of the visitors. From nowhere a squirrel dropped onto Clarks arm. For two-seconds the van was eerily silent, until Clark realized what was happening. He began to squeal loudly like a girl. Mayhem ensued. Even the Knights Protego became a tad unhinged for a few seconds despite all being seasoned warriors. The squirrel found a way to jump out of the open passenger window of the van.

Randall, the ex-cop finally calmed the group down, ensuring them it was "just" a squirrel, and everything was okay. Clark, however, took offense to the notion, arguing that he was the one who had been assaulted by the small rodent. "Man! You are crazy. Do you know how much a squirrel can mess you up?" The entire van burst into laughter. Scooter sarcastically agreed. "He is right...those squirrels...they are vicious little creatures." Lt. Cruz, finally able to get his laughter under control had to respond. "Yep Clark...those squirrels...they are monsters." The van once again rolled with laughter. Clark, half-embarrassed, half-amused added. "Are you trying to tell me if a squirrel ran up your leg you wouldn't scream just like I did?" Lt Cruz calmly answered him. "No, I am not saying that at all. I am sure it was a very poignant moment for you. But...in all fairness to the squirrel, I would like to point out, that in the history of mankind...there has never been a horror movie made where the villain was a squirrel. There have been movies where giant rabbits were the monster." One of the KP in the back of the van shouted. "Night of the Lepus!" Cruz continued. "There was a movie where frogs were the villains. There was even a movie where worms were the bad guys."

Another KP shouted. "Squirm!" The van vibrated with laughter once again. Clark pouted. "Well...I am just saying. Squirrels will mess you up!" The group continued to snicker as they drove past Reynolds mansion all lit up with its white washed stucco appearance.

They drove around for a while longer before deciding to head back to the campsite and their sleeping bags in anticipation of a fun day. Randall, with the knowledge there was no law enforcement on the island, took the opportunity to push the van to its max speed. Once they reached Hog Hammock and turned down the dirt road toward their campsite, he slowed appreciably, but still progressed at an aggressive pace, until...he saw the huge silhouette of an enormous bull in front of him. He swerved, and the van slid into the ditch. Clark and Scooter noticed two smaller masses, cross in the headlights before the van came to a stop. "What the heck was that?" Scooter asked. None of the other men responded. Clark asked. "Did any of you other guys see those two shapes?" Lt Cruz and the other four men just sat uncomfortable and quiet. "All I saw was a two-thousand-pound speed bump" Randall looked back to watch the bull amble away at a leisurely pace. "Those weren't bulls!" Clark added. "They were two stocky smaller looking things. Almost looked like two fat midgets." Lt. Cruz answered up. "You guys probably just saw two wild boars or something. I read where there is a fair population of those on the island."

The group got out of the van to push it from the ditch before making their way to the campground. Two of the KP decided to retire to their sleeping bags, but the others took seats around the fire. "Ya know, they say Sapelo or Blackbeard Island, I can't remember which, has the second highest concentration of alligators in the United States." Scooter provided. The rest of the men just looked at him and shook their heads, while from the woods appeared a mangy dog that wandered up to the fire in search of food. "Hey there buddy!" Randall coaxed the dog over and patted him on the head, reaching over to their pot of beans, spooning out a portion onto a paper plate. They all watched as the mutt chomped on the beans. Suddenly, behind them a deep male voice. "Excuse me, are you the group of men that are going to want to go fishing tomorrow?" The entire group jumped from their chairs to a defensive stance, none prepared for just how stealthily the man had snuck up behind them. When things calmed down, they saw a man that looked like the black version of Chuck Conner, the actor from the television show 'Branded'. Randall thought this was easily the blackest man he had ever seen. The only thing visible on the man were his bright white eyes and perfect teeth of his smile. Clark answered for the group. "Whew...you scared the crap out of us! How did you manage to get so close without us hearing you?" The man replied, "It's how we do on the island."

The entire group, except for Lt. Cruz, bent over, hands on knees as they recovered from the unexpected appearance. "Montel tells me you fella's might be looking for a boat for fishing tomorrow. Says you have plans to not eat unless you catch some fish or hunt something on the island down. I has a boat and thought I might see if I could make some money helping you gentlemen out. I aim to head out tomorrow morning about seven if any of ya's wants to come with me."

Clark thought about it. "You know what? We might just take you up on that. Will your boat take all eight of us?" The man looked at them, seeing only six of them. Cruz responded to his confusion. "Two of our guys have already called it a night." Clark added. "Is there any chance you can get us over to Blackbeard Island?" The Chuck Conner look-alike offered. "I don't see why not. It might leave her low in the water, but if we go slow, I don't see why it wouldn't get you there. "The man started to walk away. "My name is Moses. I will be back at daybreak if ya still want to drop a line in the water." And just as quick he was invisible again. Clark, Cruz and Randall sat back down in their chairs. Cruz was shaken due to having been caught completely off guard by the visitor. "These island folks have skills." Clark asked. "How long do you think he was there before he made his appearance?" Cruz guessed. "He could have been there before we went out in the van. He was mighty stealthy." Clark yawned prompting them all to stand and head to their tent. "Seven comes early."

Chapter 4- Return to the scene

Disappointment was the only feeling that Jewell could connect to as he stood back observing the unsoundness of the PVC pipe frame for the awning, he and Rock had created for the purpose of protecting them from the brutality of the Nevada desert sun. It was obvious that they had miscalculated the size of the pipe it would take to support the parachute with the center pole drooping to a height considerably less than the planned twelve feet and the eight-foot outer poles hanging like limp penises. "It appears you were right. We should have bought the two-inch stuff." Rock grimaced a sarcastic smile to admit he had been wrong arguing with Jewell about the material requirements. He took his turn at standing back, admitting that the multicolored parachute did not stand as proud as it had the first visit that they had made to Burning Man, however...it was functional and that is really all that mattered to him. Agent Capone watched as his four KP detail quickly erected dome tents for them all to sleep before dispersing them out into the crowd for protectionary purposes.

Rock and Jewell erected a tent that was considerably larger than the other KP, then busied themselves inflating air mattresses. Jewell seemed lost in inner thought as he seemed to be staring off into the distance. Once Rock noticed, he stuck his head outside the tent to follow Jewell's gaze and found him transfixed on the vision of a young naked woman rinsing the dust from her body inside a fiberglass shower enclosure that the festival-goers next to them had brought for that very purpose. The woman was obviously completely comfortable in her tight skin. Capone snickered at the ex-stripper. "Somethings never change do they Jewell?" The cocky Puerto Rican enjoyed the view for a few more seconds before responding. "Nah...things have changed for sure, but I guess that doesn't mean we can't appreciate the beauty of a naked woman. I am pretty sure even you can relate to that."

Capone gazed over at the woman, but could only shake his head with acceptance, knowing full well that of the four friends of Rock Razie, he considered Jewell to be his 'diamond in the rough' with respect to his training toward becoming a Knight Protego. He just seemed to have a knack for understanding what it took to provide service to his new higher calling and Capone was extremely pleased with him.

Jewell asked. "So, Rock! How are we supposed to find this medicine man?" Rock shrugged, "I don't know, all I really have to go on is his name. I would imagine we should immerse ourselves into the festival, begin asking folks if they know anything about this 'Gogondo'." He looked over toward Capone for any fresh idea. The leader of the KP replied bluntly. "Don't look at me, you and I have two entirely different missions. Trust that we will have our eyes everywhere around you to ensure there will be no such trouble as the last time we were here." Rock smiled at his paranoid colleague before grabbing a soda from their cooler. "Fair enough, once we are set up here, we should start mingling and see if we can collect information." Jewell smiled and agreed.

Thirty minutes later, they finished the last details of setting up their camp and Rock looked to Capone. "I guess, it's time we see what present day Burning Man has to offer." Capone nodded his approval, coinciding with his glance around the perimeter to ensure his men were properly embedded. Rock asked, "I assume you will be following us?" Capone blank-faced him. "A fair assumption. You will never know we are there!" Rock knew that to be true as he led Jewell away from camp. Each of the two friends were dressed similarly, in khaki cargo shorts. Rock sporting a black t-shirt, Jewell remained topless as they walked up the gridded dusty avenue toward the interior of Burning Man. The surroundings were very much as the last time, where eye candy was displayed with every slight turn of the head, both stationary and mobile with playa vehicles costumed up in every imaginable way.

Fifty-yards up the road, they encountered a kissing booth, this one smaller than the one Rock had met Paul at the last time they came to the festival. "Hey there...care for a kiss?" A middle-aged woman with dirty blonde curly hair asked the two friends. Jewell confidently shoved his only unscarred cheek towards the lady, but she pushed him away with one finger on his lips, turning to her assistant, a middle-aged man, and signaled him to duty. The man puckered up. Jewell, rather than become the butt of Rock's next smartass comment, took control of the situation by grabbing the man's head and smacked him square on the lips as if it were no big deal.

It did not go unnoticed by Rock that two seconds after the kiss, Jewell spit when he turned his back from the booth. Rock chuckled at his prideful friend. The big man respectfully declined a smooch for himself as they headed up the narrow dusty lane. As the sun quickly faded along the desert floor, the playa became vibrant with lights and music springing up everywhere.

Just ahead the men discovered a hundred-foot long line of people, Rock asked those standing there. "What's going on here?" A festival-goer on stilts and naked save a small thin and hanging loin cloth, painted the patterns of a giraffe, answered. "They are serving fresh cooked French-fries up ahead." Jewell looked up to where the front of the line seemed to end, noticing a forty-foot inflatable replica of a bottle of Heinz ketchup, where camp volunteers appeared to be handing out cones of potato wedges. Rock knew Jewell enough to know he didn't feel like debating what was about to come, so he just succumbed and walked back to stand in the rear portion of the line. Jewell's face brightened to indicate his thrill.

After the line moved twenty feet, the two friends began to chat with a nice young couple named Jeanie and Samuel from Florida. They were dressed in industrial styled steampunk costuming, snuggling while they waited for the starchy treasure. "You guys look like a loving couple." They learned that the couple had just joined a fun theme club called the "The Billion Bunny March" and had been given a pink set of bunny ears to solidify their membership. "What made you want to join them?" Rock asked. "Oh, we have known for quite a while that the best way to succeed at making friends here at Burning Man and enjoy the culture is to just immerse, and since almost everyone is in costume, we look for any opportunity to do the same." The couple apparently believed that the costume made them more approachable to others. Rock looked to Jewell. "Too bad we didn't bring any costumes with us." Jewell frowned. Samuel leaned over and whispered to his wife. "If you guys are interested, we have costumes from last night if you would like to borrow them?"

Jewell's face brightened and a watermelon sized grin appeared upon his face. "What kind of costume?" He asked. "Clown" Samuel replied. Rock snickered as Jewell looked down at his feet...dejected. "Poor timing." He mumbled thinking back to what had just happened the day before in Atlanta. "I don't believe that grumpy clown from yesterday would prevent me from having some fun here with you. I refuse to give him that much power." Rock turned to the couple. "I believe we will take you up on your offer."

Eventually the four made their way to the front of the line, where they got their opportunity to munch on some freshly fried potato wedges. The two men followed their new friends back to their campsite where they collected the Clown outfits, with hat and red noses included. The couple recommended they stop at one of the many face painters to have clown makeup applied. Rock and Jewell proceeded back to their own tent to dress in the darkness. Jewell stumbled his way oddly up the entire dusty lane, prompting Rock to ask. "What in the world are you doing?" Jewell looked back to his bigger buddy. "I am being a clown." Rock looked at him blankly. "I don't want a chunk of pie to smack me in the face." Rock gasped as they located an artist who cheerfully gave them clown faces. Once the artist finished, Jewell asked him to take their pictures to remember the situation, handing the man his smart phone. When he was finished Rock snugged in behind Jewell to look at the picture. Both men shrugged their shoulders when they saw the results. Neither man had noticed what color the costumes were, having dressed in the dark, but the flash of his phone showed the girlie pink and lavender costume color's and the artist had matched that with the same color scheme on their faces. Beyond that, however, was the positioning where Jewell had leaned over to Rock making the picture almost looked as if he had his head on Rock's shoulder. "Good lord! Is it possible to look any gayer than we do in that picture?" Rock blurted. Jewell laughed at his big friend. "Well...I won't tell if you don't?" Rock walked away. "Deal!"

Moments later, they spilled out onto the playa floor in the center of the horseshoe shaped festival grid, toward the inner row where they could see their first glimpse of this year version of the Burning Man structure. Gone was the lighthouse/birthday cake base from the last time they had visited, this year the man stood alone and much taller. A large sign located directly beside them for a huge theme camp captured their attention. It was called "Camp Jersey". The member participants wore black and white cow costumes, the men outfits with horns, the women with udders. Rock chuckled as he turned his head to see a few of the women on top of a marvelously polished wooden circular bar, dancing and shaking their udders at the menfolk. "Howdy partners!" A particularly attractive woman shouted as she stood just inside the massive theme camp tent entryway. "You guys look like you might taste funny." She offered, an obvious reference to the nature of their costumes, while she snatched Jewell's arm and licked it. "Yep...you taste funny." Rock stood amused by her boldness. "You do look like you taste funny in more ways than one." Jewell smiled widely, parading like a happy peacock to the inner portions of the tent, ensuring everyone he saw knew that he "tasted funny". It became his theme for the evening.

The two friends asked around about the medicine man for a while before exiting the bar, where they continued stopping others for information.

Wandering about the festival grounds for another thirty minutes, they noticed a theme camp sign painted in hectic dismal colors that featured the name *Subterranean Post WW3 bar*. There was a line of twenty or so revelers waiting to enter. It peaked their curiosity, so they got in line behind an attractive woman with a thick Irish accent, joined by her rowdy male friends. Rock's attention focused on her thick accent, transfixed as she conversed with her friends. "Bro...I think I am going to make use those Porta-potties around the corner." Jewell half asked, half informed his bigger friend. Rock continued to listen to the Irish woman but replied. "I am sure I will still be in the same spot when you get back" Referring to the speed at which the line was moving.

The long haired new-Yorker wandered away while Rock struck up a conversation with the Irish woman, learning that she had been in America for three weeks on holiday. Eventually learning that her group of friends, had decided to wander about some of the more famous spots in America before they returned to college in Dublin. Rock glanced to his left to notice Jewell making his way back around the corner. Something was odd in his gate, though Rock couldn't identify what it was. He looked somehow different, his hair was oddly straight and had apparently taken off his clown costume. He was wearing a plaid shirt and loincloth with matching knee-high moccasins. "What in the world?" He blurted as Jewell walked right past him, without glancing at Rock at all. The big man stood dismayed.

The Irish foursome moved up to become next in line for the theme camp. Jewell continued walking until he disappeared around the corner, like he was lost. Rock, for a brief second, considered going after his friend but decided against losing his spot in the line, instead justifying that perhaps Jewell had been unable to find an open porta-pottie and went looking for an alternative. "But the clothing?" He thought. "Where'd ya friend go?" The Irish girl asked. Rock didn't know what to tell her. "Bro...we next in line." Rock turned to see Jewell step into the line beside him in his clown costume, which baffled the hell out of Rock.

He didn't have much time to ponder though as the attendant ushered the Irish folk and two friends inside a make-shift faux elevator. "Enjoy your trip down." The usher provided as he closed the wooden elevator door. It was the only instruction provided. Once the doors closed, typical elevator music played loudly, as the walls of the "Elevator" shook, obviously by the attendants to give the sensation of deep underground travel.

Once the shaking stopped, the door on the opposite side, directly behind the way they were all faced and where they had entered, opened and the six of them spilled into a tent that was designed to give the feel of being in an underground bar, complete with dank dirt walls, a video screen playing nuclear blast scenes and views of desolation and destruction. There was a legitimate sense of what it would be like in a post WW3 nuclear event. There was of course an extremely attractive female bar tender with jawline length jet black hair, the right side of her head completely shaved with two full sleeve tattoo's running from shoulder to wrist thru her dark colored wife beater t-shirt. She stood behind a makeshift bar constructed from the hood of an automobile,

As the six new revelers entered the bar, they noticed ten or so other festival goers dancing wildly to loud alternative music. The Irish foursome along with Jewell jumped onto the dirt dance floor, reveling with the others, while Rock drifted over to the car hood. "What type of libation do you have available bar keep?"

"Bloody Mary's and Car Bomb's. It is all we serve. Which do you want?" She offered very straightforwardly.

Rock thought for a second, "Bloody Mary?" The bar tender went thru the motions, putting all the ingredients together before sliding the big man a clear plastic cup. "And what might I offer in trade?" He felt obligated to ask. My name is Rock, my jubilant friend on the dance floor is Jewell. And your name is?"
"My name is Maggie and I would accept an answer for trade!"

"Fair enough!" Rock replied. "Ask your question straight away."

The woman pushed the drink toward him with her wolf/human blend tattoo' d arm.
"Why are you searching for him?"

Rock looked at her puzzled. "Well, I suppose its human nature that most of us search for our maker in one way or another." Maggie grimaced through her own confusion. "Your maker? You thought I was asking about your maker?" Rock seemed even more puzzled. "I am asking you why you are looking for Gogondo!" Stunned, he stuttered. "How did you...uh...how could you possibly know I am looking for a man named Gogondo?"
Maggie smiled widely. "He asked me to look out for you?" Rock stayed confused. "He? Who told you?"

"Gogondo did"

Rock's face crinkled, unable to comprehend what was taking place. "Matter of fact, if you can wait until morning. I will take you to him...just meet me at center camp at nine and I will arrange things." Rock thought for a second and decided it was a reasonable plan. "Might want to drink your Bloody Mary and head back to your tent though. Word is a sandstorm, is headed this way. Ever experience a sandstorm at Burning Man?"

Rock nodded and puffed, remembering his last festival experience. He slowly worked on the Bloody Mary, allowing the revelers to burn a little of their energy before signaling to Jewell his intent to go back to the tent. Jewell, of course, followed.

On the way back, Rock couldn't help but notice the constant smell of marijuana everywhere, especially since he had only detected even the slightest trace on his previous trip. As the two friends, drudged their way back to the area where their tent was located, they passed a camp with a fifty-five-gallon barrel of flaming green-leafed material, burning gloriously in front of everyone. It reeked of pot. Rock glared at the man tending the fire. "Dude, you are burning a fifty-five-gallon drum of weed, really?" Jewell looked to Rock perplexed, as did the man tending the fire, who rose from his folding chair and made his way over to the drum. He looked inside then looked up to Rock. "That's sage, Dumbass!" A deep garnet hue of color flashed over Rock's face. He felt like such a fool for blaming the man and should have realized that he was too naive to even know what pot smelled like. But, then, Jewell didn't let that get in the way of ensuring Rock knew how naïve he was...all the way back to the tent.

The two friends woke the next day shortly after daybreak with the expected sandstorm in full force. Once Rock managed to unzip his tent, he realized that they would have to cover their faces or risk lung irritation with the abrasive nature of the silty sand in the air. Glancing around at the safe space inside his tent, he found a rag he had used to bathe with the previous night and wrapped it around his head. Capone spoke to Rock from somewhere outside the tent. "Don't worry about your safety today. Despite the dust storm, we will be using all of our technology to make sure we keep our eyes on you at all time." Rock shook his head, amazed and humbly grateful for Capone and his men's commitment to protecting him. Amazingly, since they had embedded themselves, he had not seen one of them at all...but he was confident they were constantly there.

Jewell, sporting a long thin scarf wrapped round his face, joined Rock and asked. "Weren't you washing your ass with that rag last night?" Referring to the white rag around his big friend's face. Rock couldn't deny it and just shrugged. They left their campsite and tried to navigate with extremely limited visibility, unable to see more than ten feet ahead of them. During their travels the previous evening, they had learned of a theme camp that provided festival goers with pancakes for breakfast and felt certain it might be between them and the center camp which was a thousand feet in the direction they were heading.

A golf cart startled them when it appeared from out of nowhere beside the two friends as they walked thru the sand soup. A man, accompanied by an attractive woman asked the two if they wanted a ride to center camp, which Rock politely declined. The woman naughtily insinuated to him, that she would really like some male companionship back at her tent...in addition to that of her husband. Rock declined again a final time, triggering the man driving the golf cart to speed off to continue looking for their brand of fun. Jewell laughed at his big naïve buddy. "Do you realize what she was wanting?" Rock stopped walking and stared at his ex-stripper friend before the real invitation purpose slowly soaked into his thinking. He shrugged and continued through the storm, where people crossed within feet of their path, some almost causing a collision as they worked their way down the walkways between the individual theme camps. Rock came to an abrupt stop when he almost fell into a cast iron bathtub at the edge of one of the theme camps. There inside the tub, sat a solitary individual naked man...during the sandstorm, with a scarf around his face as if he were soaking in a nice warm tub. Rock mumbled a quick sorry for almost stumbling over him and proceeded.

Moments later they arrived at the Center camp to duck inside of an enormous circus sized military tent. It wasn't until then that Rock realized that they had either missed the pancake theme-camp or it had been cancelled due to the inundating weather. He was impressed with the enormity of Base Camp. It was two-hundred feet in diameter, with enormous circus style tent dangling flaps all along the exterior three-hundred-sixty degrees around it that were functional enough to restrict the blown sand, enough so that festivalgoers were able to see across the tent with a slight dusty haze. Inside the tent was a surprisingly active crowd, with three or four hundred people scattered about performing Yoga exercises in groups of ten, hacky-sack circles where people footed small bean bags at each other. One man in the middle was swallowing fire and spitting flames as well. There were hundreds of costumes, story tellers telling tales, fortune tellers telling fortunes, people sitting around grooming each other in small trains of human groomers. *Fascinating*, thought Rock.

Finding a vacant spot though was a different story and offered somewhat of a challenge, but with patience the two friends located an acceptable spot and plopped down to a seated position to wait out the sandstorm and hopefully locate Maggie from the bar the previous night. A pair of hippies sat down beside Rock. They were pleasant enough, each giving the other foot massages while they talked of Chai tea and armpit hair. Rock just sat and watched while a naked woman plodded in front of him wearing nothing more than a very realistic zebra mask while a naked man with a matching Unicorn mask chased her around the huge tent.

Jewell decided he couldn't sit much longer, as he hopped up in search for a beverage of any type. He excused himself while Rock continued his sit with his butt-rag filter to continue removing any stray silica. He became infatuated with a young bearded man playing a metal drum called a "Gu". His music was magically hypnotic and the big man's eyes dulled, until he was jolted from a semi stupor when the 'Gu" musician began belting out a Mongolian throat song that the big man found equally as fascinating. After a brief conversation with the talented musician, Rock learned he was from a small village in Switzerland where they made a specific brand of cheese. He sensed Jewell slide up beside him as he chatted with the Gu player. Looking down briefly he noticed that it appeared Jewell had changed his shoes and clothing again. He was no longer wearing the gray shorts and tank top, rather once again showing up in the knee-high moccasins and modest version of loin cloth. While remaining massively engaged in conversation with the steel drum performer, and without looking at his friend, Rock asked. "Why do you keep changing clothes?"

Jewell simply stood silently beside him. "What do you think about this music? It is intoxicating, isn't it?" He looked up from his seated position directly into Jewell's face, only it wasn't Jewell. Rock could not have been more confused. Standing in front of him was a man that was identical to Jewell, same height, same body style, same face. Could have been his twin except for this man had straight hair and even that was almost the exact same length of Jewell's. His face was identical to

Jewells minus the wicked scar that had been created by the flesh stripper in the miner's shack two years earlier. He had the swagger almost. But...he wasn't Jewell.

Rock was stunned to silence.

"Excuse me, Maggie asked me to take you to grandfather." He spoke in the slight choppy style of a native American. Rock stopped paying attention to the swiss man, marveling as he stood looking around for his friend Jewell, who appeared making his way back with a goblet of wine. "My name is Nonie." The native American informed as Jewell walked up to the two.

"Whoa dude...you could be my brother." Jewell jabbered as he walked into the situation, giving the confused Native American a hug. Rock stared at them as they stood side by side, freakishly identical, his jaw slackened and all he could really do is gawk. Nonie introduced himself again this time to the man who had just walked up, prompting Jewell to do the same. Rock looked around everywhere, sure he must be on some sort of hidden camera TV show. "As I shared with your big friend here, I have been instructed to assist you in locating my grandfather, Gogondo!"

Rock turned his head to look around for Nonie's grandfather, reluctantly snapping out of his trance. "Is he far?" Nonie pointed out to the desert floor. "He is in his sweat lodge about a quarter of mile to the north of here out on the desert floor. Each year he comes to this festival....for those needing guidance or inspiration with determining their direction. I assume this to be your desire?" Rock shook his head. "I honestly do not know why I am here...I just know that it involves him...and looking at you I cannot possibly believe you are an accident. "Nonie led the way out of the center camp tent thru the waning sandstorm.

* *

Rock, nor Jewell, nor any of the Knights Protego mingling throughout the crowd while they kept a watchful eye on the big man, happened to pay the slightest attention to the bald man with a perfectly shaped head sitting in his gray tank top, blatantly focused on the big man as he walked from the tent.

Chapter 5- Sorry

As the sun made a sneaky appearance over the live oak trees, shielding the make-shift campground from the breezes created by the Atlantic Ocean, Moses snuck into the Knight Protego camp again, he stoked their low burning fire and generously began 'fixin' all the men a pot of stout black coffee with the equipment they had left for that exact purpose. Scooter, as usual, was the first to rise, followed erratically by the others. "Good morning, Gentlemen's!" Moses offered, receiving a complete groggy group response back from folk who were less than expert at tent camping.

Once the large coffee pot was empty, Moses loaded his guest all into their rented van, strapping their fishing rigs and bait on top as they made their way to a local's dock, rather than the dock the ferry had used the day before. There Moses removed the cover from his small tri-hull boat, pumped the gas bulb and started the engine. "I need to apologize to you'uns as I ain't gonna be able to goes with ya! My wife says I got to watch mine kids. You know yo way around the channels?" Clark puffed his chest and took the lead. "I think I do, I mean, I studied the map. I could probably navigate us where we need to go if you show me anything special about the boat." Moses took a few minutes to introduce him to the watercraft, including the depth finder, which he emphasized to Clark as necessary in these local waters.

Once Clark learned as much as he could, asked a few questions and felt comfortable, the other men loaded their equipment and cast the boat off the dock, just as Clark pulled away out into the channel. "Guys, our main goal today is to hug up to the west side of Sapelo and make our way to the north end of the island where a narrow channel named Blackbeard creek, separates Blackbeard Island from Sapelo Island. Once we navigate that channel about half way down, we can beach the boat and search for Blackbeard's treasure...or food, the choice is yours." Clark briefed the group, all the while piloting the boat out of the smaller tributary into the main channel, that led directly to the ocean.

They passed the DNR ferry that had provided them passage to the island the day before, waving at the people as they floated past as the Knights made their way up to the inner channel that skirted Sapelo. Clark couldn't help but notice how sluggish the boat reacted and how low it slumped into the water due to the weight of the eight men riding inside. For the most part, the men enjoyed the ride with sea birds flying randomly ahead, a lone porpoise surfaced fifty yards ahead of them before Clark maneuvered between Sapelo sound and another uninhabited island just west of Sapelo Island itself. The boat scooted along nicely until without warning the propeller began to dig into the mud, Clark having not seen the indications of shallow water. He quickly glanced down at the depth finder, realizing that he had failed to notice not only how shallow the water was, but also how low the boat's profile was underneath.

The boat suddenly and quickly came to an abrupt stop, almost slinging two of the Knights at the front of the boat into the channel. All the men turned to look at Clark somewhat miffed for the lack of warning. "Sorry!" He said pitifully. After a brief discussion, Scooter and Randall jumped out of the boat into knee deep water to dislodge it. Once they realized they weren't going to be able to budge, they asked the others to do the same, except Clark who continued to try to steer the boat. Eventually they were successful in floating the boat both from lack of weight inside and their combined thrusting power.

Clark used the depth finder to hunt and peck, eventually finding a slightly deeper channel between the two bodies of land but couldn't locate a portion of the small channel that would allow the boat free travel.

"I'm not pulling this boat a quarter of a mile in waste deep water, knowing there are alligators, oh...and bull sharks in this area." Scooter complained. Clark pondered to determine that with it being low tide, perhaps it would be wise to find another direction, so he directed the entire group of men to turn the boat around back toward the main channel and attempt access the island from the Atlantic Ocean.

Once the water was deep enough, they all jumped back inside and puttered east up the main channel toward the sea. They watched as a massive cabin cruiser made its way from the open ocean steadily, amazed at the sheer size of it. "Clark, it might would be a good idea to steer around to approach the cruisers wake straight on, especially with all of us in such a small boat." Scooter warned, Randall nodding his agreement. Clark took his advice, maneuvering the small eighteen-foot craft on a course to do exactly that.

The group sat or stood and watched as the large yacht produced an impressive wave behind it and that wave was approaching them quickly. "You need to be careful when you attempt to float over this wake!" Lt Cruz warned with a touch of concern in his voice, sensing a nervousness in Clark's own demeanor. The cabin cruiser plowed through the water and passed by them, prompting the boatload of men to go silent, worried as the wave rolled closer and closer.

From small boat level it looked at least six-feet-tall. "Thirty feet!" Scooter counted down the distance, "Twenty...Ten!" It was at that moment, Clark did the inexplicable, by nervously placing the boat throttle in neutral, prompting a collective "NOOOOOOO!" Wailed the entire population of the boat. Two seconds later the front of the boat dipped lower in the water due to Clark letting off the throttle. Then Scooter and Randall gasped from the front of the boat as the six-foot wave had now turned into a seven-foot-wave and washed over the boat, over all eight men, almost washing the entire crowd into the brackish water of the channel. Three of Moses fishing rods floated out over the sides. Eerie silence ensued. Every member managed to stay inside the boat somehow...but every one of them was completely and utterly drenched.

A small hum originated from somewhere inside the boat as the boat's sump motor came on to begin pumping water from inside back to the channel, while they stood as if posing for a still picture and the only sound detectable was a small meek voice that originated from the middle. "Sorry..." Clark said...for a second time this trip.

The proud Knights Protego stood limp and soaked as they all looked behind the boat watching debris that had been washed overboard. The borrowed craft listed to one side with all the water inside and was in real peril of sinking should its passengers not make wise decisions. The KP cooler of drinks bobbed in the brackish waters behind them, a two-thousand-dollar professional camera was bobbing a strapped floatation device. It would have been useless to try to rescue it from the salt it had been soaked in. The residual loss of equipment was limited to fishing items and various and sundry trash floating behind them.

After a brief discussion, the men made the decision to not attempt to retrieve any of the material but to head back to the dock, hopefully to mitigate the boat from sinking beneath them.

They arrived at the dock safe and sound, then loaded up the van to head back to the campsite where they held another group discussion, deciding to split up. Obviously agitated with Clark, Lt. Cruz decided to take the remainder of the Knights Protego fishing, while Randall, Clark and Scooter voiced the desire to use the van and trek out on a search for land-based food. The entire group appeared to be on the verge of becoming hungry.

Scooter chauffeured the van as he and his two friends, dropped off the remaining Knights at a campground at a place named Cabretta Island Beach access. The friends followed the others to the beach on the east side of the island, helping them to get settled into a full day of fishing. The weather was beautiful, temperatures in the eighties as the three friends tromped their way back to the van. Clark made a flimsy argument that it was his turn to drive, which he won without much dispute. They sped off up the dirt road headed for the north end of the island looking to poach anything with four legs or wings.

A short while later, the van entered an area thick with massive Live Oaks, laden with Spanish moss. There were sable palms scattered beneath them all over the wooded area as far as they could see. "This place sort of reminds me of the jungle in the movie Jurassic Park." Randall geeked-out his thoughts.

Sixty seconds later the fauna made an abrupt change from ancient hard wood trees to a plethora of pine trees lining both sides of the dirt road. "What is that?" Scooter noticed something odd in the road a good distance in front of them, pointing to guide Clark's line of sight. Randall recognized it first, despite the fact he was in the second row of seats. "That is an alligator." Scooter found it difficult to believe. "Noooo...out here in the middle of the forest? We haven't seen water for half a mile, nothing but pine trees and small undergrowth." Clark's eyes widened. "OOoooo....let's catch him and eat him." There was not a great amount of thinking to occur after his statement. He depressed the accelerator to quickly catch up to the gator before it decided to run away. However, the reptile continued to lay in the middle of the road, stretched to its full length from one side of the dirt road to the other.

Clark slid to a stop about twenty feet from the dinosaur looking critter. The van doors flung open as all three men jumped out of the van with no firm plan other than to subdue the gator.

Once the animal recognized its situation, it bolted toward the tree line, over a ditch, before turning toward his three attackers. He opened his mouth to display the cotton white membranes and the sharpness of his formidable teeth, deeply hissing at his assailants as he waited on their next move.

Clark, the instigator of this hunt, skidded to a halt, stood straight up and looked to his friends with adrenalin pumped wild eyes. Common sense made them all suddenly realize that they really had no weapon, no duct tape, no rope, nothing. Just six hands and whatever skills they could muster to overwhelm the creature. It became blatantly apparent their lust for adventure were simply not going to be enough to meet this challenge, prompting them to walk back to the van and hop inside.

They continued their travel, but at a much slower pace, hoping to see if they could find other smaller prey that they might possibly be capable of handling. A few moments later, the van emerged from the pine forest, to a narrow land bridge with water on both sides of the dirt road ribboning over between the marsh looking lagoons. The area was fantastically beautiful as two salt marsh fed ponds with birds flying everywhere, might be. The friends searched the ponds to see if they could locate any other game...even perhaps smaller gators.

As they crept across in the old van, the land bridge continued to narrow until Clark became uncomfortable with the driving conditions and asked Scooter to exit the van and provide him some guidance on how to continue safely. Scooter did as he was asked, popped from the passenger seat and proceeded to the front of the van, motioning for Clark to make small adjustments to his driving tactics. Randall sat inside impatient and uncomfortable, eventually deciding he might be of more help outside the van.

Shortly thereafter, they reached an area with very little margin between the width of the van and the land bridge causing the travel to slow dramatically.

"Whoa...whoa...whoa..." Randall barked from the rear as the left back tire began to slide off toward the pond. In slow motion, much like any scenario where disaster is about to occur, the heavy van cascaded to slide down from the six-foot bank, twisting in a vulgar manner sideways into the pond. Clark freaked out from inside the van, panic bulging from his eyes, his arms trying desperately to turn the steering wheel of a vehicle plunging without any wheel firmly on land. His two friends stood with shocked looks on their faces, unable to do anything that might be considered help.

When the fan landed, it didn't splash, didn't displace a great deal of water, there was no great horrifying noise, befitting a catastrophe. As a matter of fact, the end of the incident was as anti-climactic as any of the three could have possibly imagined.

The van simply lay half submerged on its side. Scooter and Randall, standing on the land bridge, watched as Clark frantically attempted to slide the passenger door in attempt to exit the vehicle. He was drenched from the ordeal, due to the driver's window having been rolled down before the tumble. Scooter and Randall jumped from the solid ground onto the side of the van to assist, pulling Clark out. The three leapt back to the land bridge. Clark looked down at the van, stunned and more than a little scared. "Well...that did not go as we planned." Randall nodded, Scooter stood with a look of indignation. "Nope, I imagine Miss Dorothy is not going to be a happy lady."

Clark sighed. "What do we do now?" Scooter shook his head. "We have plenty of daylight left, but there is no way we have cell signal this far out. We could walk back to that Cabretta landing thing or maybe just try to find our way back to Hog Hammock or...we could just explore the north end of the island on foot. By my calculations we can't be more than a mile from the very end."

Again, without a great deal of thinking, they decided to plod ahead and explore.

They walked for an additional twenty minutes before re-entering the jungle-like huge live oaks with spooky moss dripping down like candle wax. Other than the road itself, the only signs providing any type of information, were several two-inch plastic round blue numbers on some of the trees at inconsistent distances. The markers made no sense to the friends, but forty-five minutes later they reached the north end channel that led to the ocean. Hiking down out of the trees toward the water, they noticed millions, perhaps billions of oyster shells scattered about on the beach, which just so happened to create a hazardous hiking environment. They noticed a deer carcass off to the side, with only a slight amount of meat remaining...and smelling hideous. "I think we can eliminate that as a food source." Randall offered.

They decided to travel west down the dirt road, away from the foot shredding ocean path simply because it was the more inviting of the two. A quarter-mile later, they noticed a structure off the road to the right. It was interesting enough to tempt them to drift through the trees and investigate. Once they got close enough, they determined it was a structure, eight to ten feet tall, made from oyster shells plastered together on the walls to form a round shaped dwelling of some type, complete with inconsistently shaped and placed windows. They guessed it to be thirty-foot in diameter with no roof whatsoever.

They quietly walked around it to the rear, where they noticed it had decayed and fallen to the ground on the backside. "This must be one of those shell rings I was reading about," Clark reasoned. His friends nodded agreement. "The book says these things are fifteen hundred years old. Which if you think about it, kind of blows the theory that Columbus discovered America, doesn't it?" They decided they would backtrack, then proceed east, toward the northern tip of the island.

A half an hour later, they entered an area of lush vegetation immersed in differing shades of green before eventually escaping into a clearing with two large vegetation covered, thirty-acre ponds separated by another land bridge, like the one where they lost the van earlier. "What the heck is that?" Scooter pointed, noticing something odd on the surface of the pond to his right. Randall squinted to see what his usually paranoid friend was talking about. "Looks like a floating log bridge to me." The friends stood curiously, wondering who would have constructed a log bridge to span the pond and why? As they continued to walk toward the log bridge, down the land bridge, Clark stopped them again. "What the hell? That floating bridge is moving." His friends peered carefully at the bridge. "Wait! That's not a bridge, those are alligators." The men stood, jaws agape, baffled by the most unusual sight any of them had ever seen. They watched several hundred alligators lined up side by side in a perfectly straight line...and they appeared to be slowly pushing their formation toward the friends. "How does that happen?" Clark barked. "What in the world could

possibly motivate alligators to collectively make a formation?"
Randall suddenly howled as he pointed toward a walking trail on the
far side of the pond. "What the...what...tha?" They all gawked as two
small extremely dirty forms skirted the edge of the pond bounding
toward them. "Are those...dwarves?" Scooter mouthed, as the
creatures pounded the surface of the black soil, quick-stepping their
way around the pond toward the uninvited men. Once they got close
enough, the friends noticed the dwarves, their beards full of mud and
dragging the ground, appeared to be about four-foot tall and almost as
wide with craggy, deeply rutted faces and facial expressions that were
nothing if not extremely serious and agitated by the appearance of
three apparently unwelcome men. There was no doubt they were
storming from across the other side of the pond to intervene.
Randall, without a plan, began the evacuation...and his friends did
their best to catch up with his exit from the area.

Chapter 6- Dream Time

      As they tromped out over the dried-out lake bed floor that is called the playa, Jewell leaned over toward Rock. "Dude, he doesn't really look that much like me, does he?" Rock turned to his prideful friend. "To be honest, you two could be twins. You need to ask your mom some hard questions the next time you see her." Jewell gazed over and studied the Native-American look-a-like from head to toe. He partially had to accept that Nonie did look like a rougher version of himself and that if it weren't for the wicked scar that ran the length of his own face, it would be tough for most folks to tell them apart.

Looking back toward the festival grounds, Rock began to realize just how far they had walked. Far enough from the horseshoe shaped campground to where the other festival goers were nothing more than distant vague mirage-like images floating around on the horizon. "Old Grandfather is only a short distance from here." The Native American provided the others. Twenty-minutes later they arrived at a sharp mountainous rise. Nonie led them to a rounded mud-covered hut with a large fire burning to the side. "Old Grandfather says he first built this sweat lodge over a hundred years ago with dust and his sweat. He tells me he has seen many things here." Jewell noticed smoke wafting from a stove pipe located near the middle of the ruddy creation. "Who is this 'Old Grandfather' dude you keep referring to?" Nonie didn't reply to Jewell, thinking that the name should have been an indication of who exactly he was.

Once they got closer to the sweat lodge, Rock could see it was oddly placed in that it was built partially from a grotto in the mountain side, the other half was constructed of saplings covered with animal carcasses, some extraordinary looking mud and other materials the two friends could not possibly identify. "The Apache word for this is *inipi*". Nonie explained. To the rear of the construct, directly behind the mud hut and toward the mountain, Rock noticed a large stash of green vegetation. He assumed it was 'sage', since he had just learned that 'sage' was a thing, and at the very least he now knew what the green material wasn't.

As they walked up to the *inipi*, another Native American man, this one perhaps ten years older than Nonie appeared from behind the hut. "Dude, is that your grandfather, he looks young?" Jewell asked. "No, his name is Montu...he is the lodge keeper and a student of Old Grandfather." They watched as the man tended the fire outside, meticulously moving honeydew melon sized stones around to different positions inside the fire. The smoke from the sweat lodge roof wafted into Jewell's eyes causing him to squint. "Man...it looks hot inside that thing." His scarred faced grimaced with the thought of sitting inside of it. "It is fairly cool inside, more so than you would think." Nonie attempted to calm is worries, as he guided them to the small opening covered by an extremely thick animal fur. Jewell yelped. "Dude, what is that?" Nonie anticipated the question. "Buffalo!" Jewell looked over to Rock with awe. "You get me into some of the craziest stuff...buffalo...are you kidding me? I thought they were extinct or something."

Montu, the other Native American man came running to the hut opening. "Before you enter, you must shed your white-man clothing." The lodge keeper handed the two friends their ceremonial garb, a ridiculously small piece of leather underwear. "If you will..." They each stood gawking at the scrap of leather. " That is all?" Jewell complained, odd behavior considering his former profession as a male stripper. "No...that is not all. You must ensure you have no metal...false teeth...watches...anything that is not from the earth." Jewell being his cocky self, smarted back. " Oh...we do not want to upset the Great Spirit or anything." Nonie looked at Jewell unimpressed and rebutted his claim. "Or...you will suffer a nasty burn if you have any of those materials on your skin. It is called a sweat lodge...not a cool down and chill lodge." Jewell realized he was distinctly out of his element here amongst those who had lived in the area for millennials.

After each had changed into their smallish loincloths, Nonie handed them leather sandals, while Montu dipped foot long sage brushes in water and began to gently lash them on each of their bodies. Jewell looked to Nonie for an explanation. "He is preparing you for your experience, your journey so to speak." Rock looked at Nonie suddenly surprised. "We are participating in a ceremony?" Nonie took a moment then to look at Rock...again unimpressed. "You could say that...yes!"

Montu reached to pull the animal skin covering away to allow his visitors to enter. Rock dipped his head inside. His first impression was that the size of the sweat lodge appeared larger than he had imagined. Then he noticed the largest dog he had ever seen, standing on the other side of the tent across a round rock fire pit in the center of the lodge, glaring at him. The dog didn't present itself or seem aggressive at all. It was just huge enough to intimidate anyone that encountered it and despite the dim lighting, appeared tan in color with a black masked face with droop skinned jowls that flowed around his head. The dog had a long sliver of slobber hanging from his mouth that almost reached the ground. Once Jewell ducked inside and his eyes adjusted to the darkness, he was unnerved with the fact he was facing a creature that was perhaps much larger than himself and he refused to take his eyes from the dog. For once in his life Jewell was quiet, not wanting to draw attention to himself.

Nonie ducked in behind the two men. "His name is Dog. There is no need to be scared. Old Grandfather once performed a ritual for a breeder in Canada. They gifted him an English Mastiff puppy, and that puppy is Dog. He will not harm you. If you will, please take a seat in front of the pit." Montu entered and circled around to the rear of the pit, where the two friends were surprised to learn that a tattered and frail older man stood with his back turned. Despite the lack of lighting inside the sweat-lodge, Rock perceived that the man had unbelievably wrinkled skin.

Gogondo slowly turned to face the others, dangling a gently smoking foot-long sage whisk, raising it to wave in front of his waist as he made his way toward the firepit in the center of the lodge. He oriented himself inside the lone shaft of light stabbing its way through the top of the mud-covered hut. Rock noticed that the medicine man kept his left hand cupped across the left side of his face, covering his left eye. His other eye appeared to gaze out over their shoulders behind them. It looked as if it were twice the size of what Rock thought an eye should be and was blistered white and opaque. The old man appeared to be blind. Rock noticed the skin on his hand was paper thin and craggy, his fingers flattened and widened. They reminded Rock of large tongue depressors. In the lone shaft of light, the big man noticed the color of his hands, a muddy dark brown color with thick and long fingernails. As Gogondo shuffled toward the pit, he mumbled a melodic chant with strained breath. "Crooked Finger, if you would take a seat!" He instructed as he waved his smoking sage at the two. Jewell looked to his friend with confusion. Rock raised his finger that he had broken as a young boy and wiggled it to show his friend. "How did he know about that? I thought he was blind?" They both looked at the old man curiously.

Gogondo answered Jewell's question in monotone simplicity. "There are many ways for a man to see." His words caused the two friends to focus intently on his raspy voice. Gogondo lowered himself to the ground gingerly. The two friends followed Nonie's example and sat down as well, crossing their legs in front of the fire pit. Rock noticed the medicine man's long straight black hair with sporadic barely perceptible individual silver strands spilling down over his shoulders. His face vastly contrasting the slight coloring of his hair, was deeply wrinkled and resembled the bark on a pine tree in texture but was paper thin.

Jewell was infatuated with the old man, his vision transfixed as he watched him methodically position himself to a sitting position that was ripe with esteem. Skillfully fumbling within an animal skin pouch slung around his shoulder, the ancient old man withdrew a hand sized stone chalice, that was the size of a coffee cup and placed it on a large rock directly in front of him. He then produced a large feather which he placed on top of a rolled animal hide to his side. Gogondo murmured softly in a language neither of the two friends could ever hope to understand.

"Old Grandfather says welcome to the both of you. He has named you Crooked finger and the other Wounded Bird!" The friends looked at each other. Gogondo, once again, pointed to Rocks right hand pinky, before motioning for Jewell to approach him. The New Yorker looked to Rock for guidance. "Old Grandfather would like for you to go to him." Nonie clarified. The ex-stripper slowly rose and moved to where the old man sat. Gogondo motioned him closer. Jewell nervously bent down to one knee in front of the ancient old man, who slowly brought his flattened finger to the one-inch scar running the length of Jewells cheek. He gently rubbed the non-damaged portion of Jewells face with his oversized thumb before motioning for Jewell to return to his seat, before he began a very faint, beautifully melodic chant.

Rock glanced over toward Nonie for any instructions he may have missed, lost for what he was to do next. "Old Grandfather is chanting instructions for your dream experience. I will interpret." Nonie listened for thirty seconds. "He tells of a spirit journey. He says that you will have two paths unveiled for you. One will be your path of service, the other a path of action. He says that your journey will show you many things. He asks you to pay attention to even the slightest detail...because it all matters. He tells me that once you are finished with your journey and we sit here in the lodge around this fire, you must speak the word for each of your paths that you have experienced, for the purpose of solidifying the vision."

Neither of the friends could comprehend what was occurring. Nonie recognized their confusion. "Old Grandfather is about to send you on a spiritual journey with the aid of a special combination of ingredients called *Gump*. This *Gump* has been created by substances that he has collected for many years. He alone, knows the recipe for his *Gump*. The ingredients will be placed between your lip and teeth and will help create your journey." Jewell's eyes brightened. "Dude...he is going to get us high?"

Nonie dropped his head to look at the dirt beneath Jewell's feet, disappointed. "Not exactly! It is difficult to explain; just trust you will be safe. Dog also has a purpose on this journey." He glanced over to the creature sitting dutifully across the fire pit. "He will assist in preventing evil spirits from harassing you. Old Grandfather will also watch over you and perhaps invest himself into your adventure." Jewell looked over to Nonie. "Are you going on a journey as well?" Nonie shook his head negatively. "NO, this is your journey. You are dressed for the experience. I am not."

Gogondo mumbled something undecipherable to the group of men. "I understand Old Grandfather." He nodded and stood to leave the sweat lodge. "Where are you going?" Jewell asked uncomfortable with the idea of being left alone with the spooky Gogondo. "Apparently, I was mistaken. I must change as I will be a part of this experience as well." With that, Nonie exited through the opening. Rock stared across the fire pit as Gogondo continued to hold his hand above one eye while making conciliatory moves toward the pit with the feather he had retrieved and placed in his other hand, all while continuing his hypnotic chanting. The big man noticed with slight surprise that Gogondo wore metal earrings the shape of upside-down cleft notes, along with tarnished silver rings on the hand covering his good eye. At least Rock assumed it was his good eye. He noticed how defined Gogondo's cheek bones appeared, jutting from his face prominently as if to contradict the deep creases running from the inside corner of his eyes to his fantastically wrinkled skin. It was a face of wisdom. It spoke of honor, of knowledge. It exuded trust.

Sunlight spilled into the lodge as Nonie joined them, wearing just a loin cloth and the leather sandals, sitting directly beside his look-a-like. Montu entered as well, shuffling cherry red rocks from the fire outside into the sweat-lodge pit in the center. Once he had brought three rocks from outside, Gogondo reached to his rear, using a long-handled cup that he dipped into a large stone bucket to retrieve a liquid that Rock assumed must be water. He sprinkled the cup of liquid over the hot stones, immediately producing a steaming atmosphere. Rock, at once, found the simple act of breathing to be burdensome, the sudden steam forcing him to slow his inhalation in order to tolerate the temperatures traveling down his nasal passages. Glancing to Jewell, he realized he was not the only one struggling as Jewell breathed in shallow gasps. The entire interior of the sweat-lodge became murky and the friends were unable to see anything with certainty.

Rock was startled when Gogondo, unexpectedly had moved to directly in front of him, pulling on his lower lip, tucking a quarter sized amount of *Gump* between his lip and gum. He sensed the old man doing the same thing to Jewell, and then to Nonie, before sensing that he worked his way back to the blanket he sat upon. Montu, the assistant, then closed the flap over the lodge entrance. The men became mostly deprived of their sense of sight.

They listened closely, but the medicine man once again surprised them by speaking in perfect English. "You must find your path, I will accompany you, but it is for you to find the things of meaning. In short time, each of you will experience a deep resting sleep. It is important for you to remember those things of meaning. When we re-convene at the end of your journey, it is essential that you describe your path of service...and your path of action with one-word descriptions. These descriptions are the intent of what you are about to experience. The one-word description is the key to bringing meaning to this experience. Once spoken...the journey will then have meaning. You may not realize the meaning at that time, but the words for each are the keys to remember, they become the contract that binds you to the experience." Rock could feel himself swaying without consciously trying to do so,' To and FRO', slightly bumping into his friend next to him, who also was now swaying, though not in complete synchronization.

Gogondo spoke softly but with hypnotic synchronicity, dragging each of his ancient words, thick with medicinal magic and his wonderfully melodic tone. Nonie began to talk in a monotone manner. "When I was a boy walking through the woods, my father would share with me to remember the things that should be remembered and forget those things that should be forgotten. My first spiritual travel was at the age of eighteen and on that day...on that journey I was much as you are at this moment. I did not know...what I did not know, so I became frightened. But...I was also brave and while in my dream state, I saw myself walking in the forest. As I walked, I came upon Mr. Fox and he did not speak to me. He only stood and watched me. Then I came upon Mr. Bear and he did not speak either, but he did wave to me. At least I thought he waved to me, but I turned to see he was not waving to me...he was waving to Mr. Horse behind me. I jumped to mount Mr. Horse and began to ride like the wind through the forest. We rode as fast as any man and horse could ride. Until we came upon a light in the woods. It had turned from green, to yellow to red...then Mr. Horse stopped suddenly, and I was tossed from his back. He looked down at me and taught me the lesson as I attempted to regain my breath. *You must slow your life to see the signs...do not be in such a hurry.* My path of action became one of patience and I practice my path even today. You each will find your paths today."

Those were the last words Rock heard before he awoke and stood in a vast field of flowers.

Chapter 7 - Scurry

Clark had to stop his sprinting due to the feeling that his lungs were about to pop. He bent over, placing both hands on his knees. Then his friends caught up to him, gathering around in a huddle and joined him for a shared struggle for breath. "What did we just see?" Clark wheezed uncomfortably. It was a few minutes before either of the other two could reply. "I can't say for sure..." Scooter gave an attempt, "but I know this...we do not need to even think about making another attempt to investigate without Cruz and the others. Alligators...do not act like that." Randall continued to look behind them, absolutely spooked by what he had seen and expecting the dwarves to appear at any moment. "Alligators? Did you not see those nasty midgets coming after us? Hell, there arms were as big around as my legs. I recommend we make haste down this dirt road." The other two didn't need a lot of convincing. Once they gained a manageable level of breathing control, they marched swiftly down the road, each taking small nervous opportunities to glance behind them every so often.

It took them an hour and half, but eventually they made their way to the beach where the other Knights were fishing. Lt. Cruz noticed them first, still quickly walking. "Boy...when you guys go on an excursion, you certainly do not seem to have a great deal of concern for the comfort of your brothers here."

Cruz pointed to the other men, patiently standing behind their fishing poles. "Any luck?" Clark asked, the anxiety from the unusual events of nearly two hours earlier drained by the long walk from the north end of the island. Cruz pointed to the large bucket they had brought. "A couple of sea trout, a nice flounder, but we mostly caught a dozen or so baby hammerhead sharks. Those things are everywhere, we probably let another dozen go back into the ocean." Randall nodded his head with appreciation, asking. "Any of your guys know how to cook these things?" Cruz responded. "I believe one of our guys might just impress you with his skills." He looked over to the Knight nicknamed Einstein, who nodded back to the friends as he jerked the rod in his hands to reel in another small hammerhead. "We probably have plenty for tonight, if you guys want to go ahead and take this bucket to the van." The three newest Knights, eyes widened. "About that...we sort of lost the van." Cruz halted packing up equipment. "What do you mean by lost the van?" He waited for an explanation. Clark shrugged "We were trying to cross a land bridge and it got away from me and spilled into one of the ponds that we were trying to cross." A look of exasperation washed over Cruz's face. He sighed as he signaled for the other men to wrap up their fishing adventures.

The men began another hour-long march back to Hog Hammock and their camping sites, while the three friends shared their harrowing story to the remaining members of their group. Once back at the campground, Lt. Cruz collected his satellite phone and made immediate contact with Ft. Knox to inform them of their situation, while the others prepared for supper, cleaning fish, preparing the fire pit, facilitating pots and pans. The agent named Einstein, who reminded Clark of the actor Gary Busey, with his mussed hair, methodically began preparing the fish supper, barking out commands for ingredients as the others sat in their camping chairs.

Lt. Cruz sat in his folding chair, chatting with Randall about their odd experience during the day, when he received a call on his satellite phone. Scooter watched him intently, Cruz just sat listening for minutes, before he ever had the chance to respond. "I understand. Contact me if anything changes." Cruz scratched his head as he looked over at the other men, unsure just how much he should tell them, sighing, before providing them all an update. "I have requested that Ft. Knox provide us satellite images of the north end of the island. Their scan failed when apparently every image they gathered came back completely distorted. None of the efforts to clear the picture have been successful. Headquarters believe there is some type of shadowing or cloaking mechanism here on the island that prevents them from any type of recon action. Thus...they are incapable of collaborating your story." He looked at the three friends. "We have encountered this type of cloaking efforts before, but it is usually a sophisticated electronic signal that is normally only used by the more tech savvy organizations around the world...the Israeli Defense League, British Intelligence, KGB or I guess now it is called the SVU. Usually those types of groups only have this capability. So, while Ft. Knox continues their research, we have been instructed to continue our vacation as if nothing happened."

Einstein finished preparing the meal and placed plastic plates with different varieties and portions of fish, French fries and coleslaw on the table, encouraging each of the Knights Protego to enjoy the bounty. Once they all had filled their plates, Einstein filled his plate and sat down to enjoy his work. "Oh my god!" Clark clamored at the quality of the man's cooking. The fish had been sautéed in a butter/garlic/wine sauce that rivaled French cooking he once had eaten. Randall and Scooter nodded their agreement at the superiority of the food. Einstein lifted a soda their way to acknowledge the compliments, "It was my mother's recipe from four hundred years ago."

Just as Clark finished his meal, a tow truck crept up the road to the campsite dragging behind it nothing other than Dorothy's van. Moses stepped out of the truck. "You gentlemen's misplace something?" Clark jumped up from his chair and scurried over to hug Moses. The van still draining and soaked, he was shocked that Moses had even known they needed help retrieving it. "We have eyes pretty much everywhere on the island. A few of our local young men, informed me that you could probably use some help up toward the north end.

Surely, Montel warned you about the North End of the island, didn't he?" Clark looked sheepishly to the others. "Umm...we were lost." Moses smiled. "Lost huh? Well, all we can do is warn you, but to give you some advice. The island itself tends to handle any shenanigans that might occur here, best if you keep to this end." After Randall and Scooter dug thru britches to pay Moses a healthy tip for helping them, he turned his tow truck back toward Hog Hammock and puttered on down the road. Scooter jumped inside the van to sit in the soaked seat where he attempted to start it...and remarkably succeeded, prompting an impromptu cheer from the entire group.

Later as sunset approached, the Knights Protego gathered around the camp fire. The three newest members of the KP continued telling their versions of the story for what had happened on the north end of the island. "Ft. Knox has done us a favor. They have approved us to carry our weapons henceforth given the inability to monitor us by satellite." Cruz shared, looking to the more seasoned Knights Protego. "I would add though that we should be discreet with the need to carry them. The islanders have already proved that their version of intelligence on this island is far superior to ours. They may disapprove of our weapons, but I am sure you would agree that most of us have been around long enough to recognize a weapon worthy situation." He made sure the three newest members realized he was talking directly at them. "Until we gain some further clarification from Ft. Knox, I believe it would be wise if we keep our adventuring to Cabretta beach and fishing for the time being." The group all nodded agreement, even the three friends.

During the evening, before they retired to their sleeping bags, plans were made to retrieve more bait in the morning from the Hog Hammock store before they would head out to the ocean and all eight have a tournament with prizes for the most fish caught, and the biggest fish caught. Once agreed, the men turned in for their second evening.

****

Deep inside Rock's dream state, he found himself walking upon a clearing out on the playa, only unlike the playa there were millions and millions of two to four-inch holes in the dried-up lakebed as far as his eyes could see. There didn't appear to be any consistency with respect to size and shape of the holes. Some were oblong, some egg shaped, others perfectly round. The only consistency was the sheer numbers of holes in the ground. He walked over the holes with the sensation that it was unacceptable to look down into the holes, having the feeling that he was only allowed to recognize that they were there. It felt as if he had walked for some unknown length of time, while avoiding stepping in the holes. Abruptly, the scenery transitioned into a deep dark forest. He continued his walk through the forest wondering why it was as dark as it seemed, stopping to look at the surrounding trees. He noticed that they were black...and he wondered if there had been a recent fire that may have discolored them. He reached out to touch the tree to see if it had been burned...but there was no soot or charring. This puzzled him greatly. It appeared all the trees were the same type...all had black bark. Noticing a sapling, a machete suddenly appeared in his dream induced hand, obviously indicating that he was meant to chop a tree down...so he did. He selected a smaller sapling and whacked away at the base and in two whacks he held the sapling in his hand. Holding one end of the sapling he looked at the wood inside the bark, which was also black. Looking back out over the forest he thought how he had never seen a black colored tree before.

Off in the distance, Rock heard slow methodical native American chanting...and the further he walked...the more significant the chanting became, causing the forest images to leave his mind. And then...he came to realize that he was regaining consciousness.

Though it was a major struggle, he attempted to crack one of his eyes open to the darkness that was the sweat lodge and managed to barely see the image of Gogondo, waving sage smoke around the lodge with his feather. Coming out of his dream, he felt as relaxed as he could ever remember. As he further regained his senses, he came to realize that he had slumped over and his head was now resting on Jewell's hip, who had also slumped over toward Nonie next to him. The big man inhaled greatly then slowly opened both eyes fully, which caused Gogondo to stop chanting and shortly thereafter, Montu slung open the animal fur covering over the sweat lodge opening allowing cooler air and a small amount of light back into the hut from the fire outside. Jewell and Nonie stirred around the same time, slowly regaining all their faculties as they sat up, groggily resisting their re-introductions to reality.

"I trust you had good travels?" Gogondo asked them, his voice a muddled masterpiece for what a medicine man should sound like. Montu produced a ladle of water from a bucket he carried into the lodge with him, providing the first dip to Rock who sipped graciously, then the servant ladled another cup over the big man's head, which felt divine in the steamy heated hutch. Montu did the same for Jewell and Nonie, before scurrying over to Dog and providing the canine water in a bowl before slipping outside to take care of other duties. Dog lapped up half the bowl before lying with his head on his paws staring at the three men across the fire from him.

Gogondo spoke again. "On your journey, you should have experienced two different happenings. One of those visages was your path of service...it most likely was the first experience. The second and final happening you encountered was your path of action. For you to solidify those paths...you must speak of these journeys...then name them with one word. Would either of you like to speak first?" Jewell, despite the annoyance of being told the same instructions three times now, appeared on the verge of bursting if he wasn't allowed to tell of his experience. "Dude...I was walking down a path...and like all these dudes were surrounding me...like maybe twenty…or fifty…I mean…I couldn't count them all but the weird thing was…they all had like…wing thingies. All of them…and I couldn't tell if I was safe or not…but…these dudes had wings…" He blubbered.

Gogondo nodded acknowledgement of his story without any change in his own expression. "Continue…" Jewell proceeded. "Well…then things got really weird. I turned to look behind me and like the winged dudes were gone and suddenly the ground in front of me had turned to red dust. It was weird man…this dust. I reached down to pick up a handful of the red dust and it was like bloody baby powder." He grabbed some dirt from the ground surrounding him. "It was not like the playa floor…it was red fine dust…I walked on this dust for what seemed like hours. I was very hot…and very thirsty. Then…a red dust mountain just appeared in front of me from out of nowhere. Oh, and I also saw the silhouette of a dude on a horse on top of that mountain…it looked a lot like Gogondo. Then…next thing I knew I was waking up."

Gogondo admitted, "Indeed, I joined you for a portion of your journey. It was I atop the horse on the red dust mountain. Had you made it to the top, you would have seen a blood red waterfall on the other side. Given that…you must now name your path of service…and your path of action." Jewell looked to Rock and Nonie for assistance. "Ummm….uh…Winged-Men…is my path of Service? And red-dust is my path of action?" Gogondo blew sage smoke heavily in the direction of Jewell, the aroma settling on his skin.

"So, it is!" Gogondo added. "Usually one word is all that is needed...but it matters little."

Gogondo looked to Nonie who was anticipating his turn. "Old Grandfather...my journey started out much the same as his...I saw above me the largest eagle I have ever seen. He flew just above my head and was larger than a buffalo, perhaps twice the size. He did not attempt to harm me, it was as if he was curious about my journey. Then, as I journeyed the playa floor. I came upon a bone shard. I picked up the bone and continued my journey only to find an animal skin. I picked up the animal skin. The bone and the skin did not appear to belong to anyone, and I felt as if I was meant to collect them. Then I noticed a small rock formation surrounding me formed into a circle. It also felt as if I should be in this place...this rock circle. I laid the bone and the skin inside the circle and three seed pods appeared. Then I awoke."

Gogondo measured his words. "I visited you on your journey as well. I too saw the great eagle. And I saw the rock formation, but it was not a small rock formation. In my journey I saw you standing in the center of a very large circle formation." He paused before asking, "Your words?"

Nonie, having had a spiritual journey in the past understood. "Collector for the first journey. Seedpod for the second."
Gogondo wafted sage smoke over Nonie.

Rock then shared his journey dreams. He named his paths, "Holes" and "Black Wood'. He as well, was anointed by sage smoke.

Montu abruptly rushed into the sweat-lodge. "Your presence is requested outside!" Everyone else in the room turned to Gogondo, but Montu looked down to Rock sitting cross-legged on the ground. "Me?" Rock pointed to his chest with a look of confusion toward Jewell and Nonie. They all got to their feet and stiffly made their way toward the hut opening, then beyond to outside, surprised by the fact that it was now dark, an indication they had been in the sweat lodge for many hours. In front of them stood the Knights Protego, no longer concealed to protect Rock. Between his protectors, knelt a man on his hands and knees with blood trickling down his bald-head. "What have we here?" Rock inquired, noticing the Knights were very much on-guard and at high alert with the man in the middle. Capone broke the silence. "We discovered this man following us during our trip to our present location. Over time it became obvious his interest revolved around Rock, such that we decided to intervene. He resisted of course." Capone indicated callously as he pointed to the lump developing on the man's head. Rock looked down at the man. "Is this so?" The bald man hesitantly looked up to Rock. Initially in the darkness and with the light of the fire pit flames flickering over his face, Rock didn't recognize him...until he spoke. "It is so!" He replied, awkwardly attempting to get to his feet, causing the three Knights surrounding him to gather close to his side. Rock stood stunned. "It's you...still here two years later? Or have you been following me the entire time?" Capone seemed surprised by Rock's recognition of the man, but quickly understood the situation he was dealing with. Jewell looked largely confused. "Who is this dude, Rock?"

The descendent of Jesus glared down at his persecutor, the man who had attempted to kill him the last time he visited Burning man. It was Yusef. "You should recognize him, you booted him from the Galleon two years ago, to save my life. He is also the same man that ordered the torture that created the scars on your face and back." Rock anticipating Jewell's reaction, snatched his friend by his long curly hair and pulled him down butt first onto the dusty surface, to prevent his vengeful lunge at the bald man. "Why did you do that? This guy is a murderer." Jewell admonished. Capone uncharacteristically stood back, allowing Rock to handle the situation, confident that he could protect the savior's descendent from his present position regardless of any reaction by Yusef. "So, why are you here? Is your hatred so strong for me that you cannot give up your duty? Or have you perhaps been ordered back to complete what you failed to do last time?"
Yusef looked back at him conflicted, as though he struggled to answer. "I heard a voice!" He offered. Jewell barked back at him. "Yeah...you heard a voice alright, you heard us yelling after you to come back and get your ass kicked." Rock pulled his friend back to his feet and not in a delicate manner, looking directly into Jewell's scarred face.
"That is not who we are...at least...not any longer." The big man turned

back to Yusef. "The things you have done to me and my friends were horrible. What did you expect to accomplish by finding us?" Yusef raised his arms to place both hands on his naked head. "I only want the voice to stop." Yusef indeed seemed upset. "For the last two years, at least ten or twelve times a day this voice comes to me...it is relentless...repetitive. I can find no relief." Capone chimed in with a monotone voice. "What does this voice say to you?"

Yusef looked to Capone with dread. "It says...follow...learn." Capone looked to Rock. "Follow who? Learn from who?" Yusef looked down to the ground. "The voice never says who, so I do not know. I only know these words and I am here because I can only assume that I am being commanded to follow this man." He looked over at Rock, who seemed incredulous with the bald man's claim.

Yusef shifted his attention to Jewell. "You are the man that kicked me from the galleon. In the fall, I fractured most of my ribs. I knew that I was in serious trouble and attempted to find my way back to the Sanhedrin rescue airplane awaiting me out on the desert floor. While struggling my way to the escape vehicle, this voice that I speak of came to me for the first time." There was no deception in Yusef's tone. It was easy to tell he believed what he was saying. "It was so strong that I collapsed. For a few moments I was able to ignore the voice and rose back on to my feet and continued my way back to the Sanhedrin. There they would take care of me. But then, again the voice came...it was so strong...and so bold that I collapsed once again, and I must have

Page | 85

lost consciousness. When I recovered, I watched as your entire group boarded a private jet off in the distance. It was at that moment that somehow I knew I would never be able to return to the Sanhedrin...and as far as I am aware...they have not searched for me."

Yusef seemed to be talking to himself as much as telling his story to the group. "Though I expect none of you to believe me, why would you? Even before I committed those horrible acts two years ago, I felt a force deep inside tugging me away from the Sanhedrin. As a leader, I felt disturbed by what I was being asked to do and at the same time bound by my duty. You must understand, I have been raised to perform these things against you. I have known no other way from the time I was a little boy. So, I followed my duty despite the inner turmoil. After your jet left the desert floor, I eventually made my way to the small town of Gerlach where I gained employment in a gypsum factory, contemplating my next move. The voice would not allow for me to follow but one path. So...I waited, hoping, praying...that someday I would have a chance to do what the voice was instructing me to do." Rock looked over to Capone for any type of guidance but received none.

Gogondo slowly made an appearance from the sweat lodge, with fragile deliberation making his way directly over to the bald man. He reached up to place his wrinkled flat hands on Yusef's face, dropping him to his knees as if struck by lightning. "What is it that you want from these men?" He began to chant rhythmically. Yusef began to bawl! Nonie made his way to Old Grandfathers side to support him while he stood. The medicine man moved his hands to Yusef's cheeks and quickly jerked his face, forcing the bald man to look directly into his milky-white eyes causing Yusef to spew sorrow laden spittle over the ancient one, unable to tear his look from Gogondo' s bizarre eyes.

The Native American slowly turned to the others. "I sense good in this one...untrained...raw goodness. I also sense a dread from having failed...for betraying some unseen code. He is a tortured man. It is this that tortures him. He is lost...and is searching for someone or something to help him." Capone looked at Gogondo impressed...as did Rock. "So...what should we do with him? Let him go?" Gogondo looked back to Rock, then to Capone. "My talent is merely the seeing...and my path of action is of patience. You do not want advice from me...it is not my strength. I believe you know someone who is much wiser...and has many, many more years than I. Seek advice from him."
Rock looked to Capone, who immediately began to contact Paul on his satellite phone. A moment later, Capone whispered into the phone, nodded several times...then walked over to Rock and handed it to him. "Yes?" Rock responded. Paul instructed his student. "You must decide what to do with this man?" Rock breathed deeply...looking off into the distance as the others watched him. "Well...to be honest Paul...his story sounds a lot like yours. All the way down to the fact he worked for the Sanhedrin, just as you did." The Apostle replied. "Fair

enough...instruct Capone to bring this man to me. I am in Athens."
Rock asked, "Athens, Georgia?"

"No...Athens Greece. Capone knows where I will be located. Leave
immediately, I must learn about your dream experience as well." Rock
handed the KP leader the satellite phone and sighed before giving
commands. Gogondo provided other information, "Nonie, is to follow
you, as long as you will have him. This much I saw...on his dream
journey. It is his destiny." Rock looked to Nonie, who proudly took a
position next to his new look-a-like friend Jewell. "Ever been to
Greece?"

Chapter 8 - Blackbeard Island

Scooter and Randall carried most of the bait as they tromped their way down Cabretta beach, while the other KP set up their folding chairs, fishing rods and sun covers to settle in for a day of relaxed fishing. Clark finished hauling his equipment and decided to stretch, snorting in a healthy amount of salt-sea air. He turned his head to look to the north past the channel to Blackbeard Island, doing the same looking south down the length of Sapelo with the realization that there was not another living soul joining the Knights Protego on the Sapelo Beaches today. Thinking it wise to stick with his buddies, he jogged over to Cruz to inform him of their plans before making the short walk over to the channel that flowed between the two islands.

The friends set up their own fishing gear, then plopped down in their folding chairs and waited...and waited...and waited as they watched the Knights Protego haul in fish after fish from their locations further down the beach. "Dang it...we aren't catching anything over here." Clark became extremely impatient, looked over to Randall and Scooter. "When are we going treasure hunting over on Blackbeard Island?" His two friends perked up at the suggestion. "I brought our mini metal detectors." The three men grinned at each other, mischievously. Clark looked back over his shoulder at Lt. Cruz...who was busy reeling in something large.

Randall took the initiative. "Let's go now." They excitedly jumped up from their chairs, kicked off their sand shoes and strapped the metal detectors to their backs, before sprinting for the flow of water between the islands for a swim. Halfway across the channel, Scooter noticed a shark fin only twenty yards to the right of them toward the ocean. It caused him to inadvertently gulp in a mouthful of the salty channel water. He squawked a warning to his friends before becoming deathly still. Seconds later the shark swam beneath him. "Clark that shark has got to be twelve feet long." His friends reacted in a totally different manner, both squealed then swimming like hell toward Blackbeard Island with frantic abandon.

Something bumped against one of Clark's legs, causing him to stop. While he treaded water, he looked around to locate the man-eater. "Guys...I have to admit something...this scares the poop out of me. What were we thinking?" Another bump on his lower leg caused him to nearly elevate out of the water and swim in near hydro plane fashion. Scooter was the first to make it to the other side as he climbed up out of the water and laid on the beach thoroughly exhausted. Moments later Clark and Randall joined him, wallowing up onto shore like walruses, happy to be away from the swimming menace.

Moments later, once they all were able to breathe with some semblance of regularity, they rose to glance back toward Sapelo for a quick check to determine if their panic had been noticed by Cruz or the other KP. With no indication of the KP looking toward them, they turned back toward Blackbeard Island and the trees and scrubby growth on the left, beach and Atlantic Ocean on the right. The men removed their mini-metal detectors from the water bags they were stored in and extended the telescoping handles. They began to waive them around the sandy soil as they walked up the beach toward the trees.

Clark looked back to notice that Lt. Cruz had finally turned his attention back towards them. Clark waved to him that they were okay. "Suck up!" Randall grumbled toward Clark, playfully. The three friends went in different directions to continue their treasure search, each scanning out individual ways way up into the scrubby trees toward the center of the island.

An hour later, they gathered back together to share what they had uncovered. "I found a few musket balls and a belt buckle from at least a hundred years ago." Randall bragged, holding them out in both hands. Clark shared. "I dug up a metal fountain pen and a button." Scooter looked at them both with a wide victory smile. "I found an old watch...it's not working but it must be a least ninety years old." Impressive enough, but he wasn't done. Scooter wow' d his friends, holding up the shank of a long-barreled pistol. "I also found this." He held it up in front of their faces. "The wood is rotted off, but it might have belonged to ole Blackbeard himself." Clark gawked like a school kid at his find. "Well, not what we were hoping for but still kind of cool. Want to keep looking?" Based on their success, Scooter and Randall nodded affirmatively. They separated and once again spread out through the trees.

Clark wandered deeper into the woods than the other two, and fifteen minutes later noticed a small vine engulfed red brick building with a submarine like door attached as an entrance. The top was covered with vegetation and he could see the door was slightly ajar. Randall and Scooter noticed it as well and drifted over toward his location. "What do you think this is?" Randall quizzed as they walked directly up to the structure. Clark shrugged his shoulders, reaching for the door handle to open it. Before he even touched the handle, the door was flung open and a scraggy man with disheveled grey hair knocked Clark to the ground as he exited the brick structure and bolted away from them toward the woods. Scooter and Randall stood stunned as they watched the lanky man dart awkwardly through the forest like his hair was on fire. Scooter scrunched his face and addressed his friends. "Fella's, I hate to tell you this and I certainly could be wrong...but I believe that was our good friend Harry Moorer." The other two looked at him, mouths agape, given credence to his statement being a distinct possibility.

****

Exiting the Acropolis Metro station with a full entourage of protection surrounding him, Rock could sense the aridity in the atmosphere. Capone made sure in a methodical method that he personally placed himself between Rock and the bald man, especially considering that Yusef was untethered. In addition, his men herded Yusef to the front of the descendant of Jesus, where he was fully in the line of sight of each

Page | 92

member of the Knights Protego with the unavoidable exception of the two men on each side paralleling the Sanhedrin assassin.

Rock noticed that there were several dozen additional KP around him attempting to ensure there were no unexpected obstacles for them. He could only assume the dozen extra agents were borrowed from a European branch of the KP. There were also additional agents who had been placed behind them to ensure an unsavory did not sneak up from the rear.

Capone and Rock were to meet the Apostle Paul on a rock formation near the foot of the famous Acropolis. They stopped to discuss their situation with respect to locating Paul and despite all the special efforts of the additional protection provided, a stocky man directly out in front of the group snatched a purse from an elderly woman and sprinted down the street, directly toward Capone. The leader reached inside his jacket for his weapon, expecting the thief to run him over. Unexpectedly, the Greek villain lurched, feet up as the back of his head smacked the stone walkway directly in front of the KP leader and Rock. The thief released the purse, rolling around in stunned misery as two of the agents hoisted him and frog-marched him down an alleyway toward local law enforcement headquarters.

Once the scene calmed down a bit, Rock realized that it had been Yusef who had clotheslined the man trying to escape with the purse. Rock looked to Capone impressed, then they both looked to Yusef with a nod of appreciation. "I was an assassin, not a thief. We were not animals. We served our duty...not evil. The old woman has worked hard for her belongings. She does not deserve to have them ripped from her such as that." He bent over to pick up the purse, dusted it off and made his way to the elderly woman to hand it back to her.

Capone, while not disappointed in Yusef's action, was not completely happy with his agent's inability to control the bald man and he nodded an indication their way to tighten up the formation.

The group continued their walk up the path that led to the Acropolis, the amazing hill featuring the Parthenon with its majestic pillars, along with other temples to one Greek God or another. Yusef, Rock, Jewell and Nonie were all barely walking as they gawked at the majestic and larger than life display of ancient architecture. "How old is that structure?" Rock pointed to the temple on top of the hill, directing his question toward Capone. "Nearly twenty-five hundred years, give or take a decade." Capone then provided more information. "We would usually meet Paul in his office in the National Archaeological Museum just over to our left. Something must specifically be on Paul's mind if he has chosen to meet us on top of the Areopagus." Capone spent the remainder of their walk, attempting to provide insight to Rock about Paul's special link to the past with respect to the rocky outcropping they began to climb, with it being where Paul challenged the people of Athens over two-thousand years ago concerning their "Greek Gods" and their worship of pagan idols.

The area surrounding the Acropolis was a place of immense beauty. Capone explained that he had learned this place was one of the Apostles most favorite. Paul felt his speech to the people of Greece catapulted his newly founded spreading of the teachings of Jesus Christ and the Christian religion into prominence. As they stood on top of an uneven and rocky hill overlooking the more ancient parts of Athens, Capone continued. "This rocky outcropping is called the Areopagus. It was a favored place for Plato and Socrates to teach and ponder theories, as a matter of fact, Socrates was imprisoned for heresy not far from where we are walking now." He pointed through an orderly wooded area of pine and olive trees. "Just through those trees is the cave where Socrates was held."

Rock was awestruck with the thickness of history in this place. His head on a swivel turning to soak in every angle of the area with all its fantastic beauty. Moments later they arrived at the top of a short span of steps before a short climb placed them on the veritable top of the rocks of the Areopagus, where Paul stood standing with hands behind his back looking out over the city of Athens, deep in thought.

Once he noticed them, he sauntered over their way, hugging Rock sincerely before doing the same to Capone. One by one each of the Knights Protego that were close enough to touch without leaving the rocky outcropping, received the same treatment. He then turned to Yusef, who looked at Paul like he was a god. His eyes reached deeply into Yusef's. "The last time we met, you attempted to kill me...but you failed." He looked around at the agents, surrounding him. "Why does this man stand before me?" Rock spoke to explain. "He says he has been tormented by a voice. One that has haunted him from the moment his attempts to assassinate us were thwarted two years ago."

"A voice?" The old man's eyebrows rose. "And what does this voice say to you?" He looked to Yusef for an answer this time. Rock answered instead. "It said to follow him and learn from him?" Yusef blurted out in his pseudo Hebrew accent at nearly the same time as Rock, only with more conviction and meaning. "Follow him...learn from him!" Paul looked to Yusef, then slowly back to Rock as the situation seemed to turn oddly awkward. Rock attempted to add some content. "I would assume the voice is referring to me." Yusef added. "I have not understood what the voices were asking me to do...until now...until I watched you just now from the top of this most fantastic place." At that very moment, Yusef looked like a child. "I was confused when I was taken custody by your companions." Yusef looked down to Rock and Capone. "There was no relief when I was under their control, but just now...walking up this path, and seeing you upon the hill, I now understand. My path is...the same as your path. You were Sanhedrin...and so once was I. But I now understand...I must learn a new way...as did you. The voices were referring to you. I must learn from you and follow you. That is all very clear to me now. If you will allow? I will do whatever it takes. I feel like I must realign myself for the remainder of my life. And you are my vessel to do just that."

Paul went to him and rubbed his head, pulling his face up and looking through the tortured man, pleased with what he was seeing. "Perhaps there is a path for you here...I understand you. I understand the voice you are hearing as I hear it frequently. But...I will warn you this, you must serve penance." He motioned for two of the Knights, tossing them a key. "Take him to Socrates prison for the time being. He has much to learn. Apparently, as do I. Is there anything you would wish to say to those you have harmed?"

Yusef turned, tears of relief in his eyes as he looked back to Jewell, to Rock, to Capone. "There is nothing I can say that will ever repair the damage I have imparted upon you. I can only hide behind my sense of duty at the time, regardless of how ignorant I was." He looked to Jewell's scarred face. "You were collateral damage...an end to a means toward that same duty. I humbly apologize to you for the permanency you suffer." He continued to Capone. "I apologize to the leader of my then enemy. Had I known then what I know now, we would not have been bitter rivals, but collective souls and I hope one day we will share the same cup." With that said, he was led away toward the cave.

Paul crossed his arms and watched him until he was out of sight, then he turned to Rock.

"My good friend...Lets change the mood. I must hear about your spirit dreams. While I had other duties to attend, I can share with you that I had differing dreams of my own. But first...you must introduce me to our new friend?" He looked at Nonie...then to Jewell...then to Nonie.

"That is incredibly fascinating." He waved for Titus to bring him a cotton swab, encouraged Nonie to open his mouth, collected a sample and sent Titus away for genetic evaluation purposes. "My assumption is this was Gogondo's idea?" He insinuated the fact that Nonie had joined the group. Nonie spoke up. "Yes, Old Grandfather believes that I am a part of this spirit journey." Paul smiled. "Excellent, welcome."

The entire group, minus the KP, sat upon the rocks and looked out over the old Athenian Agora marketplace. Rock told of his dream and Jewell shared his before Nonie provided the final piece of the story. The Apostle learned about the holes, the red dust mountain, the black wood forest, the winged soldiers, the great eagle, three seed pods, blood red waterfalls, rock circles. Paul soaked in the entire tale before feeling compelled to reply. "And Gogondo? Rarely does he participate and not add to the story."

"He watched us from above on a large horse. He confirmed parts of our journey and had us put a name to them." Nonie provided.
Paul shook his head, then stood. "We must go back to my office in the Museum. I have something there I need to provide you with." He looked to Capone. "My good friend, if you wouldn't mind giving these young men a tour of the Acropolis. I am sure they are dying for an opportunity to be regular tourist. As for Yusef...he stays with me."

****

The entire group of Knights Protego entered the conference room smiling, following their brief tour of the Acropolis. Paul sat at end of a huge luxurious executive conference table with a dapper stranger who sported a thin well-trimmed beard. "How was your tour?" Paul cheerfully asked. Rock nodded his head appreciatively. "I have to admit...it is pretty dang awe-inspiring to be walking around a structure built some twenty-five-hundred-years ago. This place makes the history of the United States seem sort of insignificant." Rock stopped himself, noticing the man next to Paul, before adding. "I guess you wouldn't understand?" Paul shook his head in mock disappointment. "I'm not quite that old my friend."

Paul looked to his left. "Allow me to introduce someone, for those who do not know him. His name is Dominic." He nodded to the man sitting next to him, dressed in a perfectly fitted and nifty Italian silk suit. Rock noticed the man looking directly at him as if awestruck. He smiled back appreciatively. "It should be obvious to you that Dominic is Knights Protego, but for those that do not know, he is actually one of the original twelve Knights Templar, much like Capone. He is based here in Athens, where he coordinates our affairs in eastern Europe, from this very Museum. He is responsible for ensuring your safe journey from the airport and for the duration of your visit here to Athens. He oversees seven hundred people in this area alone." Looking closer at the man, Rock finally found his crusted cross-emblazoned boots that all KP wore. "It is a pleasure to meet your acquaintance." He spoke directly to the descendent of Jesus. "We are thrilled to have you here in Athens."

Dominic looked at Rock's entourage, obviously familiar with his friend Capone, but unfamiliar with the two men who looked very similar. Rock introduced his friends. "This is Jewell, he is a longtime friend and a new member of the KP." He walked over and placed his hand on Nonie's shoulder. "This is Nonie, a member of the Apache tribe back in the states." Dominic smiled appreciatively at Jewell, rising from his chair to give the bawdy ex-stripper a brotherly bear hug. "Welcome my young friend, it is a considerable pleasure to have you in our proud ranks." He wandered to the front of the table. "I would like for you each to take a seat as we discuss a few items Paul would like for us to cover." Dominic, a little taller than Nonie and Jewell, with a distinct local Mediterranean look, shook Nonie's hand before taking his seat.

Once everyone except the four protective agents at each corner of the room had taken a seat, Paul began the meeting. "The first item to discuss would be the new development with this man Yusef." Paul looked to Capone. "Dominic and his interrogative staff have...shall we say, "interviewed", him for the last hour and a half. He is presently located in the confines of the museum. Dominic's staff believe and have made me feel comfortable that there is a real possibility he is telling the truth. We also feel that he may be a very valuable asset in our efforts to protect our friend Rock Razie, with respect to recent activity within the Sanhedrin. Therefore, our plan going forward will rotate around submitting him to a unique set of physiological and psychological vetting techniques, where we will collect data as to whether he could be trusted inside of our organization...and certainly most importantly if he could be trusted around Rock. Subsequently, with respective positive results, we would then place him in specialized training. Presently, he appears to be an advanced counter-intelligence trained individual and would be a high value tool within our organization." Dominic nodded his agreement. "Very well!" Paul finalized the plans with the nod of his head.

"The next agenda item is the collective spirit journeys of our young friends." The group spent the next fifteen minutes recanting their 'Drum' induced dreams.

Dominic stood, peacocking his dashing dark silver suit, typical of an Italian socialite as he addressed the crowd. "We have used Gogondo many times in the past. His spiritual guidance for situations, where we have previously struggled with ideas, has provided positive results. The Apostle informs me that our treasurer, Mr. Moorer, has been missing for a time now. We believe these journeys provide clues to help us investigate his disappearance, with the following disclaimer." Dominic glanced at Paul, skepticism framed upon his face. "Gogondo's methods and these experiences tend to be delivered in the form of riddles. From what we have heard just now, and this is just my opinion, I believe the most significant item in your dream state is that of the red dust and Paul and I have discussed this issue. This may be our starting point." He motioned to an agent at the door entrance, jotted a note on a pad and handed it to him, who quickly exited the conference room.

Two of Dominic's men jostled Yusef into the conference room, his hands bound in front of him by thick nylon straps. He was invited to sit on an exterior chair away from Rock. "We will continue to evaluate the remaining elements of what we have learned today from your spirit adventures." He looked to Rock. "The holes and the seed pods, the rock formations are all curious elements that we have not previously experienced. However, the winged men and giant eagles are elements that we have had to follow up on in the past." Dominic ducked his head to whisper a brief private discussion with Paul before making closing comments. "Rock, we would request that you travel to Naples Italy to meet with a contact that may provide clues in deciphering your spirit journeys."

Rock smiled at Jewell, greatly appreciating the opportunity to travel. The agent Dominic had sent away, returned and handed the Italian leader a note, which he in turn handed to Rock. "This is your contact, He is known as the Vicar of Duomo di San Gennaro. His name is Cossimo Baboccio da Piperno. I believe he will prove most helpful." Paul smiled and stood, pointing to the door for Rock and his friends. Yusef spoke un-expectantly. "Not that I would expect you to believe me, but...the Sanhedrin do not typically perform functions in Naples. The local mafia tend to be powerful and erratic, but very controlling. Sanhedrin agents typically find it extremely difficult to operate with any measure of success." Dominic and Paul each nodded with pleasure. Paul responded. "Thank you Yusef, that is very useful information. Rock...you have been under much stress lately. I want you to relax and tour Mount Vesuvius and Pompei. These are places of both mystery and history that you should enjoy seeing." With that the meeting disbanded and Capone ushered them out of the conference room.

Chapter 9- Island Hop

      With the wild man running frantically off through the moss-covered live oaks and surrounded by a fair number of sable palms, the dumbfounded threesome stood not knowing what they should do themselves. The stood stunned and silent, trying to determine just exactly what it was they had just experienced. "Tell me if I am crazy...but didn't that look a whole lot like Harry, didn't it?" Scooter expressed his observation. Clark carefully reached to open the heavy iron door, halfway expecting something else to escape. He pulled with both hands as all three men peered inside the dank compartment. What they saw was tattered bedding, a makeshift mattress of sticks, candles, other inane objects...and a book.

"Is it possible he was living in here?" Randall reasoned out loud. Scooter walked around the entire structure to check it out. "This looks like it was actually an old crematory, a brick oven of sorts, used to dispose of human bodies or quarantined and infected birds or something at one time or another through history." Randall added. "Mercy...what in the world do you think is going on here?" The men chattered amongst themselves, before deciding it was their responsibility to find out. So, they trod on through the fauna to follow in the same direction as the man that they tentatively assumed was possibly their confused friend.

Traveling in a northward direction, they eventually discovered an old road bed covered with sable palms with sword-like green plumage pointing inward toward the road, as if warning the friends not to stumble from their narrow path unless they wanted to feel the sting of mother nature. The entire area was inundated with low hanging live oak limbs that hosted eerie looking moss. Randall said it first, "That Spanish Moss gives me the creeps." Scooter interrupted him, "Technically, that isn't Spanish Moss, its Ball Moss. See how its shaped in a wad." Clark and Randall stopped and stared at their friend? "You are absolutely a genius on 'who gives a shit' topics. Why would you even know that, Scooter?" Randall challenged him, anxiety and emotions still on edge from the unexpected appearance of the scraggy man from inside the brick dwelling. "Well, when Clark said we were coming here, I just thought it would be a good idea to study up on everything we might encounter on the island. " Clark, clearly amazed at his odd friend. "Stop...stop...we don't want to hear another word about this moss." Scooter was incapable of stopping though. "It is not like the moss is killing the trees. It picks..." Randall fired back..."One more word and I swear that I am going to smack you." Clark and Randall plodded ahead, continuing their way up the trail. Scooter shrugged at their impatience, then simply fell in behind them.

Up ahead, Scooter's usually keen eyesight, detected some movement. He stopped to discern that it was the gangly odd-acting man scurrying across the road, toward the west. "Harry!" Clark saw him as well, so he yelled. The man appeared oblivious to them, so they jogged after him until they reached a spot where he had bolted into the thick underbrush. Able to detect the faintest trace of a path, they darted into the forested area after him. A few minutes into the thicket, Randall looked at his arms and noticed that they were bleeding from being sliced by the sharp tipped palm tree blades.

Several more minutes passed before they reached a clearing just wide enough to allow them a clear view of what looked like their good friend Harry Moorer paddling a primitive looking wooden canoe. "Is that thing carved out of a tree trunk?" Clark asked. They watched the wild man make progress with help from the high tide pushing across the salt marsh away from Blackbeard island, toward Sapelo. Which was perhaps fifty yards on the other side. He seemed to be looking for something specific up and down the banks on the other side.

Scooter's eagle eyes spotted a second canoe jutting out into the channel from the thickly forested Blackbeard island bank. The trio darted toward their discovery, jogging clumsily along the edge of the marsh until they reached the canoe, tugging mightily to slide the primitive mode of transport out into the channel. Once they floated the canoe and awkwardly climbed inside, they discovered it only had one paddle available. Clark seized it, tossing two large sticks he had found to his companions. As they slowly and meticulously paddle/poled their way down the channel to where they had last scene Harry, they became extremely unsettled with the sheer number of alligators lurking in the surrounding water. "There must be a hundred of them!" Scooter sounded worried and that was before he noticed several shark fins along the same water trails with the alligators.

Once they located Harry's canoe abandoned on the banks of Sapelo, they grounded their rustic canoe just beside his, quickly pulling their canoe out of the water, before giving chase to their tattered and obviously confused friend, darting in and out of trees without the advantage of an established road bed to guide them. They struggled to keep a constant view of their friend, who was running at a surprisingly frantic pace still fifty yards ahead of them. His once white shirt now turned gray flapped in the aftermath of his fleeing, but minutes later they sensed that they were indeed gaining on him...gradually. Thirty yards...thirty seconds later, twenty yards. Suddenly, their wild looking friend did the unexpected and turned to square up to them, bending over slightly at the waist, opening his mouth as wide as he could and yelled. "GO AWAYYYYYYYY!"

The friends stopped in their tracks, stunned and confused by his odd behavior. Then they heard an unusual humming noise develop to their left. A monstrous black pulsating cloud appeared from the forest floor and meandered its way toward them. They squinted as they watched helplessly while the cloud overtook and enveloped them. Clark was the first to be swallowed by the black cloud. He went wild waving at the mosquitoes as they coated his arms first, then his face, lips...every square inch of his skin was being covered by mosquitoes. They even invaded the inside of his mouth, of his nose...attempting to land on his moist eyeballs. He couldn't help but panic as the incessant buzzing noise nearly drove the grown man insane when they attacked the inside portions of his ears. In a massive panic he turned to run away, but sprinted face first into a large live-oak tree limb that was horizontal to the forest floor and fell back, striking the ground like a sack of potatoes, knocked unconscious by the unforgiving tree.

Scooter, experiencing the same discomfort reacted differently. He dropped to the ground, equally overpowered by the pesky mass of black insects. But with his panic-driven haste, he franticly covered himself with clumps of the ball moss and half decomposed palm fronds and other debris lying along the island floor next to him.

Randall simply turned and sprinted away and out of the cloud, running like what little was left of his sparse hair was on fire. He darted from side to side...in a pattern learned at police academy many years back, trying desperately to escape the miniscule blood suckers, until he could reach Blackbeard's Creek...where he promptly dove head first into the water between the two rustic canoes to escape his tormentors.

Scooter waited for fifteen minutes but it seemed like hours, before he was aware that the mosquitoes had completely disappeared...just as his erratic friend Harry had done. He slowly and hesitantly uncovered himself, his body a massive whelp of bite marks covering all his exposed skin and even portions of his skin covered with cloth. The bites didn't itch as much as they ached from the amount of biting that had occurred, his skin pocked and splotchy all over. He sat up and ran his hand over his bumpy bitten face, then looked around. He searched to find Clark laying face up next to the tree with a wicked bluish knot on his forehead, along with similar massive amounts of mosquito pocks all over his body. Scooter dragged his own aching body over to the tree, to help Clark sit up, groaning with his friend as he coaxed him to a more conscious state. "What happened?" Clark slurred. Scooter held out his arms to show the damage done by the mosquitos, which prompted Clark to remember the attack as he instinctively swatted all around for the now dispersed cloud of pesky insects.

"Where is Randall?" He asked once he realized the ordeal was over. Scooter looked around the forest floor, while he tugged on Clark to pull him to his feet. "Last I saw, he made a sprint back toward the canoe." They wandered back to the spot where they had landed on the Sapelo side bank, noticing Randall's metal detector at the creek bed. "Did he shuck that when we got out of the canoe...or?" He looked at the channel where alligators swam menacingly around the area at the back of the canoe. Clark sat heavily and asked. "Tell me he didn't jump into that water?" Scooter shook his head sheepishly worried, unable to disarm the notion his friend might have done something so drastic and certainly it appeared he had done so. They attempted to re-enter the canoe and walk back to the rear to search for their friend, but an enormous alligator bumped the back of the boat, jarring it almost over on its side. They quickly changed their minds. "What are we supposed to do?" Clark looked to Scooter who made his feelings perfectly clear. "I am not getting back in the canoe." Realizing conditions had changed, they stood ten feet from the edge of the channel and looked intently for any sign that their friend was safe. After twenty minutes of nothing more than dread, they decided to walk back to the Cabretta Beach area where Cruz and the other KP were located figuring perhaps they were wrong, and Randall had simply run away toward the same.

Two hours later, they staggered back onto the beach exhausted for the second day in a row. The other four agents ran to assist them as they crumbled onto the sand before the concerned agents. "Where is your friend?" Einstein asked. Once Clark regained enough energy, he explained what had happened, sharing the story, about Harry, about the chase, the canoe, the mosquitoes and finally about Randall possibly diving into the water to rid himself of the pests. Lt. Cruz rubbed the three-day bearded stubble on his face, before reaching into his communication pouch for the satellite phone. He contacted Ft. Knox, again...for the second day in a row.

****

Capone, half expecting Rock's wife, Raw-knee to call as she did about this time most days, signaled for his men to take a break once he saw Rock position his cell phone to his ear. surprised the man he had responsibility for guarding had reception this far up the trail that led to the summit of Mount Vesuvius.

"Hey babe…how are you and the rest of your tribe doing today? Your boisterous son sure misses you greatly." Raw-knee lovingly chided her husband, who perpetually felt guilty for not being around them more. He shared the events of the past few days, telling her about the spirit travels, the trip to Athens and apologized for not making a point of contacting her sooner. "We have just been so focused on this adventure and about what we have dreamed, ahh...I don't guess that is a good excuse though. How is Rocco?" Referring to the name they had given their son, bypassing the Apache tradition of naming him after the first thing she saw following his birth. Especially considering it was Rock's teary-eyed face that had dominated her vision following the son's arrival.

She playfully responded. "Apparently, our son is full of his father's mischievousness and destined to spend a life of punishment handed out by his mother. Oh, hey, speaking of dreams, I need to share mine from last night with you. I dreamed that you were in the center of a big temple with some type of huge columns and you were in distress. You or someone was being held down by something...or someone. And...there were these black trees all around you." Rock laughed at her. "Funny you should mention that, considering we were just at the Parthenon, at the Acropolis. Capone gave us a tour. It was pretty awesome, but nobody held me down there." She remained silent for a second. "No, it wasn't the Acropolis. It seemed like it was more rounded...like...like...Stonehenge. It was shorter with much thicker columns. But I clearly remember the black trees. Those were odd." Capone nudged Rock for him to continue his hike to the top of the volcano. He finished his call, promising to call her soon. "Gotta run babe, my lungs are about to pop hiking up this trail on the side of Mt. Vesuvius. Give my boy a hug for me."

Four lung purging breaks later, they made it to the top, looking out over the Tyrrhenian Sea toward the Mediterranean. Once he got into position, to look down inside the volcano, there were several steam vents to indicate just how active and live the volcano was. Jewell was exhausted and while in decent shape, his lungs had never made a two-thousand-foot ascension in that short of a period before. He leaned over inside the mouth of the Volcano. "What makes this so special? It's a hole in the top of a mountain?" Capone told him the story about how the volcanic eruption that had destroyed the Roman city of Pompeii around eighty A.D. and described how many people in the area died. His bawdy friend queried. "No chance this thing could blow with us up here on it?" Rock shrugged his shoulders. "It is a very seismically active area."

A few hours later they toured Pompeii. Nonie asked the most questions amongst the group, fascinated by the culture and how they had lived those many years ago. The entire group became somber once they had an opportunity to see the plaster casts of some of the people who refused to flee the mighty eruption and whose bodies had been trapped inside the mud and ash from the volcano, producing voids in the compacted ash as the bodies had decomposed. These odd cavities allowed paleontologist to fill them with plaster and create ghostly replications of those that had perished...preserved in the positions they met the volcanic dust. The bodies had been consumed, but they were brought back in the immortal form of morbid statues, preserved forever. "I can feel their souls still screaming through all of the mayhem of the eruption." Nonie spoke his sorrow. Rock looked up to Vesuvius and shook his head. "They had to have seen it coming...and couldn't do anything about it, what a shame!" He stared down at the sculpture of a three-year-old, perfectly formed as it slept and the volcanic ash that roasted him alive before preserving his remains for eternity.

Once the Pompeii tour was finished, Rock and his entourage traveled back to Naples where they were inundated by traffic as they tried to locate a place to try pizza in the place legend suggested pizza was invented. Rock noticed that every car parked along the side of the road had their sideview mirrors folded in to prevent travelers from knocking them off. The driving culture was unlike anything he knew of in the United States. Automobiles were inches from crashing into the side of the KP van. The people of Naples were driving Capone nuts with their miniscule proximities...that and the sheer volume of traffic and the apparent lack of respect for other driver's personal space. Even Jewell was frazzled, despite being conditioned to accept impolite driving from his days in New York City.

Eventually, they made it to an area where they could exit the van and found themselves a cozy restaurant inside one of the quiet corridor's that Capone had visited before. Against Capone's recommendations, Rock decided he wanted to sit outside on the streets using all four of the restaurant's exterior tables. "There is no way this place can make a pizza better than New York City!" Jewell proclaimed, sounding entirely defensive, Capone took the liberty of ordering a Margherita pizza and a glass of wine with an Italian salad for everyone in the entire group. He was slightly edgy in that he was allowing his men to relax a little bit while Dominic's team of the Knights Protego took up the watch for them. The white wine arrived first, a wonderful local brand and the entire group was delighted by the taste. But...then the pizza hit the small three-person tables and they dug in excitedly. Jewell's eyes rolled back in his head. "Oh, my Gawd! This is unbelievable." Capone just smiled and nodded at him as he snuck a bite or two, while he continued to monitor the street for any type of unusual activity. He noticed that Dominic had stationed agents at each corner and they in turn scanned up each ten or twenty story building lining the streets of Naples. Just as he would have done.

He received an unexpected text on his smart phone. "Cossimo says he cannot meet us until six p.m. this evening. Looks like we are going to have to find something to occupy our time." Jewell tugged a tourist pamphlet from his back pocket. "I saw this cool pamphlet about some sort of Under City Catacomb tour close to where we are now. Apparently, the people of Naples used to escape down inside them during WW2 when the bombing occurred."

Capone looked to Rock and Nonie. Each shrugged, appearing to be conducive to that event. He notified Dominic of his intentions to allow him time to set up a protective cover to get them to the area. Capone paid for their food and began to make his way down the inviting streets of Naples. Before they left, Jewell hastily ordered a to-go cup of the Pizza sauce. Rock and Capone looked at him with amusement. "What? This stuff rocks man. It is what legends are made of...I am going to sip this gravy while we walk around." They shook their heads with amazement before heading toward the Catacombs.

As normal, Capone made sure he positioned himself just ahead of Rock, nervously eyeing balconies where women, men and children watched the group as they clamored up the stone roadway toward the church. Seemingly from nowhere, Dominic suddenly appeared with his silver suit and dapper look, signaling for Capone to join him in a private conversation. Rock stood looking around. He suddenly became very aware of the numerous eyes of the people on the street, that were watching. Jewell wandered over to whisper. "Are you noticing the amount of attention we are collecting?" Rock nodded to affirm. Nonie eased over to add. "My people believe that fear is the venom of a predator's sting and it causes the prey to become unfocused on survival. We should take action to avoid their gaze."

Dominic and Capone huddled with the others. Dominic spoke to them in hushed tones. "It has become very apparent that we have attracted the attention of the local mafia, the *Camorra*. They are not overly sophisticated, but they have the largest group of watchers of any mafia group in the world. If they have noticed us, they will attempt to intercede at some point and determine our intentions. It would be wise if perhaps we take a few evasive moves." He nodded his head toward three different windows where men stood solemnly...watching. "Up ahead is the entrance to the underground Catacomb tour, it is smart for us to kill some time and leave these streets. We will be much safer under the street, at least until the Vicar unburdens himself."

Capone immediately signaled the group to follow him thirty meters up an enclosed street where the right side opened into a courtyard. There a small fountain stood with a placard on the sidewalk for "Catacomb tours". He engaged a young woman named "Gina" and was told that a new tour would begin in seven minutes or when twenty people had purchased tickets. Dominic didn't hesitate, he paid for a private tour for his entire group. Gina seemed thrilled when he tipped her more than she had made all day and as soon as a church tower bell rang to indicate it was four p.m., she began the tour.

Initially, she took them to the souvenir shop to discuss articles created either from the catacombs or from the surrounding area. She then led the group down a hidden corridor which opened into a very narrow but well-lit stairway carved from stone with a metal railing that dropped downward a hundred and fifty feet but appeared as if it traveled forever. The entire crowd descended while Gina spoke about the history of the catacombs, describing how the early Greeks in the fourth century B.C. had built them and how subsequently the Romans conquered the area and built organized aqueducts that provided water for many centuries for the Neapolitans. Once at the bottom of the staircase, they were able to stand upright for most of the tour through craggy tunnels, dank and withholding of light until eventually they arrived at a huge opening that was once a subterranean theatre where the Roman emperor Nero had performed. The theatre held an audience of potentially thousands for any play that might be occurring in Roman empire days. The men found out it was rumored Nero had a private dressing room built here.

Dominic, a compulsive micro manager as were most of the Knights Protego leaders, seemed to be positioning security personnel inside the tunnel system. His men invisible to Gina who was only slightly aware of the men that he had paid to take the tour. The group passed through tunnels that were nearly too small for some of the larger men like Rock and Capone, to keep from struggling to fit through comfortably.

As they exited one of the tighter crawl spaces into a wide expansive area, Gina began to discuss an experimental challenge for the people of Naples, , which were described as an experimental challenge to grow various species of plants using the artificial light source down in the catacombs. These plants would be grown without the slightest trace of pollution. The experiment was called the world's first Hypogeum Gardens.

As she spoke to the group, Nonie noticed a shadow moving back inside the opening for one of the adjoining caves. He wandered over to investigate, creeping low to enter a barely three-foot tall crawlspace that opened into another huge cavernous room....where all he could see were holes in the wall everywhere. A fragile ninety plus year old man appeared to be slowly but diligently digging into the sidewall of the room with a small three-pronged digging tool. Nonie ducked back into the tiny crawlspace from where he had come, to where his group were standing. He ambled over to Rock. "I believe you must see something." Rock looked down at him, wondering whether he should be suddenly concerned, but followed Nonie to the opening. He ducked down to crawl on hands and knees, ensuring that he made Nonie aware that he was not a fan of the tight constraints of the small entrance. Regardless, he wiggled his way into the next cavern behind Nonie. Capone and Dominic noticed Rock crawling away, they rushed over to investigate with Dominic becoming flustered, realizing he had not anticipated such a move from Rock such that he had not positioned any of his men to investigate this portion of the tunnel system.

Because of that he dropped to the floor in his silver suit and quickly joined Rock as he slithered into the hole. The remaining members of the group and Gina did the same. Once inside, they all watched as an old man in tattered clothing finished digging one of the thousands of holes in the sidewall of the large cavern. Rock spoke softly to the man, his hunched over elderly shoulders turned facing away from him. "Why do you dig the holes?" The old man, while slight of hearing was unaware that he had company. He stumbled slightly, shocked by the sudden appearance of the group, having been so focused on his task, not to notice them arrive. "I am so sorry!" Rock added, while Jewell and Nonie rushed over to prevent the old man from falling. "*Mi hai spaventato*!" He rasped. Dominic translated for the others. "You scared him!"

Rock looked to Dominic. "Ask him why he is digging?" Dominic asked. "*Perche stai scavando*?" The old man explained to Dominic as Jewell and Nonie continued to support him. He shared that he had been searching for a locket that he had given his wife during World War 2. He explained how, as young lovers they, like most of the other Neapolitans, were forced to enter the catacombs in order to escape Allied bombing raids. It was during one of those periods that he proposed to her and promised his undying love for the rest of their lives. He had given her a locket to seal the love they shared. While they were forced to take shelter during the air raids, she kept it in a hole in the side of the cavern to prevent the Nazi's from taking it from her and to hide it from her father, who would have been furious to learn she had a husband. He shared that, two months later she was killed when a bomb was dropped directly into the cavern and caused a collapse that buried all the holes where locals stashed their belongings. He claimed that as she lay dying in this very cavern, she asked him if he would find her locket and place it on her grave. She said it would give her comfort and she would never regret having loved him.

The old man wept even today as he told the story. Once he calmed, he spoke of spending nearly seventy years searching for the lost locket. He had never remarried, never experienced any other love. He admitted to being completely and wholeheartedly committed to locating the locket. "Le ho Promesso!" He whispered at the end of his explanation. Gina interpreted this for the group with tears welling in her eyes. "He promised her!" Rock had to choke back a tear of his own as he looked to Jewell, tears streaming down his face, obviously moved by the Italian man's dedication to one woman, something he had never been able to do and only now could even begin to understand.

Help him! A voice boomed deep inside of Rock's head. He closed his eyes and located the *INEFFABLE NAME*, something he had learned to do with relative comfort over the last two years. He whispered to himself, *Help him.* He then opened his eyes, walked to one of the tens of thousands of holes about three feet from the floor and not more than twenty feet from where the old man had been presently digging. He reached inside as far back into the hole as he possibly could. His longer than normal arms obviously able to reach farther than the old mans as he dug for a few seconds before locating the chain of the locket, pulling it out, dusting if off with his shirt. He walked over to hand it to the old man. The entire group inside the cavern gasped, including Capone and Dominic. *"Mi Chiamo Discenzo Umberto! Grazie! Posso solo supporre che tu sia stato inviator da Dio!"* The old man bawled with appreciation. Gina continued to stand with her eyes watering. She blubbered out. "He said, he could only assume you were sent to him by God!" Jewell finally recovered enough to speak. "Dude, you just fulfilled your spirit act of service...the holes. Remember the holes!" Rock nodded and smiled with sudden recognition of that fact.

Once the old man had an opportunity to collect himself, he stood and proudly straightened his back, sauntered over to Rock and handed him his three-prong digging tool as a trophy. Rock smiled widely and attempted to find somewhere to place the awkward tool. The inadequacy of his pockets prompted Nonie to take the tool from him and place it in his large rawhide pouch that hung at his hip with the strap draped around his neck. "Thank you!" It was all Rock could say to the fragile old man, who reached up on his tip toes to kiss Rock on each cheek, then turned away and awkwardly scurried to the small cavity to exit the cavern...and the catacombs, with all intent on fulfilling his promise to his lost love.

Dominic stared at Rock with reverence, having been informed but not fully convinced that he was in control of the INEFFABLE NAME, until that moment. *"Ho visto abbastanza miracoli per un giorno"* Dominic forgot most of his group did not speak Italian. "It means I have seen enough miracles for one day. Shall we visit Cossimo?"

A brief discussion with Gina led Capone to suggest they make their way through the catacombs and exit up near the Cathedral of San Genaro on Via Duomo, the city street directly in front of the entrance to the Cathedral where they would meet Cossimo, the man Paul had recommended. Gina led them through the necessary catacomb branches until they reached a stairway that they climbed to find a thirty-foot ladder with a panel at the top. Gina instructed Capone to activate a lever at the top of the ladder and the panel would move for them to exit. Capone climbed the ladder, rotated the lever, watched the panel open into a warm wooded and vanilla scented antique bedroom. The bed rotated to allow them access from a hidden access portal, into and out of the tunnel. He climbed out, then positioned himself to assist the others as they exited into the bedroom. "Whoa! This is nice." Jewell seemed impressed. Gina explained that the bedroom was San Gennaro's bed in the past, then she slipped back down the ladder to return to her business of escorting tourist through the catacombs.

Before the crew closed the hatch, Dominic whispered direction to unseen guards below to ensure the group were not followed, then positioned the bed over the trap door.

They exited the room and made their way down to the street and maneuvered to directly in front of the magnificent Neo-Gothic shaped entrance to the Duomo di San Gennaro with its straight lines and jutting angles at the top. They proceeded to the massive brown double doors, contrasting the grayish-white granite material for the façade.

Once inside Jewell could not contain a well-earned "WHOA!" His voice echoed thru the cathedral, prompting him to shush himself. Dominic chuckled, "It is appropriate that you lower your voice, however, we are the only individuals in the cathedral at this time. Cossimo will meet us momentarily." Capone's KP and Jewell, each made the sign of the cross before they wandered around the cathedral soaking in its staggering beauty. The beautiful lit archways lining each side of the cathedral hid several ornately decorated naves, a ceiling filled with spectacular art, funneling the eyes to the other end of the cathedral where a statue of Saint Januarius on the High Altar of the chapel sat amid gold, silver and gems from the thirteen-hundreds. Nonie, usually unimpressed with the finer things of life, was awestruck at the beauty of the place as he gawked at the garish artistry and lifelike busts of cherished Italian religious figures.

Dominic wandered to the front of the Royal Chapel of the Treasure of San Gennaro to see if he could locate the Vicar, while Rock motioned Capone over to ask him a question. "We never talked about it...but why are we actually here?" Capone nodded his head toward Dominic at the other end of the church. "This chapel is famous for one thing.

There is a mystery concerning a popular religious figure in Naples many years ago, named Januarius. He was a bishop here around the year three-hundred A.D. and he was decapitated because he refused to renounce his Christian faith in another city. A woman by the name of Eusebia, with help from a couple of priests, supposedly collected two vials of his blood along with his skull and bones and brought them back to Naples where they lay today in the crypt directly below where we stand now. The enigma is that the containers of blood remain here and on certain occasions this blood that is over seventeen hundred years old and has turned to dust...turns back to liquid." Rock pondered the story. "And Paul believes there is a connection with Jewell's spirit dream about red dust and the waterfall?" Capone nodded his head, appreciating Rock's summation. "Dominic, Paul, I and a few other original Knights believe they are both somehow tied together, yes! The people here in Naples sincerely believe the liquification signifies good fortune for the locals. The blood is contained in two ampules inside round white-gold host carriers with a cross topped crown and a handle on the bottom. On specific dates and a few special other odd times, the blood turns from a dried powder to liquid. This happens sometimes three times a year and is the event we are here to discuss with the Vicar." They sauntered up towards the front of the church past a double row of fifty or so twelve-foot-wide warm wooded church pews for parishioners to worship from. Jewell gawked the entire way, not only amazed at the amount of detail each individual column contained, but also the ceiling that was covered with intricate religious imagery. It seemed that every fifty-feet, there was another nave where yet another cathedral was embedded, one of which had twenty-foot tall bronze gates.

In every direction that the men turned they viewed yet another sculpture, painting or ceiling painting that rivaled any of the world's finest of art. At the very front behind the altar was an enormous statue of Januarius appearing to approve of their presence while surrounded with fifteen or twenty angels. Jewell whispered to himself. "Winged Men", referring to his spirit-dream path of service.

Rock noticed Dominic, standing at the top of a rose and gold colored age-tested marble staircase descending from the main cathedral altar. He was speaking with a man dressed completely in white. The holy man watched Rock as he walked up the steps to the front of the altar and proceeded with Dominic to where Rock stood. "Rock...allow me to introduce Cossimo Baboccio da Piperno, he is the Vicar of the Cathedral of San Gennaro. We have detailed to him your abilities with respect to your special religious power and have asked that he show you the dried blood of the Patron Saint of this cathedral. He has agreed in principal but insists that he be allowed to perform a questioning of your sincerity." Rock smiled, slightly unnerved by the request from the holy man. "Of course, what questions do you have?" The Vicar with his stereotypical rutted Italian face, studied the big man. Rock could tell that he took his responsibilities to the church extremely serious.

Cossimo breathed in deeply. "I will allow this solely out of respect to Paul and Dominic. The handling of the ampules containing the blood of San Gennaro is usually relegated to that strict structure of the chain of command inside the Catholic deices. Look me in the eyes and tell me that you mean absolutely no harm to our treasures or anything else you are about to see here this evening." Rock stared back, a gentle smile lighting his face. "I mean you, nor your glorious treasures any type of harm." Again, the Vicar breathed in deeply. He pointed toward a nave they had already passed, the one with the huge twenty-foot-tall bronze gates. The entire group retreated toward those gates. "This is the Royal Chapel of the treasure of San Gennaro. Within you will see one of the most magnificent collection of statues, busts, wall and ceiling art, crowns, jewels and other treasures, gathered on earth. To the Catholic church this treasure is unparalleled with the notable exception of the Vatican treasury itself." He marched to the gates and looked around at the crowd. "The church would appreciate it if you touch nothing and I trust Dominic and Capone will ensure there is no harm done on your part." The two original Knight's Protego nodded their concurrence. Rock couldn't help but notice just how well-spoken the Vicar was, with barely a trace of Italian accent in his voice. He inserted a large metal key into the bronze gates, quickly stepping to the side to activate a digital code on a keypad located to the right of the gates. Nonie stood in complete amazement as the gate opened slowly by itself. Once the gates retreated, Cossimo walked the remaining hundred feet into the chapel toward the altar. Lights in the chapel automatically illuminated the magnificent surroundings. Life sized statues were elevated up around the exterior of the altar made of bronze. Just below most of the sculptures were silver reliquary busts of past Bishops and other significant employees of the holy church. Stucco's, frescos and paintings lined the walls and ceiling. "This is easily the most beautiful place I have ever seen in my entire life!" Claimed Jewell. Nonie, overwhelmed, couldn't even begin verbalizing his feelings.

Cossimo, lifted a small golden theatre rope barrier and proceeded to climb up onto the altar, ducking down to unlock an apula that looked like a silver bust of San Gennaro, where he reached inside to produce a round gold and silver item containing a vial filled with a reddish/black looking dust. "This is the blood of Saint Januarius. Three distinct times a year in ceremonial form this blood enters a liquid state. It is this miracle that is celebrated by the people here in Naples. On numerous occasions when this miracle has failed to occur, a terrible blight would come to the Neapolitans that live in the area. It is known as the miracle of San Gennaro."

Dominic added. "Rock, we ask for you to hold the ampule." The big man strode to the altar alongside Cossimo and took the religious phial into his hand. The blood immediately liquified. At once, a deep dirty rumbling ensued, and the entire cathedral shook as Rock held onto the artifact to ensure he didn't drop it. Cossimo immediately dropped to his knees in prayer. Capone and Dominic both looked at Rock with wide-eyes, while Jewell and Nonie simply looked around trying to figure out what exactly was happening. Capone and Dominic each whispered into their ear-pieces, attempting to collect intel. Cossimo stood to collect the ampule from Rock and placed it back into the silver bust from where he had retrieved it. He motioned for Rock to leave the altar and immediately signaled for Dominic and Capone to a side conversation in one of the alcoves of the Chapel.

The two Knights shook their heads at the information given. Cossimo finally broke the silence. "For many centuries the men who have guarded this cathedral have kept the traditions of the blood of Gennaro. But there has always been withheld a secret. Mr. Razie, if you will follow me, I think it is time to share that secret with you."

He locked the Chapel doors after they closed, before walking back to the Main chapel and led the entire group down into the *Cripta di S. Gennaro.* Cossimo became very serious as he walked past a marble statue of a priest kneeling toward a small red urn inside an enclosure. The urn was elevated over the floor with an iron gate preventing the public from accessing. Inside the enclosure, outlined in sturdy marble columns was a red carpet that rose up the four steps to the platform where the urn was mounted along with a bust of San Genarro protectively watching over the urn filled with his own bones. To the left of the urn, the Vicar operated a small marble lever, which popped open a small door on the papal hat of the magnificent statue forty feet behind him. He walked back over the statue and reached up to move the papal hat slightly to the left where a parchment was visible. He retrieved the parchment...then read it, before handing it to Dominic. The Knight Templar read the parchment then handed it to Capone. Rock paced nervously but eyed Capone with irritation, until the KP leader with his crew-cut looked over to him." It reads in Latin, so I will have to loosely interpret it." Nonie and Jewell stuck their noses up where Capone stood. *"Cum fluit sanguine, et ait Vesuvio. Intelligatur quod habuerit*....it means... when Vesuvius speaks and the blood flows, only then shall he possess what is meant to be." Jewell stood dumbfounded but that did not stop him from injecting his opinion. "Whoa! This is some straight up Indiana Jones shit right here!"

With the reading of the note, Cossimo then shuffled his way into the small enclave at the left of the statue to position another smallish marble switch, causing yet another small marble drawer to open beside the Urn. Cossimo scurried over, opened the gate and reached inside the drawer to collect an oblong blueish glass bottle containing what looked like more dried blood. "Our parishioners know only of the two containers of blood, and that is by design, however, those who have stood watch as tenders of the treasure of San Gennaro know this vial as the 'sacred phial'. This legacy has been passed for seventeen hundred years.

We have no knowledge of the purpose for this third vial. It presumably is for the recipient to understand." Dominic listened to his headset. "Thank you." He turned to Capone. "I can confirm that indeed,

Vesuvius did belch a small amount of lava from its crater." Cossimo then turned to Rock. "Then it is my responsibility as Vicar of the Cathedral of San Gennaro, that with integrity I gift you this vial. The blood of San Gennaro has never been in a liquid state while Vesuvius flowed. May you use it for its sacred purpose." He handed the vial to Rock and the blood inside immediately turned to liquid as he rotated it from one side to the other, marveling. The vicar also retrieved a small wooden box from the marble drawer and had Rock place the vial inside for safe travel. Rock looked around and gave the box to Nonie for safe keeping. Nonie placed it into his leather pouch.

Before they left, Cossimo, Capone and Dominic knelt to express appreciation for the newly received gift...and magnificent abilities of Rock. Capone sent the four agents ahead to clear the path to exit the Crypt. Then they proceeded to leave the church.

Jewell having run past the first four KP, was the first to exit the Cathedral, followed closely by Nonie. They cascaded down the front steps of the Duomo. Once the two leaders of the Knights Protego exited, Dominic continued positioning his men for Rock's safety, but as the big man came through the huge door, a group of thuggish looking heavily armed men seemingly seeped from every crack of the adjacent alleys. They appeared from nowhere...and everywhere to line up in front of the Cathedral, intent on stopping the unknown group of men exiting their local church. The men silently threatening the group with their shotguns, rifles and hand guns. None of the thugs were smiling.

Jewell reacted first, pulling his small hidden automatic weapon from underneath his coat as Capone's other four KP ran past him to form a line of protection, pulling their weapons as well. Capone glanced to Dominic who intently whispered into his own collar. Capone recognized the situation as an ambush by the local mafia and he tried to calm the situation. *"Non vi intendiamo male, ma dobbiamo passare!"* He asked the men to allow his group to pass and insured the intent thugs that they meant them no harm. The mafia members brought their guns to shoulder level. Dominic looked up to the roofs of the buildings surrounding them, for his men, counting ten of them, but they were improperly aligned.

Uncomfortable with the situation, he asked Capone to stall the mafia. *"Perché ci affronti?"* Capone asked the men why they were confronting the group. A bald man in ruddy clothing and in his late forties stepped to the center of the group to speak. *"Hai rubato parte del tesoro di San Gennaro. Non possiamo permetterlo."* The man accused the group of stealing treasure from the Church of San Gennaro, stating that his men could not allow this. Capone realized that this situation was not improving at the very moment. As soon as Dominic had enough men in position, they would neutralize any threat rather than take the chance of allowing Rock to get hurt. He also knew that Dominic would do so without asking for his permission, considering it was a shared responsibility to ensure Rock was safe in Dominic's part of the world.

Capone knew full well his own duty, but he also knew that it would be a bloody mess if he couldn't find a quick solution. *"Non abbiamo alcuna parte del treausre di San Gennaro!"* Capone boldly made the claim that his group of men did not have any part of the treasure of San Gennaro. The bald mafia man called Capone a liar and demanded a search of all the men who had exited the Cathedral. Capone looked back to Dominic who stood straight and nodded back to him that his men were prepared to take down the mafia gang. *"Non possiamo permettere che..."* Capone informed the gang leader that he would not allow the search. The Knight Protego leader was conflicted. He did not want the dozens of locals to die...but glancing up to Dominic's men on the roof, he realized that if he looked back to Dominic one last time, they surely would.

From an alleyway tucked up beside the Duomo, an old man wobbled up the street feeding two dozen plump pigeons flittering around behind him, following him down the street as they collected seeds he pulled from a bag, tossing them to the sidewalk. He appeared to not realize that he was walking directly between the organized crime gang and the Knights Protego. Dominic whispered into his collar for information. "This man is the same old man from down in the catacombs." The old man looked up to see Rock and his entourage, then turned his head to notice the unruly gang with weapons challenging them.

As quick as his elder frame could carry him, he placed himself directly in front of the bald gang leader and turned to him. *"Questi uomini sono bravi uomini... tu li lascerai."* The old man rasped out to the mob indicating Rock and his friends were good men and that the locals needed to leave them alone. The mafia leader raised his shotgun and stepped forward to press his weapon directly into the old man's forehead, causing a small cut to the feeble man's thin skin and a tiny trickling amount of darkened blood to flow down his face. *"Prima ti ammazzo, vecchio sciocco."* He promised to kill the old man first. Jewell and Nonie both advanced toward the old man to protect him, scattering the pigeons into the sky, the look-a-likes skidded to a halt when the other gang members directed their weapons at the two of them.

Confusion occurred once the pigeons took flight, because they didn't disperse and flee like one might expect, rather they hovered ten feet behind the old man. The mafia leader relaxed his finger from the trigger of the shotgun, noticing the birds. The mass of pigeons began to slowly transform. At first, they took on a ghostly translucent discoloration, then appeared to be increasing in size. Right before every human being's eyes, they all transformed into winged-men...and retreated to spread out. They positioned themselves in between the gang members and Rock at the top of the stairs. Capone, Jewell and the gang stood directly in front of the now unnerved gang members. In unison the winged men reached full size and took the shape of angels, as they spread their wings.

Each member of the mafia gang dropped their weapons and ran away from the celestial confrontation, except for the bald man who stood alone with his gun pressed to the old man's head. "*Non ho paura di te!*" The old man slurred that he was not afraid of his attacker. Unsure of his next move, the mafia leader glanced to Dominic, suddenly aware that the man with the silver suit was looking up toward the rooftops of the buildings surrounding him. He dipped his head to see not less than ten laser beam points rotating around his chest area and while he couldn't see them, he was sure there were more on the top of his head. Slowly, he dropped his weapon, raised his hands and fast walked down the closest side alley.

When the old man turned around, the pigeons had returned to form and begun to strut around to look for more food. Capone breathed a deep sigh of relief as he and the other Knights kneeled out of respect for the angels. Jewell and the others quickly joined in before they waved goodbye to the old man. "What did I just see?" Jewell could no longer hold inside his question. "Intervention!" Rock interjected. "If you needed any evidence that there is something bigger in play than just us making a spirit journey here. Those were not just ordinary angels." Jewell looked at him dumbfounded? "Ordinary angels? You act like you see angels all the time. Have you ever seen an angel before?" Rock had to give Jewell credit as he chuckled. "No....

nope...never seen an angel before this today. "

Dominic and Capone were both feverishly busy on their communication devices, Rock guessing one or both were informing Paul.

Nonie walked over to talk to the pigeons. He came back with a disappointed look on his face. These are not like birds in our country. Some Apache speak with animals. I am one of those that have that skill, but these birds are incapable of communicating with me." Jewell sprinted down to talk to Nonie. "They aren't birds, they are angels, but not even normal angels, Rock says they are special angels or some crap." Nonie looked at Rock and challenged the statement. "Crooked finger says he has never seen an angel. How does he know they are not normal angels?" Jewell barked back up to Rock. "Yeah...if you have never seen an angel, how in the world do you know they are not normal angels?" Rock shook his head. "I don't know how I know. I just know. I think the angels have a rank system and these are not just basic angels. Somehow, I just know." Jewell rubbed his chin, justifying. "Some of that big brain stuff that Paul has been telling us in our Knights Protego training."

Capone waltzed over to the others, watching as his other four agents automatically formed a defensive formation around Rock and the group. Dominic joined him. "We are safe for now. Paul believes this display of angels is a big deal. He has done some research on your spirit dreams and wants us to meet him in Malta. It's a small island between Sicily and North Africa. We are to meet him in Medina, tomorrow at 10 a.m. in the courtyard of St. Paul's Grotto. He wants us to stop and pick up non-descriptive clothing and warns against wearing anything displaying the Knights Protego." Capone looked especially at Jewell and his Mark Nason cross-crusted boots. "Paul would like for Rock and myself to engage some of the locals to find out what the political climate in Malta is lately. Oh...and you two..." He pointed to Jewell and Nonie. "He wants you to put your hair in a man-bun and put on a baseball hat or something. He says these people are as sweet a group of individuals as you will find in the world...but...they are very...very suspicious, and very intelligent." The entire group looked somewhat bewildered. Dominic directed them down an alley to make their way to an 'outside of town' shopping center and then toward the airport.

Chapter 10 - Grotto

Captain Trace Bonner had been called a helicopter pilot for most of his adult life, having flown many missions for the very elite of Navy Seal teams. He had even taken quite a few jobs for the mysterious group he now carried in his oversized egg beater. The men in his helicopter called themselves a curious code name…"Protectors" squad. He was comfortable with the fact that he didn't know much about the Protectors other than they were just as elite as the Navy Seal teams he ushered around the world, maybe less filled with death and destruction, but they were indeed equally as impressive as the best of the best the United States Navy had to offer, with both groups seeming to have unlimited resources. Due to the sensitive nature of the Protectors missions, he rarely found himself surprised with where or what they were being tasked to do. However, he had to admit that his current task had him somewhat perplexed.

He had been directed to transport a seven-member team with his UHC 751 Heli to a small island off the coast of Georgia, where he was pleased to learn that an old acquaintance of his, Lt. Dan Cruz, was the Alpha dog for the team on the ground. The two, having gone thru basic training, had stayed in touch and even interacted on smaller missions throughout their careers, until it seemed Cruz vanished once he was selected to some type of top-secret operation. From that point he had sort of lost contact with Cruz. "Trace Bonner, UHC Seven-fitty- one, contacting Protector One, come in Protector One."

Lt. Cruz paced the sand impatiently at Cabretta Landing, agitated that he had not been given the 'go-ahead' to proceed to the north end of Sapelo for the purpose of checking on the newly 'Knighted' colleague, Randall, who was missing. Bonners voice scratched out over his radio, as Cruz noticed Clark and Scooter pacing impatiently up and down the beach, Cruz knew they felt as if they were unnecessarily waiting for word from command back in Ft. Knox to continue the search for their friend. "Lt Cruz here. Trace Bonner...Is that you? Long time no see old friend." The pilot responded. "Roger that...it has been exactly that."

Cruz continued. "Good to hear from you. What is your ETA?" He released his finger from the key of his walkie talkie. "Presently, we are beating the air down the coast line, just north of Blackbeard Island. Matter of fact, you should soon be feeling the pulsating pressure of my blades scattering the sand on your beach any moment now." Cruz looked up the beach to notice the helicopter making its way, slightly over the ocean. "It would be most appreciated if you could touch down and pick us up here on Sapelo." Cruz requested. "Sorry...that is a big negative good friend. There are two problems with your request, first...my craft is as full as a Krispy Kreme doughnut box. I have seven agents in the rear cargo sections. Second...my orders were to find Sapelo and do a recon flight over the north end of the island and allow these guys to gather intel on anything they might see at that location before I dropped them off with you there at Cabretta. There was no mention of joy riding in my shiny toy." Cruz rolled his eyes and sighed with exasperation. "Yeah...figures...see you momentarily."

Cap'n Bonner flew his craft to the very south of Blackbeard Island, nodding his head in an awkward salute toward Cruz before he pulled his bird up and navigated back to the west toward Sapelo. Thirty seconds later he was staring down at the channel separating the two islands. There even from his present altitude, he noticed the considerable alligator activity. Just as he crossed the creek, he viewed out over the canopy of trees toward the north end, he came in from the east, when a massive bird like blur rose above the tops of the trees, hovering just above as it opened its huge gaping mouth as if to scream. The helicopter pilot was clearly startled by the enormous size of the flying creature. The closer he approached, Bonner realized the creature looked more human than avian in nature.

 Suddenly the instrumentation on his control panel went hay-wire, with analog gauges pulsating oddly from the high data range to the low, multiple alarms resonating underneath the buzz of his blades. Because of the result of whatever was happening to his electronics, the chopper began to list terribly to the right. Even with his expansive amount of flight experience, Trace felt certain that his craft was going to crash, to the point where all he could hope to do was stay elevated long enough to determine where, in his judgement, would be a suitable place to perform a controlled wreck which would minimize the damage to the aircraft and prevent or limit loss of life from those on board. The dense wooded nature of Blackbeard Island below gave him little feeling of comfort or relief. Without panicking, he struggled to operate his craft to force a landing on the sandy beach...or even the shallow ocean. Even though the helicopter rotated awkwardly at angles it was not supposed to operate, Trace managed to clear the tree-line knowing all that he had to do now, was to prevent it from drowning them or flying apart to cut them to pieces. Struggling mightily with the control stick, he positioned the helicopter to veer into the sand at the southern-most tip of Blackbeard Island. He intentionally positioned it to where he collided into the sand at an angle where the rotating blades broke off and immediately imbedded themselves into the beach without being slung all around dangerously. After the initial shock of the crash, Trace turned to the shaken men in the back and recommended they exit...immediately.

****

Cruz watched as the gigantic eggbeater careened out of control , emerging from over the tops of the trees of Blackbeard Island. He gathered his men to him. "They are going to crash. Be prepared to take action once this occurs." His men started into the channel between the two islands. "Stop...wait just a minute. We do not know whether he is going to be able to control his craft and even if he is capable, we do not know where he might want to land it. It could be anywhere...it could even be over here. Once this situation resolves itself...then we will proceed." His group of highly skilled soldier types could only sit and gawk as the helicopter pilot fought to steer craft out from over the tree-line. Following a large thud, the flying vehicle smacked into the beach right at the shore line, prompting Cruz to signal his men, who swam to assist the crash victims.

Once they arrived at the scene, they were surprised to see eight men standing shaken, thirty yards away from the smoking helicopter. Lt. Cruz approached one of the agents, Corporal Fitzgerald, trying to ensure the others were okay. "Anything in there that would help us or that we need to help you retrieve?" Each of seven 'protectors' shook their heads negatively. Fitzgerald spoke up. "We were told to fall in line with your team as soon as our intel mission was over. We collected no information due to the issues with our vehicle. We are here to support your efforts."

After his original team verified each of the crash participants were indeed okay, Cruz provided them information. "One of our own has gone missing on the adjacent island. Randall, one of our newer agents." He continued, informing the new team mates from the helicopter the operational experiences and odd occurrences of the previous time on the island. Trace spoke up, informing Lt. Cruz about the oddity he had experienced that led to the helicopter crash. "I guess in retrospect, we should probably have seen that coming. Ft. Knox has had trouble with any sort of satellite imaging due to some strong type of cloaking or jamming device on the north end. So far, we have had little success with our communications devices being functional there. We may possibly have some type of EMF situation."

Cruz made contact to inform Ft. Knox with the latest information. After a few minutes he glanced around to give the group instructions. "Gentleman, our goals from here on out are the following...Priority ONE is to locate our missing agent. Our next priority will be to search for and locate our treasurer, Harry Moorer, if indeed that is the real situation." He glanced over to Clark and Scooter about the second priority. Thirdly, we are to investigate the origin of the odd electronic disturbance." Cruz peered into each agent's eyes to warn them. "There appear to be unexplainable happenings here...do not make the mistake of assuming that you know what is going on. Question everything. Things may not be exactly what you think they are."

He nodded his head for his men to begin their journey to the north end, stopping to address his old friend Trace. "You have always wanted an opportunity to tango with this dance team. I was told to give you a choice. You can stay here on the nice sunny beach or you can grab your backpack and weapon and fall into formation and follow my lead." Trace made haste to collect those items and ran to get in line behind some of the others. "Try not to get yourself killed." Cruz gave his last less than friendly warning.

- -

He sat, wearing a mustard colored T-shirt with a sumo wrestler on the front, not to mention the jeans and a pair of tennis shoes, as he wondered just exactly how ridiculous he looked. Capone stewed as he sat sipping on a small cup of coffee, hating his nonconventional attire. His crew cut hair and perfectly shaped head made it difficult for him to envision even remotely being considered a normal tourist. Either, he just didn't believe, or he hoped nobody else would believe that he was in either case. It amazed him how uncomfortable he was, rarely wearing anything that was not typical of a Knight Protego. He would have refused had Paul not insisted that they loosen up their appearance, knowing how perceptive the locals of Medina were with respect to those that visited the area.

Glancing around the courtyard in front of the Church of the Grotto of St. Paul., he noticed two of his more dependable agents, ambling around just as he was in plain clothing. They were followed on the other side of the courtyard by Rock, Jewell and Nonie. Rock wore a charcoal gray tank top and cargo shorts as usual, at least he normally looked the part of the tourist. Jewell wore a black leather vest and shorts with hiking boots and a trucker hat with his hair tucked up sloppily inside. Nonie wore a plain plaid shirt, jeans and flip flops on his feet that made him look sort of awkward. The three made their way over to a table away from Capone. Rather than sit with the others, Jewell proceeded over to 'Vince Bar' to see what was available, moments later returning with two coffees' and one tea.

The Church of the Grotto of St. Paul located across the street from the restaurant, was built in a Baroque style with three sharp angled spires that reached to the blue billowing sky. It had arched doors made from rich brown and warm looking wood. With Rock seated and in full view, Capone took a glance around the courtyard at the twenty or so local men between their late fifties to early seventies, drinking coffee, tea or any other libation that was deemed appropriate. Capone had been forced to detach himself from Rock and the two look-a-like men for discretionary purposes to prevent them from all being seen together and to give him a broader oversight position for which to protect Rock with more efficiency. He was always uncomfortable when he wasn't personally within a ten-foot radius of Rock, but he realized Paul's suggestion had sound reasoning this time.

Looking around the small village at the highest point of Malta, he couldn't believe that he had never been to this location before, considering it was one of Paul's favorite places in the entire world. Paul had shared stories about how he had become shipwrecked in around the year sixty after being imprisoned by the Romans and sent to Rome for judgement of made up crimes. On the way toward Rome, while being escorted, the ship he was traveling in entered a tremendous storm, veered off course and crashed onto the shores of Malta. The Apostle had spent three months teaching the lessons of the fallen/risen savior and subsequently healed an important dignitary on the island. Today, the island was estimated to be ninety-eight percent

Christian and basically idolized the Apostle Paul from his time here. Paul had returned and spent much time on the island over the years, but lately had felt the need to return in disguise, something Capone found odd because not a soul alive could recognize him today, or at least he didn't believe it was possible. But...it was Paul's thing. Capone looked down at his watch with growing impatience. *Where is he?*

Directly across from Rock's table, sat three old men, playfully chatting about their 'old man' events of the day, something about a female tourist observed snatching artichokes from one of their fields, chuckling about the sincere fact that all the woman had to do was ask the owner and they would have given them to her...especially given how pretty she was. Capone used his considerable judging skills, something he was quite expert at given the number of years he had practiced it, thinking that the old men seemed joyful...honest...and calm.

He watched as Nonie enjoyed their gleeful conversation as well, figuring with his simple nature that he was probably admiring how the old men seemed to love their lives...and appeared it gave him a tremendous amount of comfort that they emitted that feeling freely. Jewell engaged the old men. "Yoh...is that St. Paul's church...the church with the Grotto?" The men smiled at him, relishing his textbook Bronx accent, one of them replied. "It is...but the Grotto entrance is not open until tomorrow morning...probably around nine a.m. Where are you from and if you don't mind me asking...why do you hide your hair up under your hat?" Jewell looked to Rock who suspected all along that keen eyes would unravel a sad attempt to conceal their identity. Jewell tugged the hat off and allowed his mane to escape from underneath. "I am from the Bronx, in New York City...this is my friend Rock. My other friend is Nonie, he is one of the indigenous people from our country. Hey!" Jewell got a look of surprise on his face. "...you speak English." The three men snickered. "Yes...English is our language. This island was once a British colony...Soooo..."

Rock interrupted. "What do you know about this Grotto of St. Paul. What is the big deal with it?" The older and probably leader of the three Maltese men, looked at the other two. "Well...legend says the Apostle Paul was shipwrecked on this island and slept, studied and prayed in the grotto beneath this church for the duration of his time here. He is held in great esteem for teaching our ancestors and giving them purpose and enlightened them in the ways of Christ. Some believe the Apostle is the reason this island is full of peaceful, happy people through our history." He paused and looked at the big man. "You must answer a question for me. If you lack knowledge of the Grotto, why have you come to Medina...and more specifically, why do you have interest in visiting this grotto?"

Rock looked at him and smiled, understanding the underlying reason for his probing. "We are here to learn. We heard there is mystery here on the island...perhaps even an adventure. You are men, we are men...what man could resist a little intrigue and adventure?" His words satiated the three old men, they broke into joyful sophomoric laughter as they completely understood the draw and attraction toward mystery and adventure. The old man added one last thing before turning his attention to his mates. "Ahhh...but it was more of a draw when we were younger such as yourself."

Rock invited the attention of the lone waitress as she walked by. "Excuse me Miss, would you by chance fill the cups of these pleasant and good-natured men with whatever they were drinking." They burst into jolly laughter again.

Suddenly, another older man arrived to plop down in the fourth chair with the other three Maltese men. "Enzio!" They all lauded in unison. "You scoundrel! How did you sneak back onto Malta without us at least knowing you were scheduled to arrive?" The old man gave him a quaint smile without replying as he motioned for the waitresses to bring a cup of tea. Enzio then spoke. "My good friends, what fun would it be to spoil a chance to provide you such a wonderful surprise." He patted the man next to him on the back. "I noticed my vines are in excellent shape." The man took the compliment and nodded his agreement for the condition of Enzio's vineyards. "Excellent! We will meet tomorrow morning and I can pay you what I owe for your services."

Jewell leaned over to Rock. "He must be important on this island. We should make sure Paul knows about this guy."

Nonie leaned in to warn his new friends. "This man is not who he appears." Rock scanned Enzio from head to toe. "I believe you are correct...for this *Enzio* is our beloved Paul." Jewell almost fell out of his seat, spilling a quarter of his cup of coffee on the skin of his chest. The coffee channeling down the scar left from the torture tool at Burning man two years earlier. Enzio commented on the spill. "Be careful my young friend, the coffee here is almost always certainly hot." The other three Maltese men chuckled at Jewell, as he tried to blow on his own chest.

Capone bristled and became slightly uncomfortable when another odd-looking man appeared from a side street, tall in appearance and rail thin, wearing a rose-colored suit with matching skinny tie. He stood in the six-foot-six range with an unusually long red colored handlebar mustache and matching fiery curly shoulder length hair that gave him an almost effeminate appearance. He walked directly toward Capone's table and sat down, whispering. "Paul has asked that I collect you all. If you would be so kind as to signal your crew to nonchalantly follow me, I will lead you to a more sensible place to discuss important issues." Capone, at once fully recognizing the odd-looking man, nodded toward his hidden four agents then at Rock's table, before slowly rising to follow the tall man down a side street.

Rock, who didn't want to give the appearance that he was following the others, slowly rose and entered Vince's bar to pay his bill. Instead of returning to his seat, he motioned for Jewell and Nonie to follow him down an alternate side street to decoy any probing eyes by intersecting Capone and the odd man somewhere down another street. *Enzio* watched as they all exited the courtyard.

Once Rock and friends caught up with Capone and the red-headed thin man a few blocks away, they were led down the several quiet corridors to the entrance of the Catacombs of St. Paul Museum. Entering, they proceeded up a flight of stairs into a conference room on the second floor, where Capone indicated to everyone to take a seat at the enormous conference table in the middle of the room. He introduced the odd-looking man. "Gentlemen allow me to introduce Nichalous, much like myself and Dominic, he is one of twelve original Knights Templar. He has assisted Paul on many occasions and is part of the backbone of the Knights Protego' and has responsibility over the region from Sicily toward North Africa."

The bizarre mustached man standing erect and stoic, awkwardly bowed and tipped his forehead toward the others. "Nichalous also led a group named the Knights of Malta, designed to protect the Maltese during the last thousand years. They were a vicious fighting group, protecting the sick...or those in need of hospital care. As such he has since disassociated himself from that group once Paul called him back to service many years ago." Nichalous nodded to the crew welcoming the KP with a higher than normal pitched voice. "Trust that you are safe here on Malta for my men are all around you. You may never see one of them...but they are there as appropriate. It seems we have some significantly important company in our presence." He looked directly at Rock. A soft knock at the door caused them all to turn and watch as 'Enzio' entered and removed his fake beard, wig and clothing to reveal himself as Paul. He replaced the clothes with his all too familiar plain smock.

Paul got straight to business. "Let us not waste any time. It is wonderful to hear tales that we have encountered some unusual adventures in Naples without any harm." Paul looked around at them all. "Life is that way...for sometimes we seek adventure...and at other times, adventure seeks us. I hear that you have each had the opportunity to witness a very rare event, at least rare in the last fifteen hundred years. The appearance of these angels is distinctive, and I believe it is significant. As a matter of fact, I believe it is an indication that there is some higher purpose that none of us have yet to realize being displayed. We now must focus instead on determining what needs to be done."

"Nichalous has graciously offered to sponsor us on our quest here on the island of Malta. Without bragging, allow me to provide you with a little history of myself and this island. Many years ago, I was shipwrecked here while a prisoner of the Roman guard as they transported me to Rome for trial purposes. Once on the island, I had the opportunity to meet with the local leaders and shared with them the story of Jesus. They became greatly interested and asked for evidence of his power. It just so happens that while sitting around a fire discussing his many miracles, a rather large Asp slithered up beside me and sank his great fangs into my forearm. I ripped him from my arm and killed the monstrous snake, thinking this creature might harm others. The island leaders were saddened and prepared for my death knowing that no man had ever survived such a bite. But...as is my curse, I will never be allowed the sweet rest of death for my attempting to kill Mary Magdalene and I survived, without even having been afflicted with discomfort from the poison. This became a sign of power the leaders were looking for. Subsequently, I was asked to heal one of the chief leaders in their chain of command. I went to him and with God's help, he recovered from a severe malady. From that day forward the people of this island have given my name high praise. Obviously, I never wanted the praise, it was not for me, but for God...and Jesus."

"Having said that, as you can tell, almost everything on Malta has my name on it, and I am convinced it would be most unlikely that anyone could recognize me after two-thousand years. If the statues are any indication, it is obvious they have no idea what I looked like to begin with." He stopped to catch his breath. "This place is one of my favorites in all of Gods nations. The people here are simply wonderful and if you spend any amount of time here you will recognize that fact, if you haven't already."

Paul then took his seat at the head of the conference table. Rock decided it was his time to talk. "So, what are we doing here Paul?" The

Apostle signaled for one of Nichalous agents to fetch him a glass of water. "We are here to retrieve two Items that I believe will be beneficial for the remainder of this quest. Do not be mistaken, this is truly a quest. I know not what we are looking for and I know not where the answers are, nor what we need to find. But...the significance of the twenty or so constitutional angels cannot be underestimated." He bent forward toward the table for emphasis. "I repeat this to you all. There is something of significance here that we must accomplish...and if we are being honest, it isn't something that I must do...but a task the three of you must complete." He looked at Rock, Jewell and Nonie. "You three were given the clues in your spirit dreams and now you must use those to solve a riddle of sorts." Rock looked disappointed. "So then again, why are we here?" Paul looked slightly shaken. "That night that I killed the snake, twenty or so constitutional angels appeared to me. They took possession of that very snake, they severed its head and threw it into the Mediterranean and in a few days later, they returned. They produced the snakes hide, tanned it before my very eyes and encrypted it with a message that I was not allowed to read...nor capable. The angels then took the snake hide...and hid it in the catacombs below where we sit at this very moment. There is a map in my grotto in a locked away passage and only I have the key. This map should lead you to the snake hide. I can unlock the grotto passage, but the three of you must find the skin inside the catacombs." Jewell stood excitedly. "Then what are we waiting on?"

Paul smiled at his newest team member, "We must wait for darkness to enter the catacombs. While the people of this island are very sweet and seem quite docile...they are marvelously intelligent and a suspicious folk. If they see a large group of men enter the catacombs, they will want answers. And...I am not prepared for those type of questions." Paul began to reassemble his disguise. "I will meet you in the grotto at eleven pm. Nichalous will guide the three of you..." He looked at Capone. "...the four of you, to the grotto to meet me."

Hours later, Nichalous led the remaining KP through quiet and dark narrow cobbled streets toward a small visitor center for St. Paul's Grotto. There he unlocked a glass door, then prompted the other men to slide into the ultra-modern building before the red headed original Templar Knight locked the door behind them. He then led them through a turnstile, down a flight of modern granite stairs into a cave like structure resembling a museum with busts, altars and ancient paintings on the curved walls. The group made a left turn where they suddenly appeared at the entrance to St. Paul's grotto. A life-sized statue of Paul stood and the apostle himself standing directly beside it. The statue, which was far smaller than actual height, seemed to humor and at the same time disappoint the Apostle. The beard and hair were extremely long and in the statue's hand Paul was holding a parchment. He looked at the crew, shaking his head. "In two thousand years...never once has my hair...or beard been that long." He shrugged. "At least they have the smock about right." He pointed to the flowing robe the statue replicated before exiting the chamber of the grotto.

Over beside the wall, he moved the handle of a sword located on a ceramic tile. "CLINK". Rock turned back to look at the statue to see that a necklace with a key attached had fallen around the statue's neck. Paul made his way back to the statue, removing the key, before proceeding to a three-foot metal grate blocking a smaller statue to the right of the statue of St. Paul.

He gritted his teeth to remove the heavy metal grate, then handed Jewell the key. "If you would be so kind." Paul pointed down the smallish four-foot-tall tunnel that led back into the darkness. He withdrew a glow stick from the pocket of his tunic, snapped it, shook it then handed it to Jewell. "This task is well suited for a man with your skills and size....perhaps you and your look-a-like friend could assist me. Approximately forty feet down this passage is another locked metal grate. There you must unlock the grate and you will find a square stone inside, move that stone and procure the map from beneath the stone?"

Jewell and Nonie eagerly ducked down into the passage and did exactly as Paul instructed, the Bronx native yelling back to him. "There is no map beneath the stone!" Paul stepped back, seeming to search his memory. Nichalous offered. "Paul...I was here with you when you placed the map. It should be there." Paul sighed. "Yes, it should be, but that was seven hundred years ago. Obviously, the museum curators have been very curious and relocated it. "He sighed. "We must find the snake-hide." Nichalous again offered. "Would you prefer that I assign

some of my people to assist in searching the catacombs." Capone shook his head negatively. "No...we must protect Rock as a priority. We need to leave your men in place." Rock stood scratching his head. "How hard of a task can this be? How big are these catacombs?" Paul blew out a big breath. "Whew! They are extensive. The people of Malta sought shelter here throughout World War 2 to escape the Nazi bombing raids. They were at times down here for months."
Paul gestured. "Then we should begin. This serpent hide will not find itself."

He led them back through a set of well illuminated tunnels and an opening labeled as WW2 shelter. They wandered a twenty-foot diameter tunnel, eighty yards back toward where the city, with cross-corridors intersecting every so often that appeared to be just as long as the main corridor with other intersections and living quarters. The shelter was an enormous maze. At one intersection, Paul stopped to ponder. "There are two hidden entrances into the catacombs from these shelters, one of them is located directly down this long corridor." He pointed to the left. "The secret entrance is deceptive in that it appears to be just another long...dark narrow passage but it travels for forty meters until it opens into one end of the catacomb." Paul enjoyed that he could remember his way amongst the maze as well as he did. "If I might suggest, Rock take Jewell, Nonie and Capone down this hidden corridor to search for the hide. I will take this corridor with Nichalous and the remaining Knights to search another segment of the catacombs." He looked at Capone. "It is approaching midnight. We cannot spend longer than five hours before we need to leave the catacombs. Meet us at the upstairs conference room at that time...with or without the hide." Capone nodded his understanding.

Taking the lead for his group of wanderers, Rock entered the corridor to his left, walking ten steps before he stopped to look back to the other three as if pondering something in his own head. "Nonie...you wouldn't happen to be trained in the skill as an Apache tracker, would you?" The Native American man nodded affirmatively. "I am a tracker." Rock smiled and looked at Jewell, who had no idea what was transpiring. "Would you so kindly do us the favor of leading us to find this snake-skin." Nonie quickly removed the trucker hat allowing his long silken black hair to dangle below his shoulders. He saw confusion on Jewell's face. "My people believe our hair is an amplification of our consciousness. It is why trackers do not cut their hair. It helps us pick up on micro-sensations, vibrations and other feedback provided to us from the earth. It is these things that help us locate that which we seek." Jewell allowed his jaw to drop with wonder, before he snatched his own hat off and allowed his hair to dangle as well.

Nonie then dropped horizontal to the dirt floor of the corridor, touching the surface with his hand delicately. He lowered his face to floor level and 'saw' the surface, allowing his hair to drag on the loose limestone dust, inhaling deeply to make use of all his senses. He withdrew a long slow breath to engage his sense of smell, then dipped his tongue to the surface to include taste. He selected a pinch of the dust and placed it in between his teeth and lips. He looked up to Capone. "There are a number of people walking above us on the surface at this time." Jewell gawked at his new friend, looking up to see if he could detect anything. Nonie then quickly stood, leading the others swiftly down the corridor. Rock smiled at Capone with satisfaction on his face.

Near the end of the corridor, they located a small entrance to the sprawling catacomb, inspiring the Apache to drop to the floor once again, examining the trail within. He looked up to eye Capone and Rock curiously. "This access will be very tight for the two of you." He crawled away into the dark and narrow corridor, challenging even his smallish frame with respect to ease of access. Jewell followed him quickly. Rock half stooped as the passage was only a little more than five feet tall. He found that he had to turn half-sideways to fit due to the width of his shoulders. Capone followed using the same coping skills as his bigger charge. Jewell and Nonie had to wait inside a few minutes before Rock and Capone slithered their way awkwardly through the passage.

The catacomb was illuminated with incandescent lighting supplied by electric cables, apparently, installed by the museum as part of the St. Paul catacomb tour process.

The corridors inside the catacomb had a distinctively different layout than the main passageway, tending to be much shorter in height and each corridor seemed to involve a roundabout not unlike one of the many on the island that helped control traffic. There were outshoot smaller grottos to each side of the main corridor throughout the catacombs, each contained a round limestone flat table, carved from the floor, where it seemed inhabitants would tend to prepare meals and partake of social activities. Spinning around those spaces were rectangular carved stone sleeping quarters that rotated about the main area, containing crypt like structures for burying the dead. This same pattern of living space grotto connected to dozens of similar grottos throughout the catacomb.

While leading the group deeper into the catacombs, Nonie continued to provide information to Capone and Rock by reading the path, commenting as to how many people had traveled and how recently in which areas.

The four traveled hundreds of feet back into the catacombs along a straight stretch of corridor, before Nonie stopped suddenly, dropping to search the walls. "Many people have traveled this route...but for some reason it appears they simply stopped here in this section of the corridor. Very few of those continued past this point." Jewell squeezed past Nonie to inspect the area few had traveled, disappearing around a bend in the corridor. He reappeared moments later. "Nothing special back there that I could see." Nonie, deep into tracking skills, ran his fingers over the stone underneath the limestone dust directly underneath where he stooped. "These people seemed to turn toward this wall." He ran his hands up along the wall until he located an abnormally round shape carved niche about waist level. Crouching slightly in front of the niche, he gently blew the dust away from around it, noticing something inside.

Rock knelt with Capone to get a closer look. "There is a hole with what looks like a button inside." Nonie cleared away the remaining loose debris. Rock asked Nonie. "May I?" Nonie stopped cleaning the carving and moved to the side. Rock nervously stuck his finger in the hole to depress the button. Nothing happened. "Did it feel like you activated any type of switch or anything?" Jewell asked. "Not at all. The button didn't move." Rock felt that whatever this button mechanism was, had to be important. "Capone, you want to try to open this weird thing?" He did the same as Rock had done, only harder. The button would not budge. Rock scratched his head. "Surely this is not a co-incidence that this unusual carving, button or whatever it is….is here in this wall where so many people have turned?"

Capone shrugged. Rock sighed and looked to the other side of the corridor where it appeared another unusual carving located at about the same height. "Well…" He looked back to the original button. "Maybe they used this to hang a pole or something. We must be on the wrong track." He motioned for Nonie to continue his scouting deeper into the corridor.

Shortly, they entered another living space, where Jewell took the lead, noticing tile looking artwork painted on the floor of one of the rectangular sleeping compartments. Prowling on ahead, he startled the others when he yelled. "Ahhhhhh.... skeletons...skeletons." Rock' s heart pumped mightily as he hustled up to beside Jewell to find a fully preserved skeleton lying as if it were a sleeping human being. Searching further, they found partial or full skeletal remains in each of the next few sleeping quarters. They eventually found the main communal area for this portion of the catacombs, where, as expected, there was a limestone eating table. Inspecting the area, Jewell located a small waist high compartment that was dark inside. Using the flashlight feature on his smart phone to shine inside, he could see a variety of bones and dust that seemed randomly scattered inside. Jewell picked up, what looked like a leg bone, six to eight inches long and held it in his hand, turning it to inspect it. "Rock, dude, take a picture of me holding this." Rock didn't really understand why his friend wanted a picture but optioned to oblige him. Jewell smiled as he rotated the bone in his hand to take the souvenir picture. The flash bounced off the walls. Rock decided to check the picture to ensure his friends success with the apparent souvenir. "That's the answer!" Rock stated while looking at the picture. Capone ducked his head to look at the phone screen. "It's a bone lock!" The others looked to Rock in complete confusion. "What are you talking about?" Jewell asked. Rock seemed energized. "Nonie lead us back to the carving in the side of the corridor. Jewell, bring that bone shard with you."

They made their way back to where the abnormally shaped hole with the button was located. Once they were all around the carving, Rock instructed. "Jewell, you found the key. If you notice, that button inside is almost the same shape as the inside of that bone where the marrow was located while this person was alive. I believe it will fit perfectly into this hole and fasten around the button. Stick the bone into the hole and let's see what happens." Jewell, still utterly confused, maneuvered the marrowless bone until it fit into the odd shaped hole. Eventually three inches of the bone slid into the hole smoothly as if it belonged there. Jewell looked up to Rock with surprise. "What now?" He asked. "Rotate the bone." He was instructed. Jewell placed his hand around and slowly turned the bone. At that moment, from behind the group, a swishing noise occurred, causing all four men to turn where they noticed a two-foot tall and two-foot wide opening had opened where the other carving on the opposite side of the corridor was located. Jewell looked up to Rock's face. "How did you know that we needed to do that?" Rock nonchalantly replied. "I don't know...I just came to realize." Capone smiled faintly, impressed by, but seeming to have half-expected Rock to solve the puzzle. Nonie dropped to the floor to inspect the opening. "The passage proceeds back as far as the light will allow then angles to the right. I believe I can fit and perhaps Jewell, but I cannot imagine either of you two being able to journey back into this place."

Rock ran his hand along the top of his head, uncomfortable with the idea of having his two friends to proceed through the passage toward an unknown destination. He looked at Capone. "What do you think boss?" Capone considered the situation for a second. "This much I know, I will not leave you alone in these caves. I also believe that our purpose here is to locate something quite important. Usually for quest such as these, the situation requires extraordinary measures to be successful." Rock appreciated the notion. "Jewell, are you okay assisting Nonie?" Jewell looked back in astonishment and with a puzzled look. "Are you kidding me?" Rock nodded for Nonie to proceed, prompting the lithe Native-American to remove his large pouch and enter the passage, crawling back into the dark unknown. Jewell did the same once Nonie got the entire length of his body through the opening.

With both men Inside the hole, there was little chance even a sliver of light from the corridor could enter. "Jewell, is there a chance you could loan me your phone to use as a flashlight?" Nonie asked, prompting Jewell to wriggle his way back out of the hole momentarily in order to reach into his shorts pockets to remove the phone. He shoved it through to Nonie who illuminated the passage in front of him. Once Jewell had squeezed back into the opening, the two men crawled another fifty feet before the passage angled off to the right, as Nonie had predicted.

After another ten feet of crawling, Nonie became aware of a large dark area in front of him where the light seemed to be absorbed. The passage narrowed even more and reduced in height for the last few feet of travel, forcing Nonie to stretch his arms out in front of him and slither convulsively like a snake through the opening of a large dark room. He pushed the phone inside first as he continued to wiggle, until his body was half through the opening where he directed the phone around the walls to light up the inside. It was a dead end. Continuing in, he could see it was an approximately ten-foot squared opening and inside in the very center was a limestone box with no markings whatsoever. Nonie positioned the flash-light to look at the floor, where there were no footprints of any kind inside the compartment. This confused him greatly and he wondered if perhaps he and Jewell had stumbled upon some sort of trap. He looked over to notice Jewell trying to wiggle his way into the room much as he had. "Jewell, you might want to reconsider entering this place." He then explained to Jewell his line of thought. Jewell sheepishly, backed up a few feet to yell back out the passage to Rock and Capone about their findings...and Nonie's concern about a trap.

They two men standing outside pondered the situation, then opted to inform Paul of the findings via headset. While waiting for a reply, Rock knelt to speak into the passage opening. "Do you remember what Paul told us about this snake skin?" Jewell yelled back. "Yes...but what exactly are you referring to?" Rock cleared his throat. "Well, he said the constitutional angels are the ones who placed the snakeskin here for protection. Given what we have seen in the last few days, would we think they necessarily have to have made footprints to hide something in an enclosure?" Without replying, Jewell slithered his way down into the open room to notice Nonie sitting in front of the limestone box. Jewell joined him. "Do you think it to be a trap or do you even think we can lift the box lid?" The room was tall enough for them to stand and attempt to remove the heavy top. Through mighty grunts they manage to successfully slide the box lid to the side, where underneath, they found an animal skin rolled with hemp string to bind it. Jewell excitedly scampered over to the hole, yelling back to the others. "We have it! We are headed out."

Once they managed to shuffle their way back to exit the small passage. Rock bent down to remove the snakeskin from Nonie's hands as the Apache attempted to stand. Capone assisted the big man in removing the twine, unrolling the hide and laying it along the floor. Even with the dismal lighting there appeared to be some sort of embossing or blistering on each side of the snake hide, even the scaly exterior portion. Rock shook his head though, unable to detect any recognizable pattern from the hide. Frustrated, they quickly rolled the hide back to its original package shape and handed it back to Nonie, who placed it in his pouch with San Gennaro's blood vial and the three-pronged digging tool. " Paul, we have the snake hide in our possession. We will meet you back at the intersection where we split up." Capone communicated.

Twenty minutes later, once they met up with the other group, they rolled out the snake skin again to allow Paul to examine it. "Where and how did you locate it?" Jewell blurted out. "Man...I don't even know about you, but what is up with Rock recently? He just seems to know things. He solved the riddle of the bone lock. He seemed to know that Nonie was an Apache Scout...he just seems to know stuff that nobody else knows." Paul looked peculiarly to Rock, who shrugged back at him. "I cannot explain, I just end up knowing." Paul shared a quick insightful smile with Capone as if they had each received satisfying news. Paul then instructed. "Meet me in the courtyard outside the Grotto entrance." Titus surprised the others as he stood beside Paul, making an unexpected appearance. "Where did you come from?" Rock inquired, having thought Paul's assistant had stayed back in Ft. Knox with Bartholomew. Titus simply smiled then assisted Paul in restoring his 'Enzio' disguise. Capone's other KP agents proceeded to ensure the tunnels were clear to the surface, leading the way for Rock and company.

Rock and his crew exited from the maze of catacomb corridors up into the courtyard outside St. Paul's Cathedral, expecting it to be empty at 3:30 in the morning, but that was not the case. For as soon as the catacomb search party spilled out into the courtyard, other men showed up with them, each wearing knee-length white or silver tunics with eighteen-inch red crosses that flared at each of the four ends. The men slowly emerged from each of the quiet dark corridors from some other portion of the narrow village streets. "Knights of Malta!" Capone muttered under his breath. Rock looked toward his protector as he directed four of his own Knights to Rock's front. The men in tunics continued their slow approach, none wore headgear, but each of them carried a long-sword strapped to the side of their tunics and a few carried automatic weapons. Eventually the Maltese knights spread out and lined up for a potential offensive with an arched line to block any movement by Capone and his agents.

"Pray tell what business a group of outsiders might have in our humble catacombs this late in the evening?" Rock recognized the man as the older guy he had purchased coffee for earlier in the day. Glancing around he vaguely recognized each man as having been present in the courtyard the afternoon before, outside Vince's bar. Rock spoke up. "We mean you nor any of your wonderful people any harm. We were simply charged with collecting an item long hidden from the world." The Maltese man looked to his companions. "Any item found in the catacombs would belong to the people of Malta and removing it would certainly be considered an act of thievery. We take thievery very serious here on our island. Stealing from the catacombs according to Maltese law and tradition is an offense outlined as punishable by dismemberment." Jewell grimaced at the word.

Nichalous stepped dramatically out from the shadows of the Grotto, given the unexpected and unusual situation the Knights Protego found themselves in. As he walked, he spoke softly into his ear piece, his mustache bouncing up and down and before he could finish his communication, tiny laser beam points appeared on six of the members of the Maltese Knights. Capone joined the conversation. "Again, we mean you no harm, but the item we retrieved was a personal item left by a friend of this group." The leader of the Maltese Knights scrunched his head in a visible scoff. "Short of St. Paul himself sending you...there is no acceptable 'friend' that will action us to allow this group to leave this place without a fight."

Capone looked to Rock with frustration, knowing full well that each one of those men in the tunics before them, was a good man. But he also knew that the agents that followed Nichalous, up on the roofs and in the buildings surrounding them would not allow Rock to be injured. "Then show us precisely what it is that your group finds so important that you would sneak into our catacombs to retrieve?" Capone pondered as he looked to Jewell and Nonie. "Show them!" Nonie dug through his pouch, carefully pulling out the vial of blood, then the snake-hide which he handed to Jewell as he held the vial of blood out over his head. Jewell held it up in front of himself to ensure the men saw exactly what they had retrieved. Suddenly, a massive spotlight lit up the courtyard and illuminated Capone and his entire group. The Maltese Knights gasped. "You have found the *Skin of the Asp*?" Rock looked over to the snake skin, where he noticed that the vial of blood appeared to have turned to a liquid state and clung to the walls of the vial, closest to the snake skin as if magnetized that way. The leader of the Maltese men asked. "What is the other artifact?" Capone answered quickly. "That artifact was not found inside the catacombs.

That item was brought to this island by us...It was a gift from a church in Italy."

Rock sensed movement from behind him as Paul rose up from out of the grotto in disguise. Three of the knights huddled together before the leader spoke again with confidence. "We cannot allow you to leave with the *Skin of the* Asp. It is the property of the people of Malta." Enzio stepped forward between Capone and Rock, walking slowly to within feet of the leader of the Maltese men.

"Broderick...how long have I known you?" The spokesman for the Knights of Malta was shaken by Enzio's sudden appearance, but certainly confused by his question and his apparent involvement with the incident before them. "You have known me all of my life, Enzio. What have you to do with this group of men?" Enzio looked around. "These are my friends." He then looked to another of the Maltese Knights. 'Guessepio, how long have I known you?" Guessepio looked slightly older than Broderick. "Since I was a boy, I have known you Enzio." Enzio looked to each of the other local men to gather their responses, each shaking their heads to acknowledge that they had known Enzio for as long as they could remember. "Given that...would you trust me to do what is right with respect to the people of Malta?" Broderick, Guessepio and another man huddled once again. "Enzio, we respect you and we truly trust you as much as any man we might know. However, you are not Maltese and we cannot allow ourselves to be influenced in this matter."

Enzio sighed. "Then who could I muster with any type of influence to allow us to leave this place with the *Skin of the Asp*?" Enzio walked back to his friends. Broderick boldly replied. "With all due respect, short of St. Paul himself giving permission, we will not allow you to leave this place with that snake skin and we will fight until death to protect our history."

Paul/Enzio looked to Capone with frustration, then to Rock, before he slowly removed his disguise. Once the wig and beard were removed, he discarded the non-descript clothing, handing it to Titus, before pulling his normal bleached tunic over his head. The Maltese Knights stood gasping, their eyes wide with shock. Paul then walked back directly in front of Broderick and the other men. "And if your beloved St. Paul were to ask the kind people of Malta to allow him to use the *Skin of the Asp*?" Broderick's knees almost buckled, as he struggled to find words to question what was happening.

Paul smiled genuinely at Broderick. "Broderick, you are sixty-eight years old, you are amongst the wisest men I know on this earth, but in sixty-eight years you never once questioned why your good friend Enzio never seemed to age?" Broderick searched for any answer in the eyes of his companions. He could think of no plausible explanation. His breathing came in short stout bursts before the only thing he knew to do was kneel and bow his head to the patron saint. The remaining Maltese Knights shocked by the turn of events, followed his example. "Please...please...STAND! I am not your savior but indeed I promise you that I am the Apostle Paul and indeed I am a friend of the Maltese people but you must stand. I have never cared for the overabundance of attention from the sweet people of Malta. It almost borders on worship and I promise you this. It is not I that you should be worshiping. Two-thousand years ago, I thought I had made that abundantly clear. You should worship your savior and his father. I am but a messenger. I simply told the story. So...please stand." Broderick led the men as they hesitantly did as he requested. overwhelmed by what they were experiencing.

"But...but...how is this possible?" He looked to Paul for an answer. Paul stepped forward and put his arm around Broderick. "It is a long story for another time my friend." He signaled for the Maltese Knights to surround him to speak with them all. "This is what you need to know today. I am your St. Paul and I love these people of Malta. However, my motivations are as they have been since I first visited, guided by God and his holy son. Today, I find myself involved in a quest of which I know not where we are headed, but we are certain that this snake skin is the first piece of a larger puzzle and we are destined to attain this artifact. So, I ask you and your men, to allow us this quest." He looked to each of their eyes. "Perhaps if you give us a moment." Broderick asked. Paul gave a quick nod before walking back to his friends.

The Maltese Knights had a brief discussion before Broderick spoke again. "Paul, though we truly do not understand these events. We are in unison accepting you for who you are. We will allow you to take the hide...however, we will not allow you to take one of the other items your men have with them." Paul looked around to each man in his own crew. Each of them, stood wondering what the Maltese man could be speaking of. They each began patting their pockets until Jewell found in his lower cargo short pocket the lone bone shard that they had used to open the bone lock. He pulled it out of his pocket and displayed it high above his head. "I am so sorry. I did not mean to bring this, when we opened the lock, I must have gotten excited and put it into my pocket. I didn't even realize it was there." He looked to Paul, then to Rock like a kid stealing bubble gum from a gas station convenience store. One of Broderick's men approached to collect the bone fragment. "I am sure this man or woman will appreciate their remains lie where they belong." The knight was joined by a few others as they exited toward the grotto to replace the bone fragment.

Broderick looked at each of the other men, head to toe. "Then you have our blessing to leave." Paul smiled. "Thank you, Broderick, I will return within the year, again as Enzio. Perhaps we can have a conversation about our beloved St. Paul. I trust that the Knights of Malta can resist the urge to cause a sensation by spreading word of what you have witnessed tonight?" Broderick again knelt and with head bowed and replied. "Your secret is safe with this organization." Paul then nodded to Capone, who whispered into his ear piece. Three large, silver vans wheeled into the courtyard as Capone prompted the entire gang of Knights Protego toward their next destination. Dominic and Nichalous joined as well.

Chapter 11- Shell-ring

Seemingly from nowhere, a massive deluge completely soaked the Knights Protego as they strategized. Cruz determined it would be wise to return to the campground and use Dorothy's van. They knew it would take two trips to navigate as far as practical to the north end of the island. Cruz had hoped it would only take one trip, but he was savvy enough to realize they would never fit the entire fifteen-man crew in the van at one time. Once they collected all they needed from the campground back in Hog Hammock, they loaded the first crew into the van and made their way back through the moss filled live-oaked landscape, down the narrow dirt road back toward the North End of Sapelo.

Clark drove the first group as far north as the van would safely travel, dropping off Scooter, Cruz, and the original four knights. He returned to pick up the other eight agents, with Trace riding shotgun beside him in the van. Halfway back to the drop off point, Clark noticed three enormous Brahma bulls standing amongst the saw palmetto bushes up ahead. The closer he approached them, the more attention the van seemed to collect, to the point that the bulls began to charge at them. The first bull ironically, T-boned the van directly in the side with a thunderous blow, twisting the vehicle onto two wheels as Clark struggled greatly to keep the still soaked interior upright. Then a second bull struck the van, creating entirely too much inertia for him to compensate for. The vehicle tumbled onto its side and slid underneath a grouping of huge tree's. Clark, still strapped into his seat, looked over to where Trace sat, a petrified look on his face. "Really, you just were in a helicopter crash and this scared you? " Clark blabbered. "Holy Smokes brother, I think I will just stick to my helicopters if you don't mind." They both looked back in the rear of the van where the remaining agents tried to untangle themselves from the mayhem created by the bulls. The two men in the front removed their seat belts and wiggled their way to the passenger window to exit the van, positioning themselves atop to assist the soldiers inside in opening the cargo entrance in order to help them escape.

Once all eight of the men were accounted for, they did a quick scan for the angry bulls. They were completely gone. Clark, being the only man with any knowledge of where they were headed, provided information to the rest. "We are only about a half a mile from the others. If you guys will follow me." He led them down the narrow path to where he had dropped the others.

Cruz was the first to notice Clark and the others marching up the road behind him. He could only shake his head, wondering what else could have gone wrong, assuming the van must have experienced some sort of mechanical failure. Once Clark and his group arrived, they shared the experience concerning the Brahma bulls and the accident that ensued. Lt. Cruz scratched his head. "Gotta tell ya...this is the most unusual vacation I have ever taken." He promptly aligned the fifteen men in parallel for their advancement toward the north end. Cruz took one last opportunity to attempt to communicate their position to Ft. Knox and share their plans. Moments later every form of communication device they had, ceased to function.

The crew crept through the woods for a little over an hour before Clark noticed that the moss hanging from the trees and the forest itself seemed to have become much thicker. He wandered over toward Cruz and shared his observation. Cruz stopped the band of men to digest what Clark was telling him, when he noticed a small structure up ahead. He motioned Scooter next to him. "We will wait here. I want you two to investigate that small structure ahead. Return back to this position and let me know what you find." The friends confidently and covertly darted off exactly as they had been recently trained with respect to recon activities.

Once they got close enough, Clark positioned himself behind a particularly large live-oak as Scooter darted in right beside him. They peeked around the trunk of the tree. The structure was a twelve-foot diameter shell-ring, they didn't notice anyone...or anything surrounding it and made their way back to Cruz to report such. Cruz gathered his entire band of Knights around him, and in hushed tones gave commands. "I want you all to ready your weapons. We now have signs of habitability and if the stories are to be held to the truth, we may not know what to expect next. However, only discharge your weapons to protect yourself or others amongst us, unless otherwise directed." He nodded for a few of his more experienced men to take the point and lead them down the path that soon disappeared, forcing them to walk through untraveled underbrush. Clark began to sense that the canopy was becoming much thicker and the coloration of the tree bark was much darker. Instead of the lush green and gray from earlier in the day, the trees appeared darkish brown or even blackish.

Lt. Cruz abruptly held up a closed fist to halt his men from advancing. "What is that?" He whispered to Clark and Scooter. Peering ahead through the trees, they were able to make out what looked to them as an enormous black wall stretching across a hundred feet in front of them. "A wall?" Cruz mouthed with surprise. Clark and Scooter each shrugged their shoulders. The lieutenant motioned his men to slowly approach the 'wall'. The men also became aware of a one-acre pond a few hundred feet to the left of the wall. While distracted observing the pond for activity, Lt. Cruz suddenly noticed a motion from their right, where he saw a dozen Brahma bulls appear from nowhere, slowly slinking their way to the right of the band of men. The wall of bulls seemed to be lined up with consistent spacing as if they were corralling the men, or at the very least establishing a bovine wall to prevent them from proceeding in that direction.

Cruz scratched his head as he looked back toward the pond for any possible escape routes. His attention was drawn to the pond surface that seemed to be pulsating with a massive amount of alligator activity. Inching his way closer to the black wall ahead, he began to realize the wall was not a human construct at all. It was more like a stand of tightly bunched obsidian black trees, enormous in height compared to the other trees in the area, in the two-hundred-foot range. He whispered toward Clark and Scooter beside him. "This is the weirdest place I have ever experienced." He then turned toward the other Knights, noticing that their discomfort level was about the same as his. He called Trace Bonner to the front. "Have you ever encountered anything like this in your travels?" Trace displayed his inexperience in tactical missioning as he was clearly shaken by their surroundings and the odd happenings. Cruz directed Clark and Scooter to lead them around the wall for the purpose of locating an entrance.

As they slowly navigated around the tight structured dark tree-line, they could not help but notice the wall appeared almost perfectly circular and perhaps two-hundred feet wide. Eventually, Clark noticed a ruddy trail leading from the pond with all the alligators to the west. It ended up against the wall and as they got closer, they realized the trail led to a make-shift gap in the trees. Inching closer, the gap was three-foot tall and about the width of a man. Clark knelt beside the gap to peer into the opening. He could see nothing, the soil inside just as obsidian black as the trees themselves. He reached inside his backpack to locate his Maglite, turning it on to peer inside. Just inside the door, the flashlight beam was absorbed, preventing him from being able to see anything. He backed away from the opening and stood with his back to the black tree growth. "I couldn't see anything inside. It's just dark...but it does look passable. If we entered it would be with absolutely zero knowledge of what we were getting involved with."

Cruz, frustrated with the entire experience, decided. "Let's make our way over to the pond to see if there is anything to learn there." He led them through the thick undergrowth up to within ten feet of the pond, standing to see the constant movement of alligators. Scooter muttered. "I swear...there is no possible way that five more gators could fit in that pond." All fifteen men in the group stood gawking at the sheer numbers of alligators they were watching. "What do they eat?" Scooter asked plainly, insinuating there could not possibly be enough food in the tiny pond to keep all of them fed. At once, the pulsating motion inside the pond stopped as the alligators all seemed to turn in the direction of Scooters voice. Half the men in the group of Knights took a subconscious step back from the pond, unnerved by the odd reptilian behavior.

Clark and Scooter led a hasty retreat toward the black wall as the Brahma bulls pressured them from the south and east and the alligators began to exit the pond to push them closer to the wall. Cruz calmly evaluated his position. Bulls, to the south and east, Gators coming from the west. "Clark, you lead the way, let's see if inside this wall is any safer."

Clark's eyes popped open, surprised at the command. He looked over to his good friend Scooter before nervously dropping down on all fours to crawl into the black hole. Scooter quickly followed him, as they drug their AK-47's while shuffling into the opening. Once his eyesight adjusted, Clark could see a slight bluish glow as the darkness waned and the trees thinned. Just inside the outer wall of black trees was an enormous shell-ring wall about twelve-feet-tall with small one-foot diameter holes at the top of the wall located every twenty feet or so. The holes were the source of the odd bluish glow inside the gap. Clark crept up to ensure it was a shell-ring wall, touching the sharp oyster-shells surface as he sat up and yelled back to Cruz. "There is an oyster-shell wall inside." Cruz shouted back nervous with the approaching gators. "Is it passable." Scooter sat up beside him looking the other way down the four-foot corridor created between the black tree line and the shell-ring wall. He yelled back in response. "Yes, there is room to walk upright between the two walls." The two stood and began to move left around the shell wall, allowing the other agents space to follow.

Clark walked about forty-feet then looked up to one of the holes where the bluish glow spilled out into the nothingness of black wood. "Boost me up buddy, I might can reach that hole and look in." Scooter placed his back against the sharp oyster shells and held out a knee for Clark to climb up, allowing him to barely see over the bottom edge of the shell ring. "What do you see?" Scooter asked as Cruz made is way to the inexperienced Knights. The Lieutenant helped Scooter, pushing Clarks rear end up as much as possible. "I can't see much...wait...I can see...umm...umm...I can see huge granite rectangles in a sort of semi-circular shape, and blue light seems to be glowing from some source inside. Can't really tell what is near the surface or anything." Clark then scrambled to get down.

Lt. Cruz surveyed the situation, looking both ways around the interior passage loop. One of the other Knights yelled from the opening. "It appears the wildlife has stopped their approach." Cruz shook his head. "Well, at least there is that. I think we should continue to follow the inner shell-ring wall all the way around and search for an opening to the interior. Let's see what the heck we are in the middle of. How big is this shell-ring? The ones outside were ten-feet diameter max, this one must be two-hundred meters. That seems a bit much for a tribe of indigenous people to have created twenty-five hundred years ago."

Scooter looked back at the opening they had just appeared from. "It has to be at least two-hundred feet, maybe more than that." Cruz turned and cautiously continued following the inner-wall around, cutting his arm several times by traveling too close to the oyster shells protruding from the edifice. Fifty-feet later, Cruz noticed a worn travel path that entered toward the inside of the shell-ring. It was an opening about the size of a large man. He stooped to peek inside, noticing the bluish light originating from somewhere inside the ring. He sat down and scooted his way inside on his rump, once completely inside, he stood to where he saw massive twelve-foot tall gray granite stones around the entire circumference of the ring. They were in sets consisting of two monolithic vertical support stones and one perfectly matched massive horizontal granite stone on top. The stones were perhaps six feet wide and four-feet thick. Clark wiggled his way through to stand beside Cruz. "It looks like an ancient off-ramp for an interstate." Scooter joined them. "Who in the world constructed this? These stones go all the way around inside this shell ring."

Cruz raised his automatic rifle slightly, leading the others as he stepped forward through the huge stones, where he saw even larger stones, perhaps sixteen-feet tall and again, with two huge monolithic vertical stones that supported a massive horizontal stone. The stone structures were in the shape of a horseshoe, but still made from the same gray granite as the previous ring of stones. Scooter commented. "This ring is not closed in, if you look these stones are laid out like an...what is the word? Like a concert hall." Clark noticed that the tree-canopy above them separated, allowing filtered light to peer through to the center of the stone structure.

Collecting the entirety of his clan of Knights around him a little further inside the ring, Cruz stopped moving when he detected an overwhelming pungent odor. Then he saw the dwarfs. "What the....?"

He fanned his men out to the right and left behind him as he closely watched the grimy four-foot tall but extremely stocky and heavily bearded men with massive forearms, chipping away at one of six blue four-foot-tall rounded stones half buried in the black dirt inside the horseshoe. The stones themselves had some sort of glow with a blue hue and were perfectly placed inside the five huge granite stone structures. The burly beasts were using massive hammers and a thick chisel to trim away at the blue stones and each time they struck with the hammer on the stone an almost musical soothing tone was emitted. The Knights Protego raised their weapons toward the dwarves, as red laser dots appeared on the foreheads of both.

One of the dirty dwarves noticed the men during a heaving downward swing. He stopped banging and looked behind him, grunted some type of communication before he…and the other dwarf dropped their hammers and chisels and simply waddled off behind the other side of the huge shell-ring. The men relaxed their weapons and began to approach the very center of the structures inside the huge stones. Clark was awed. "Look at this soil. This dirt is as rich and fertile as anything I have ever seen." He reached down and placed a small amount between his lip and gum. "What is this place?" Scooter commented as he watched one of the last rays of the sun poke their way into the center where he now stood.

Clark noticed further movement behind one of the massive stone structures. He raised his weapon at once. He couldn't tell what was moving…but it was huge. A sudden glimpse of a massive muscled arm rotated around until as one, the group of Knights were stunned when a twelve-foot tall ridiculously muscled man strode into the semi-circular with them. The massive man wore knee high silver pair of boots and matching loin cover, with chest plated armor to cover his torso. His skin was bluish-gray, his hair golden blonde and his huge face was without blemish. The entire group raised their weapons on him. Clark broke the silence. "What the hell is that?" He spoke from a place in his past, in the times before he became one of the Knights Protego.

Once the creature came into full view, the team recognized just how muscular it was. "My God...his head is two-feet tall." Scooter tried to whisper, but the entire group suddenly gasped. For on the creatures back, he carried the most impressive set of wings, strong and perfectly groomed. The huge creature reached up to slightly lift one of the horizontal granite slabs to align it with the others, moving it with ease. Lt. Cruz's friend Trace ambled up beside him to whisper. "I believe this is what jumped up above the canopy and caused all hell to break loose on my helicopter."

As if suddenly aware of the fifteen soldiers, the enormous creature whipped around to stare directly at the line of KP. Clark's knees nearly buckled, as he realized from that look that he was not prepared for what he was seeing and he couldn't help but feel like he squirted a slight amount of pee. Rifle-fire rang out inside the shell-ring as Cruz looked over to where Trace stood with his smoking weapon. "What are you doing?" Trace barked back. "Protecting us." He alone shot at the creature a half a dozen more times. Cruz rushed over to try to stop him.

The huge creature seemed unaffected by the shots, but he glared down upon Trace and then to the entire group. He opened his mouth as if to speak, breathing in deeply to do so. Clark dropped with a thud to his seat, realizing the creature was trying to communicate something to them, but it sounded as if it spoke with three different voices and three different tones, all of which were very, very loud. The volume of each syllable of the uninterpretable language pounding on his chest like a sledgehammer. Clark began to feel very dizzy, disorientated and overwhelmed by the event. He dropped his rifle and saw nothing further but the sweet darkness of unconsciousness

.

Chapter 12- Wrist-bone

Jewell dragged a weary hand across his face, subconsciously rubbing the one-inch scar as he sat in the cool'ish late morning atmosphere at the midmorning café trying to shake some of his sleepless grogginess. Merchant Street, in the middle of Valetta, the largest city on Malta, was scarcely populated this time of the morning. He took a deep draw from his cup of cappuccino before blurting, "Yoh! Paul, what are we waiting on here?" Paul, still wearing his Enzio disguise, gave Jewell a harsh look to show his non-verbal lack of appreciation of the rude comment from the callous New York native. Nichalous, however, responded to the blunt New Yorker. "We are scheduled to meet with a church purveyor, Merrick, around the time a specific church opens. He is to provide us with a tour." Jewell wrinkled his face, clearly cranky from his sleeping arrangements from the past four hours. Once the vans from Medina had arrived in Valetta, Nichalous escorted the entire group to a second-floor barrack styled room in the gorgeous city. Most were provided bunk beds, but others were either assigned watch stations...or sat in a room corner to catch some much-needed rest following their catacomb/grotto adventure. Jewell and Nonie fell into that category due to a lack of seniority within the KP.

"That didn't really answer the question though...did it?" Jewel grumbled back to Nichalous. Paul shot him another stern look before providing additional information. "We hope to collect another artifact from this church, just as we collected the snake hide in the Catacombs."
The answer didn't really satisfy Jewell, but from experience he knew that he was at a limit for how much Paul was going to share. Plus, he knew he was grumpy from lack of sleep.
Nonie sat quietly studying the remarkable baroque buildings lining Merchant Street with their jutting angles and garish coloring. Rock noticed him staring.

"Kind of different from Apache country, isn't it?" Nonie didn't reply, just smiled and appreciated what he was experiencing. Rock had to admit, if there was one person in their group that stood out, it was Nonie, with his long straight black hair and high cheek bones and dressed in rawhide pants and a flannel shirt that was pressed against his chest by the large leather pouch that spilled down the left side of his waist.

Just then, a man dressed all in black walked up the street and straight to the table where Rock and the others sipped on coffee. "Enzio, it has been so long!" Paul jumped to his feet to give the man a hug. "Merrick, my good friend. How has life treated you?" The man stood a few inches over six-foot tall with Italian features...dark luxurious hair...rutty brown skin. "I am fortunate enough to work and worship in this wonderful church...so I cannot complain."

From the other side of the table, Rock smiled and shook his head, amazed at how successful Paul was at pulling off the deception of being "Enzio". Dominic and Nichalous rose and gave the purveyor a European kiss to each side of the cheek. "If you gentlemen will follow...?" Merrick led the way down Merchant St to the first crossing then turned right to head downhill into a large opening labeled *The Church of St. Paul's Shipwreck*.

The entire group entered to see the walls of an entryway lined with five-foot tall rich wooden armoires, each with its own special set of intricate religious themed carvings. In the middle was a four-foot tall, twenty-foot-long and eight-foot-wide table with storage drawers located underneath, equally rich wooded as the armoires. It was obvious to all that this was a room where research occurred. Rock noticed the main sanctuary of the church past the end of the room, dark and garish. Paul looked to Nonie. "Might I trouble you for the hide of the Asp?" Nonie fumbled around in his pouch to produce the rolled skin, handing it to Paul, who laid it out on top of the wooden table top and completely unrolled it. He looked to Merrick, who walked to the far corner of the room, lifted an intricate light switch to illuminate a large detailed chandelier hanging just three feet from the surface of the sturdy table. Paul spoke in the direction of Merrick, but his comment was really for all of those in the room. "Can you see any type of hidden emboldened message on the surface of the skin?" Merrick made his way over , placing his face as low to the surface of the skin as possible. "I can faintly detect an irregular surface, but I cannot say in all good faith that it is or is not a diagram, or any type of message as you have indicated."

Paul sighed, but Merrick still attempted to appease him. "We could attempt to apply a small amount of graphite dust over the skin. It is possible that would further emboss the hide." Paul shrugged his shoulders. "You are the expert in this area...try what you must, short of harming the skin." Merrick walked into the other room, allowing Rock to squeeze in with the opportunity to position his face low to the surface of the skin. "There is no doubt in my mind there is some sort of message here. I can see it...just can't make it out." Once Rock moved his head, Jewell spilled his long curly hair down on the table in the vacated spot to see for himself. "I don't see squat... Nonie...you are a tracker, why don't you have a looksee?" Nonie, replaced Jewell, but he didn't just look, he also touched, running his fingers down the entire length of the snake skin. "I do indeed feel something...but to me it is almost if there are two messages...one on this side..." He turned a portion of the skin over. "I believe another message is pressed into the outer hide. It will be more difficult to determine due to the snake scales on that side." Paul appreciated Nonie's skills, taking the opportunity to run his own hands along both sides of the hide, given the new information. "Your skills are impressive, my young native-American friend. I believe you are right..." Paul's claim prompted Jewell, Nicolaus and Dominic each to take their turns at feeling the skin. Rock took his turn at touching the skin, but when he did...a solid inner voice in his mind alerted him. *There is power in the blood.* Rock jerked his hand away immediately. Paul noticed. "Prick your hand on one of the scales?" Rock shook his head negatively and Paul dropped the subject.

Moments later Merrick returned carrying a bottle of dark gray graphite shavings. He sprinkled them up and down the length of the hide, then used a medium sized paint brush to whisk the shavings over the entire length and width of the skin as the entire group of men slanted their heads closer to the surface, attempting to read some hidden message, but the graphite had no discernable effect. Capone produced a super high intensity flashlight from a hidden pocket, shining it down the length of the skin. The light only confirmed that there was something pressed into the snake hide...but not clear enough to provide any information. "Enzio, you are welcome to usher your guest on a tour of the church. If you will excuse me though, I must participate in a ceremony on the hour and I find myself sorely unprepared." Merrick then left the group, exiting through huge luxurious doors toward the entrance.

Once he was clearly out of listening range, Paul mischievously directed. "Capone, if you would be so kind to reach behind you there on the edge of the armoire. There is a notch...inside that notch is a small round knob. If you would rotate that knob, then pull it out ever so slightly." Capone positioned himself toward the end of the large wooden structure, fumbled around until he found the device, then rotated it. Paul placed both of his hands directly under the marvelous glass chandelier hanging in the center of the room over the tables, catching an item that dropped from the center of the chandelier. He held it in his hand, rotating it where everyone in the room could see. It looked like one of the many glass tassels hanging from the chandelier but it had an odd shape to it as compared to the others. He held it up...and showed the group. "Oh...Dude!" Jewell blustered. "We are about to find more adventure, aren't we?" Paul/Enzio gave a Mona Lisa-like smile as he replied. "Gentlemen, if you will. Merrick has asked me to provide you a tour. "Nonie and Jewell quickly rolled up the snake hide and placed it into Nonie's pouch.

Paul guided them through the room toward the main cathedral. As they entered, the ceiling rose over forty feet above them and was awesome with the amount of wood, gold and gaudy silver throughout the Baroque designed chapel. Massive paintings and silver carvings were everywhere and even the floor had some of the most intricate and detailed artwork that Rock had ever seen.

Paul gave them a moment to stand gawking before he slowly made his way to the other side of the chapel. To the left was a glass case, inside was a marble or limestone column with a silver and gold bust of a man's bearded head. Paul stood slowly shaking his own. Jewell read out loud what the plaque underneath said. "The Column of St. Paul. This is the marble column used to behead the Apostle Paul in 70 AD." Paul rolled his eyes. Rock waited for an explanation. Paul held his hands out as if empty of any reasoning. "Apparently someone in the Vatican felt it was important to make a claim that this particular stone was the blunt end of what was rumored to have been my demise? As you can tell...that never happened and again...it is not even a very good likeness of me." He softly complained, still very mildly miffed by the images left behind on the island. Jewell and Rock chuckled. "Vanity is a terrible thing." Rock claimed.
"It should come as no great surprise that I have obviously brought you to this chapel for a reason." He turned and made his way left from the main alter to a small alcove filled with other magnificent art, busts and jeweled crowns behind glass cases. But all eyes turned to one piece, that was also housed in a large marble and glass display positioned upon a medium sized golden altar. Inside that glass case was a life-sized gold casting of a man's right arm with the palm facing the viewer. There was an oblong glass gold riveted viewing area clearly spot lighting the fragment of a man's arm bone at the top of the viewing area

with three one-inch diameter medallions below the bone. The hand reached for the sky and was mounted on a golden trophy block with a golden snake biting his tail at the base.

On the golden column supporting the structure was written 'S. PAULI APOSTOLI OS BRACHII'. "I assure you, I had nothing to do with this display. Apparently, one of our Pope's made the determination that he had found my body in Rome and obtained DNA samples of the bones. Now...I know a good bit about DNA and I can tell you one thing is for sure...this entire thing is poppy-cock. This bone does indeed match the bones of the grave that they found but...whose wrist bone it might be is a complete mystery to me. I can only assume the deceptive gravestone Titus placed in 67 A.D. got the churches attention and the church found the bones assuming they were mine." He held his arm up. "I have mine...so as I have stated, faking my death was the only way to encourage the Romans to leave me alone. We placed a stone plaque above a grave and made claim to it being mine." He sighed again.

"However, there is one piece of this display that I will make claim to have knowledge of." Paul inserted the glass shard from the chandelier into an unseen keyhole to the left of the glass case. Immediately the glass front of the golden arm cover, swung open exposing the gold hand with its glass covered compartment. Paul pulled the glass shard from outside of the case and inserted it into an identical key chase on the side of the golden hand. A brief pop on the backside of the golden hand, where a secret compartment was exposed, containing an ancient looking and wickedly designed key. Paul handed the key to Nonie as the curious crowd of adventurers crowded around him. He then closed the hidden compartment and slid the gold cast arm back into its case, closed the glass, before turning to Nonie. "You will need this key once we get into the crypts." Rock wrinkled his brow to ask. "What in the world are we doing?" Paul chuckled. "You will see...We have another interesting artifact hidden down in the crypt that I believe might be of assistance...or at least a little bird has insinuated as much to me."

Once the wrist bone of the Apostle was returned to its previous state, Paul led them back into the room where they had entered the church, making a left turn instead of proceeding back out into the streets. They entered a small hallway lined on the left side with a twenty-foot-long display case filled with a magnificent set of silver castings...the crowd gawked as Paul turned to the right underneath a sign that read, "Crypt".

As they entered the half cave shaped room with marble floors made to be a memorial for previous priest and dignitaries buried underneath the floor of the mostly white main chapel of the crypt.

Paul provided some context for their tour. "This is the crypt for this church and located beyond that opening..." He pointed to a square wrought iron gate, protecting a narrow passage that angled off to the left. "There is a passage that travels perhaps seventy meters back underneath the city of Valetta into the dark. Jewell...you and Nonie are the only two amongst us that can comfortably retrieve what we need. Once you reach the end of this passage, you will find a very small opening where geological plates of limestone present a two-foot-tall gap that will allow you to crawl between the plates. You, likely, will have to crawl on your belly out into this 'field' as I call it. About forty meters inside, there is an eight-inch by twelve-inch alabaster box located in the middle. It is affixed soundly to the bottom limestone plate. There is no water and there are no stones that I know of, just tiny restraints and the small alabaster container. I need you to open that box...and retrieve a small dowel that looks like stone...but it is made of wood. It looks much like a fat antique elementary school wooden pencil that has yet to be sharpened."

Nonie listening carefully, took the key to open the gate. Capone tugged on his shirt to prevent him from entering. "Take this radio with you...I have its mate. Maintain contact on Channel two...should you encounter a problem we may be able to assist you." Paul looked up and down at Capone's girth and smiled. "What? I could possibly help." Paul snickered. "Yes...possibly you could." Rock stepped up to his Bronx buddy, placing a hand on his and Nonie's shoulder. "Take my flashlight." Rock handed them a Maglite and patted them on the back. "Be careful." They opened the gate and darted into the passage, looking back once before they turned the corner.

Once his friends were out of sight, Rock turned to Paul. "What exactly are we doing. You have not even given us a clue." Paul breathed in deeply and explained. "Many years ago, I had a local boy from Medina, hide this small wooden dowel." He drew Rock close to him. "Most of mankind does not believe that Jesus was crucified because they could not locate the cross Jesus was crucified upon and there is a reason for that. The cross was taken down by a small group of Jewish entrepreneurs when they realized it may be valuable. They hid it and kept it preserved for many years. On one of the few occasions when an Arch Angel has visited me, I was provided information about the location of the cross...and purchased it from these men. Originally, I hid the cross in the same location as the Ark of the Covenant. Today, that very cross resides inside Ft. Knox. Oddly, I could not store the Ark and the Cross in the same area because they created havoc with magnetic devices and electrical circuits. I was never provided a reason or a purpose for obtaining the cross and can only assume it is going to be necessary in the days to come for a far grander purpose. However, during the period while we were moving the cross...an almost perfectly formed piece of it just fell off. I thought we had damaged the cross, however, when the Levites handed me the piece that had fallen from the main cross...it was in a perfect fat pencil shape. It cannot be a co-incidence that the wood did not splinter off. I have no idea what its exact purpose may be. In my few hours of sleep this very morning, I was provided a dream to indicate that this *dowel*, as I call it, will be useful in our upcoming quest."

"We have located the end of the passage!" The radio blared loudly, prompting Capone to decrease the volume. "Good lord…. look at this field. It is as if one mountain is wanting to lay on top of the other. Ask Paul, what prevents the top layer from falling on the bottom layer. There are no columns between the two. We have got to crawl on our belly all the way out into the middle of that thing?" Capone looked to Paul who simply nodded. "That would be correct" The radio went silent for thirty seconds. "Well…Nonie is ten feet in so I guess I am committed." Jewell grunted and the radio went silent again.

Rock squinted at Paul. "So, you have possession of the cross?" Paul nodded. "As a matter of fact, do you remember me sharing the story about the DNA project we capitalized, we realized that Jesus blood had leaked upon that cross. We took a DNA sample of the blood and used that to determine those future generations with his blood, all of which clearly defined you as a direct descendant." Rock pondered." So, Jesus blood is on this dowel?" Paul thought for a second. "No, this piece came from the very top of the cross. There was no blood on it." Rock tapped his fingers on the side of the crypt. "So…how is it going to help us?"

Paul shrugged. "This I do not know…but over the duration of my lifespan I have learned that we are very likely to find out. These feelings, dreams and voices are usually pretty cryptic…but I assure you…we are being told something."

"Found It!" Blasted Jewell over the walkie-talkie. "Making our way out from underneath this death trap." Fifteen minutes later the two men, rounded the passage. Nonie handed Paul the dowel. "Excellent, my young friend." Once

Jewell and Nonie dusted themselves off. Paul led them out of the crypt and back to the huge wooden storage compartments at the side entrance to the church.

Rock asked Nonie for the snake skin, which he unrolled full length up on top of the brown wooden table in the center of the room and beneath the chandelier before Paul turned the light on and ran the dowel from one end of the hide...to the other to measure the effect of the wood on the snake skin. Nothing happened. He looked to the others, having expected some type of reaction. "I obviously thought that would have some affect."

"Can I see the vial of blood from San Gennaro?" Rock requested, prompting Nonie to produce it from the pouch. The Holy descendant ran the vial over the length of the snake skin with no effect on the hidden embossed message, however, everyone in the room recognized the behavior of the blood when placed near the snake skin and its tendency to crawl up the edges of the vial as if magnetically drawn to the hide.

"Did the cross have any specific behavior with respect to the blood spilled upon it?" Rock inquired. Paul thought for a second. "As a matter of fact, the blood samples we collected seemed to have been absorbed into the very center of the wood...we were expecting to just scrape some off the exterior, but we could not find any detectable trace of blood on the outside." The big man pondered the snake skin again, before turning back to Paul. "May I?" He pointed to the shard of the cross in Paul's hand. Rock held it to the vial of San Gennaro's blood. The vial exhibited the exact same response of magnetic attraction to the dowel as it had the snake hide.

While no-one in the room understood what was happening, they all gawked at Rock's find. He removed the red wax seal from the top of the vial and placed the dowel on the snake skin, then tugged on the cork plug, looking to Paul for assistance in performing an experiment. Paul stood watching with a blank look

Page | 194

having no idea what Rock was doing. Slowly, the big man poured a small amount of San Gennaro's blood onto the dowel, where it was immediately absorbed by the thirsty wooden cylinder. He restored the plug into the top of the vial before turning his attention to the wooden dowel from the cross of the crucifixion, carefully rolling the dowel down the entire length of the snake skin, then stood back to see if there was a measurable result. Ten seconds later the embossed diagram or picture protruded from the snake skin, standing at least a quarter inch above the hide surface. Each of the attendee's gasped.

Nichalous, Dominic and Capone crowded toward the hide to get a better look at the results of Rock's experiment. "I know this place!" Dominic proclaimed. Rock looked at the Italian KP leader with confusion, unsure what he was looking at. To him, the diagram on the embossed snake hide looked like a picture of crowded giants squatted over a set of buildings. Dominic tapped his finger on the snake skin confidently. "This is Montserrat!" Paul crowded in for a better view. Jewell had to ask. "What the heck is Montserrat?" Paul nodded his agreement. "Montserrat is a monastery, just outside of Barcelona. These crowded human shapes above them are the rock formations of the mountains surrounding the monastery. I do believe you are correct Dominic. This is Montserrat!" Rock looked to each of them finally able to make out the shape of mountains above a clean line of the walls to a monastery.

"What does this mean?" Nonie questioned. The entire group stood around as if searching for the answer to that question. "I suppose it means, we need to go find out." Rock added. Paul started rolling the snake hide to take with them, but Rock stopped him by grabbing his hand, then spoke. "There is another side to this hide." Paul smiled then nodded. "So, there is!" The descendant turned the hide over and rolled the blood-soaked dowel over the backside of the hide and again after ten seconds the embossment swelled to provide a diagram and just like the first time, the men crowded around Rock to see what had appeared this time. Rock stood back confused looking at a round circular arrangement that looked like blocks or brick segments placed in a rounded arrangement. Inside the blocks were five rectangles not touching but shaped like a horseshoe and between the outer circle and the horseshoe shaped rectangles was a circle of smaller dots. Inside of the horseshoe was an arch or half circle of the same sized dots with one much larger dot in the center of the arch. "Well…. anyone have any idea?" The room remained silent. Rock helped Paul roll the snake hide and gave Nonie the vial of blood and wooden dowel along with the snake hide to tuck safely back into his pouch. "Off to Montserrat then".

****

A huge ball of sweat clung desperately to Clark's eyelash, until it gave up and dripped down his face while he slowly regained consciousness. He struggled to raise his arm to rub on a neck that ached from sitting upright but slumped. Dragging his hands over his face he attempted to open both eyes, until they both came into focus enough in the dank lighting to make out the muted face of his friend Harry Moorer, who stared back at him from forty-feet away with a massive curved shell ring wall behind him. Lolling his head to the right, he noticed the rest of the Knights Protego along with the pilot from the crashed helicopter, all sitting in much the same position that caused his discomfort. Looking down at his hands, he saw that they were bound together with man-made twine, his legs stretched out in front of him the same as the others.

"It is best if you just sit still!" Harry commented from across the shell ring. "Harry? What are we…? what are you doing here?" Harry peered at him, wearing tattered cut off Khaki pants and a filthy and torn white oxford shirt. "I am here because I choose to be." Scooter, freshly woken, barked his confusion at his

Jewish friend. "What is going on here? How in the world are you missing for this long and nobody has heard a word from you?"

One of the two dirty dwarves handed Harry a large clay pot full of water. "We will soon have time to discuss these things, but for now I need to care for your companions." He scurried around the wall, dipping a small cup into the pot, providing a cool sip of water for each of the men who were experiencing the same level of discomfort. Clark noticed that Cruz was attempting to stand, until he was unceremoniously shoved back to a seated position by one of the stout dwarves.

Harry spoke up. "Excuse me, if I may have your attention. I should warn each of you not to attempt to stand while you have been detained. He will not like it if you attempt to stand." Harry glanced back almost nervously over his shoulder at the curved wall.

Clark looked to Scooter's face for a reaction. "What do you mean 'HE' will not like it?" Scooter insisted. Harry attempted to explain. "My friend, you have to understand, I was invited here. You were not. I have purpose here. You do not and he will not appreciate you discounting his orders and hindering him from achieving his goals." Scooter looked back to Clark then to Cruz for any sign that they understood what Harry was talking about.

The putrid smelling dwarves continued to rotate around the interior of the shell ring, handing each man a torn chunk of bread from a hard loaf. Once they got to Clark, he couldn't eat what was offered, given the odor of the dwarves, thinking that they smelled a great deal like rotted meat.

Clark complained. "Who are these...these.... I don't even know what to call them? And do you really expect us to snack on this stale bread?" Harry provided his recommendation. "If I were you, I would dip the bread into the water. It will soften. You may be here for a while..."

Cruz decided he might have a better shot at communicating with the wild-eyed friend of Clark and Scooter. "Is there any chance you can tell me exactly why we are being held here and what this place is?" Harry ignored the question. Receiving no response, Cruz decided to look around at the entire interior of the shell ring. The walls were clustered with sharp oyster shells, the floors were simply dirt with not a single piece of debris in it. There were no weeds, no leaves, no broken palm fronds...nothing in the dirt.... just black dirt. He also noticed there was no visible entrance. "Where are our weapons?" Cruz inquired.

Harry seemed flustered having to answer questions. "You do not need your weapons here. They are all stacked in a safe location outside of this enclosure. As to the topic of why you are here, you are being secured to prevent you from interfering. This place is a containment enclosure designed to contain you and keep you safe from our protective measures." Scooter, well past agitated, yelled at his friend. "Interfering in what?" Harry walked to the far side of the enclosure, joining the dwarves. "That is not for me to say!" He looked up over the wall. A loud harmonic three voiced sound flooded the enclosure...and each man lost consciousness...again.

****

Rock couldn't help but smile, as he watched Jewell with his head back, mouth open, deep in a dream state as the train made its way from Barcelona to Monserrat. He glanced down and noticed a hawk's feather attached to Nonie's pouch, prompting him to mouth for Nonie to hand him the feather. He stretched arm out to delicately run the feather over Jewell's nose. Jewell squirmed before jerking his head away from the feather, raising his hand to swat whatever dream pest was touching his face. Rock snuck the feather to his face once again, causing Jewell to jump to his feet with agitation, clearly in danger of using a poor vocabulary choice.

Paul chuckled as he sat and watched his playful friends, before turning his attention to Dominic. "I assume that you have your men positioned ahead properly for our visit?" Dominic responded with confidence. "They were one train ahead of us and will be in various positions around the perimeter before we ever exit this train. We should be at our destination in ten minutes." Paul noticed that his phone light was flashing to signify a phone call. He whispered into the mouth piece.

Rock, listening to Paul's conversation, gave thanks. "You guys simply amaze me. You are so well organized, that I feel completely safe pretty much everywhere we travel. I want you to know how much I appreciate the work that you and all of our agents do." Dominic with barely a trace of Italian accent, stoically responded. "It is what we do!" He provided further information to Rock. "As always, Capone will be accompanying you during your visit. His men will be in your group, Jewell and Nonie will provide defense functions directly at your side. My men will be located around the peripheral to ensure there are no problems with any people with perhaps a hidden agenda." Rock smiled.

Following his brief phone conversation, Paul interrupted the pair. "There is a developing situation back at Fort Knox, concerning your friends vacationing in Georgia. We have lost communication with them following some rather odd behavior with respect to the inhabitants of the island. I have to apologize, but I feel that Titus and I must return back to the Ant Hill to support their efforts there." Rock looked confused. "The Ant Hill? What is that?" Paul chuckled. "It is our nick name for Fort Knox, due to its many expansive levels below the surface." Rock gave his mentor a stunned look before objecting. "Are you crazy? I am coming back to help you." Paul began shaking his head before Rock could even finish the statement. "No...I believe it to be in all of our best interest if you continue your efforts to solve the puzzle of this snake skin. There are far too many non-coincidences in play for you not to proceed to learn more from this spirit dream that the three of you have experienced. We will be fine without you, at least for the time it takes you to learn everything that needs to be learned here in this place." Paul pointed outside the window to the Montserrat Mountains.

He re-directed the conversation with a perfect distraction ploy. "The name Montserrat means 'serrated' in Catalonian, the language they are comfortable with here. As you can see, these mountains look just like that embossed pattern on the snake skin." Jewell and Rock stared outside at the beautiful pinkish rock formations. "They do look like clustered giants above whatever that building is below them." Jewell agreed.

"Below them is a monastery called 'Santa Maria de Montserrat'. It is an abbey of the order of the Saint Benedictine monks." Jewell gawked at the old man. "How do you know so much stuff? Dude!" Paul chuckled, looked down at his phone, before holding it out to Jewell to show him a web site. "Wikipedia...." He laughed at the New Yorker. "Capone and Dominic will protect you. When we get to the train station, I will return with the next train to Barcelona. Bartholomew will stay with you." He looked then to Rock. "If you would, once your search here is complete, just rent a jet and meet us in Atlanta or Ft. Knox, depending on our location." Bartholomew nodded his understanding.
About that time, the train came to a stop and Capone ushered the group outside. Paul gave Rock a hug, as the others took defensive positions. "Be careful my young friend. These last few days, if nothing else, have proven that adventure

can find you and your group pretty much anywhere and at any time. But...feel confident with Capone and Dominic."

Thirty minutes later, Rock found himself with a queasy stomach and a slight funk as he was funneled into a funicular gondola squeezed in between Nonie and Jewell traveling up an impressive forty-five-degree angle cable, four-thousand feet above ground level toward the Montserrat mountains and its beautiful monastery. Capone had paid to occupy the entire cable car to exclude other travelers. Jewell, his nose pressed against the glass, gawking at the beauty of a Spanish river below. Dominic shared information. "That is River Llobregat. The village below us is Monistrol." Capone whispered to Dominic, "I don't like this at all. We are extremely vulnerable at this moment and there is no defensible position up at the monastery." Dominic chuckled at his old paranoid friend. "Capone, you worry far too much. I have eight men ahead of us, they will provide an adequate umbrella of safety. Relax and enjoy the beauty."

Nonie couldn't help but notice Rock's solemn mood. "You worry for your other friends?" He looked down at his Native-American helper. "Is it that obvious? I guess it bothers me knowing that they are missing and I am not doing anything to actively help find them. So, yes it bothers me a great deal. Here we are only chasing dreams." Jewell overheard his big friend and wiggled his way to stand beside Nonie. "Dude listen to yourself. There is nothing we can do for them right now. Paul needs to gather more information, besides...you act like the things we are doing are un-important." Rock looked at his pal unsure. "I suppose." He sounded unconvinced. "Think what we have experienced just in the last two days. We three got wasted on peyote where we had these ridiculous dreams, we have re-acquainted ourselves with the dude that tried to have both of us killed two years ago. We have been attacked by the Italian mafia, been challenged by the Knights of Malta, we saw two-dozen freaking angels." Rock wrinkled his brow at the loose rah-rah speech. "And for what?"

"For what? Dude...we have a vial of blood from a man almost two-thousand years dead, a snake skin that has a magic map or two on it, and a pencil made from the cross that Jesus was crucified on. And all these things we have collected in just two days. I am pretty sure Clark, Randall and Scooter are having just as much of an adventure where they are located. But....dude...come on?" Rock looked to Nonie for any words of encouragement. "You are not alone here. We are on our spiritual journey and I am sure events are occurring as they should. I feel as though we are true and our hearts are pure." Rock could not argue the two different perspectives. "Okay...okay...let's follow this through."

Five minutes later they unloaded from the yellow cable car, strode up a small hill, and climbed another hundred feet of steps before they found themselves staring at the entrance to the Monastery. Capone's men spread out automatically in front of Rock. Dominic led the way toward the opening. Capone noticed a small group of nuns and spoke to them. *"Scusa, Ti capita di kno Dove avremmo localizzato Padre Merced"* The lead nun replied. "We speak English, Father Merced typically ventures outside the monastery this time of day for prayer." She directed Capone back toward the cable car station to where they could purchase tickets for a cog train to the top of the mountain to the head of hiking trails. As an alternative, she recommended they walk the thousand or so stair steps to the top. "Grazie!" Capone nodded and scurried over to talk to Dominic, which led to both whispering commands into their ear pieces to relocate security personnel. "This makes me nervous as crap." Capone grumbled. Jewell and Rock shared a smile due to the seriousness of their protector, until Jewell realized he was supposed to be acting as a protective force as well.

Capone sent him up on the first funicular to the top of the Sant Joan to assist in forming a human shield to protect the most precious bloodline of Jesus.

Shortly thereafter, Rock and the others inserted themselves into the cog-wheeled train which slowly rose another thousand feet above the monastery. Once at the top, Dominic could be heard re-positioning his men to return on the next train down once they had located Father Merced. "It's quite beautiful, you know?" Rock expressed his admiration as he stared down into the rectangular courtyard of the Monastery with its clean lines of blonde bricks contrasted against the backdrop of pink phallic shaped massive stone giants that made up the mountains.

The cog train stopped and the men unloaded to a set of stairs leading another hundred feet up. They slogged their way up to the top of the Montserrat mountains, appreciating the marvelous views of the backside of the mountain that overlooked the great portion of Catalonia, sitting at the mountain's feet, its walls below dropped abruptly down to meet the green fields of local farmers.

Capone directed the group up a twenty-foot-wide gravel hiking trail that dropped off to the right of the viewing platform, then veered back to the left before rising to wrap around the mountain at a relatively level pace before angling to the left again to traverse up a steeper portion of the trail. They continued until they rose above a high point and the trail circled back to the right and slightly up to within view of a small stone chapel, where Father Merced was rumored to be meditating. The group stopped below the chapel at the road while Dominic humped up a small stone path the remaining fifty-feet of elevation to open the chapel door, careful not to startle whomever might be inside.

Moments later, he exited with a medium sized man wearing traditional monk type clothing. The two strode down the path, where Capone introduced himself and his group. Father Merced politely listened as he looked over each man in the group, until his eyes fell upon Rock. "And this man?" He pointed at him un-aggressively. "I have dreamed of you...recently." Rock was unsure what to do with that information, so he responded the only way he knew how. He ignored it. "Father, we need some assistance. We are on a spiritual journey and we have reason to believe there is a secret hidden somewhere here in your wonderful monastery or perhaps in the surrounding area." He motioned for Nonie who produced the snake skin from his pouch. "Our friend Paul directed us to this ancient snake skin on which we managed to uncover a secret of sorts." He rolled the skin out on the ground in front of the priest. "The reason we are here today is this..." He pointed to the raised design on one side of the skin. Jewell elbowed Rock to indicate he had shown the holy man the wrong side of the snake skin. "Ahhh..." Father Merced exclaimed, once he looked over the blistered design on the skin. "Santa Maria de Montserrat?" The priest ran his hand thru his thick black hair, showing more than just a few isolated gray hairs mixed within.

"I understand your journey. How can I be of assistance? I know of this man, Paul, of which you speak. I have seen him on numerous occasions. I recognize his confidant." Merced pointed to Capone. "We were hoping that you might consider providing us a tour around your lovely monastery and allow us to look for clues that might contain the potential of revealing a long-lost secret." Father Merced slapped Rock hard enough on the back that activated a subconscious defensive response from Capone, who was clearly taken by surprise by the Fathers move.

"I can see no reason not to assist you in this tour. Unfortunately, we will have to wait until the grounds close for the day, perhaps three more hours, but I will gladly be your host if you will consider joining me in a modest late lunch." Father Merced noticed Capone and Dominic speaking into their ear-pieces, having already detected at least half-a-dozen of their men above him on the hills. "Invite the others as well...we will have a small feast and participate in fellowship." Capone and Dominic halted...slightly surprised. "I insist!" He offered before ambling back down the trail. "Shall we?" He expected the group to follow...and Rock led the way.

The priest led the group back to the Monastery, to a banquet room, where he dispatched helpers and arranged for the group be fed. Numerous monks assisted in delivering loaves of bread, bowls of olives and an assortment of cheese delivered to the monastery by worshippers from the town below.

Dominic sat with his men, Capone did the same with his own, while Father Merced tore off a chunk of bread and dipped it in a wine goblet before asking to see the snake hide again. Nonie rolled it out over the massive wooden dining table surrounded with bench seats. "What do you hope to find here?" Merced directed his comment at Capone. Rock answered for him. "We do not know for certain what it is we are searching for. Since we began this spiritual journey, we have found items that are highly improbable and certainly none that we expected to find. Do you know of any secrets or rumors of secrets surrounding this place.?" Merced smiled through a cheek full of wine bloodied bread as he carved a matching piece of cheese. "We typically do not entertain rumors or gossip, but...I can tell you that there have always been hushed tales concerning the brothers Venanci and Agapit Vallmitjana, who carved the marvelous statues above the atrium as you enter the basilica. The town folk below speak of a holy treasure hidden deep inside of this nine-hundred-year-old gothic cathedral. As far as I know, there has not been a discovery...at least nobody has come forward to make that claim. But...I believe that you will find the biggest mystery or secret of this place is 'La Moreneta'...a statue nicknamed *The Black Madonna*. She is named that because the wood used to construct her darkened to a black color over time without a solid explanation as to why. It being such a holy symbol here in Catalunya, the Vatican refuses to allow any type of scientific examination to determine the cause of its discoloration. It is the reason I cannot allow you access to the basilica until after the viewing of 'The Virgin of Montserrat' is complete for this day. Worshipers much like the ones in the long line at this very moment are waiting to view her. She is in the back of the cathedral where worshippers touch or kiss her hand and pray for blessings. The statue itself sits behind a sheet of glass where only her hand holding an orb that is symbolic of the entire universe is exposed. Of course, there are other mysteries surrounding the church such as the vision of the Virgin Mother in a cave down below, but this snake-skin that you have shown me, clearly indicates this monastery is the place for your search.

Just a little history, this church was destroyed in 1808 by Napoleon's troops, but the Vatican resurrected it before 1900 to the splendor that you witness here today. I would encourage you to ensure you pay attention to the impressive statues on the pedestals up above the entryway, once you enter the Basilica. They are exquisite." Nonie asked. "Does this place like many others contain a crypt?"
Rock and Jewell snapped their heads sharply toward their new friend, surprised by the boldness of the question. Merced responded. "Oh yes, there is a crypt...for the monks and priest that have served here for the duration of its existence. Today it is seldom used, the Vatican prefers to maintain a healthy flow of personnel through the hallways and these last twenty years or so, few have died here. I consider myself as fortunate to have been a resident for that time."

He looked closer at the snake-hide with curiosity. "You say there are other markings?" Capone and Rock gently turned the snake hide over to show the blistered markings on the rough scaly side of the hide. Father Merced ran his fingers along the hide, tilting his head to find different perspectives with the lack of sufficient lighting in the fest hall. "Ahhh...Stonehenge!" He commented. The entire subset of the Knights Protego stopped eating and looked to Father Merced. "What did you say?" Rock questioned with mouth half full

"Half a decade ago, I was assigned the task of educating myself about all things related to Stonehenge. I anticipated the leaders of the church would be sending me there for my studies. That is where I learned about the design present on the back-side of this snake hide. It represents what many believe Stonehenge looked like when it was completed, long before the trials of time weathered it to its present condition." Rock tried to remember what his wife had told him about the dream she had experienced concerning Stonehenge. "Hmmph!" Capone tossed him an odd look before plopping a bulging olive into his mouth. "My wife, Raw knee, mentioned that she had a dream about Stonehenge the other night...something about me being in the middle of Stonehenge...and black trees. At the time, I didn't think much about that...but I do not believe that can be considered a coincidence any longer." Jewell tossed his two-cents into the conversation. "Well...looks like we know where we are headed from here! What if we were supposed to go there first?" Capone shook his head, as always uncomfortable with the lack of quality planning as they trekked all over the world.

Two festive hours later, the group heard the bells of the cathedral ringing to indicate it was six o'clock. Father Merced rose from the table as Jewell and Nonie rolled the snake hide. Rock stood as he drained the remainder of wine from his goblet, when from inside that familiar voice hammered in his head. *There is power in the blood!* He gulped, suddenly becoming light-headed, the voice much stronger now than at other times. Dominic noticed his instability and Nonie quickly moved to ensure Rock did not collapse. "Are you feeling okay?" The Italian KP leader quizzed. "Yes, I just heard a voice. Father, do you have any water." Merced scurried over to Rock's side, placing one of the big man's arms over his shoulder. "There is a fountain just outside near the atrium. I think you will find it to be just what you need."

Nonie positioned himself under the other arm and they assisted Rock to a large fountain that was fed from a mountain spring. He placed his hands underneath the cooling stream, guzzled a large mouthful then indicated he was okay and ready to head inside. Jewell took over for Merced, who led them through one of the five large arches of brick, shuffling them onto the marble floored courtyard, where ahead and above them were twenty carved statues on ten-foot tall pedestals attached to the front entry of the church. Jewell gawked. "Father Merced, you were not exaggerating, those are pretty impressive carvings. Who are these men?" Merced smiled at the New Yorkers appreciation. " St. John the Baptist, St. Joseph, St. Benedict and various other church dignitaries."

Merced led them into the nave of the church, where inside, it rose to over seventy-foot tall, two-hundred feet long and was full of sheer splendor and extravagance with its high ceiling. It like most of the Catholic churches in Europe, was adorned floor to ceiling with incredible artwork, mosaics and paintings from some of the greatest painters in history. "I have a few chores left to complete before my day is over, so I will leave you to continue your search here. If you will notice, to the right, you will see an alabaster portal with numerous biblical paintings, directly through this portal is the throne room. You will then notice stairs leading up through a small opening to the left once you have reached the other side, up those stairs you will be funneled directly out in front of the Black Madonna. Feel free to explore the entire Basilica. I trust that I need not remind you to treat the items inside with the respect it deserves. Should you need anything, simply send one of the other monks to locate me." Dominic slapped Father Merced on the back appreciatively as he exited the nave.

The entire group began investigating each of the hundreds of paintings, ornate wood carvings, hanging candles and candle holders and the small shrines that continued into the portal with its antiseptic feeling alabaster floor and walls. The large cathedral was ridiculously quiet, so much so that everyone in the room could hear each man inside breathing, each brush against their pants leg magnified, each audible expression of appreciation for the wonderment of the art surrounding them.

As they ducked down into a lower chapel, Nonie identified the entrance to the crypts on the left with its associated stairs leading down via a corridor that had an odd small portal with inch-thick iron bars just beside the entrance to the crypts. The iron bars crisscrossed preventing any entry into a small crawl space not unlike the space he and Jewell had crawled to retrieve the snake hide back in the catacombs of St. Paul in Malta. Jewell sauntered up beside his lookalike. "Not crawling in there!" Figuring he had done enough small space navigating for one spirit journey. Nonie, however, disappeared down the steps to the crypts, prompting Jewell to retrieve his flashlight and follow.

Rock called to Nonie. "Could you leave your pouch, I may need to compare the blister design on the snake hide to something we might find. The Apache tracker jogged back up the stairs and removed his pouch carefully handing it to the big man. Dominic and Capone continued their search for clues inside the chapel. Rock reached the back of the portal, locating the stairs to the left and climbed them until he found himself staring the Black virgin in the face. "Gosh...I imagined she would be huge, looking at her from the back of the church she just appeared so large." He said to Capone who crept up beside him, as always uncomfortable with the man he was sworn to protect just roaming away from him. Rock put his hand on the glass barrier, noticing that her clothing was painted gold while she sat on a silver throne. He reached out and touched the worn smooth globe protruding from a six-inch hole in the glass barrier, wondering just how many hundreds of thousands or perhaps millions of people had touched her hand and the globe she cupped. It overwhelmed him to think of the sheer number of people searching, for meaning, in need, some desperately, for some sort of blessing...from a statue of all things. Yet, he stood in the quiet solemnness and energetic awesomeness just from looking to that very same statue squarely in the eyes. It was just her...and him. Capone breathing deeply, before squeezing up beside him to ask, "Find anything?" Rock interrupted his moment with 'La Moreneta' to realize he hadn't even searched for clues. After several moments and seeing nothing obvious, he started to walk away when the voice hammered his skull yet again. *There is power in the blood!* The words unbalanced him, making him unstable as he tried to walk away. Only Nonie's pouch loosely tied around his waist, which snagged on a handrail leading down the steps away from the black Virgin, prevented him from tumbling down the stairs.

Capone dashed down the steps to assist him. Rock looked nervously at his protector. "It was that voice again. It called to me that there is power in the blood." Dominic appeared and questioned. "Then, why don't you use the blood, it worked on the snake skin." Rock's eyes stretched wide. He fumbled inside the pouch to pull out the vial containing the remainder of the blood of San Gennaro. he held it up to 'La Moreneta's hand. The liquid inside the vial followed the hand up the side of the vial just as it had done with the snake skin. He popped the lid off the vial to pour a drop on the hand of the Virgin. The blood reacted as if it were being drawn out by a vacuum much like being sucked out with a straw. It coated the entire hand. Rock was forced to tip the opening to prevent the hand from drawing all the blood from within the vial. The Knights watched as the blood turned the hand back to the color of fresh wood and beyond that, the orb in her hand seemed turned from a dull silver'ish-gray to a replica of the earth with its blues, greens and browns of grass, water and land, coincidental with the unusual plopping noise somewhere in the distance of the dark church but easily within the doors. "What was that?" Rock looked to Dominic, who shook his head to indicate he was clueless.

The three turned their attention back to the Virgin, whose hand suddenly returned to the blackish coloration. The orb also turned to its pre-blooded dullen gray. Dominic stated the obvious. "You have found something?" Capone shook his head. "We caused something...but we know not what. Or where.?"

Jewell and Nonie came sprinting toward them, back from their exploration of the entrance to the crypts. The tracker holding a small burlap sack the size of a softball, tied and bound with a sinewy membrane. "Where did you find this?" Rock asked. Jewell took a deep breath to respond. "We were inside the crypt when we heard this sucking sound behind us near the entrance. We dashed back up the stairs to see what it was and noticed that these iron bars for the small crawlspace had simply fallen from the entrance, like they were just pulled lose. I shined my flashlight inside and saw this package. It wasn't there the first time I looked in that crawl space. I couldn't tell where the sack came from."

Nonie handed the sack to Rock, who led the group away from the statue and back into the chapel area to a large marble table with a large bust of an ancient monk. He asked. "Capone if you would allow me to borrow that knife that you carry with you everywhere?" Capone produced the black combat knife, pushing its encrusted red cross across the table to Rock who thanked him, then attempted to saw through the bindings for the sack but struggled mightily. Dominic bent over to assist him. "Appears to be bound with sheep-ligaments. They are quite tough to remove." After several moments of grief, the last of the bindings were cut and Rock delicately opened the sack to find three completely different seed pods nestled in black loamy dirt. Each of the seed pods was the size of a peach pit, one even resembled a peach seed but they were all distinctively different in color and shape. "What in the world?" Jewell barked. Rock rubbed his head and looked first to Capone, then Dominic for signs of what they were looking at. They were all completely baffled by the contents. *There is power in the blood!* Rock winced at the voice but was relieved that it wasn't quite as powerful as it had been moments earlier. He removed the blood-filled vial from the pouch and poured half of the remaining contents onto the seeds as the group dropped back, then anticipated what might happen next. But nothing happened, causing confusion in each of the adventure seekers faces.

"Well...what do we do now? What is our next clue?" Jewell asked Rock, then Capone.

Rock sighed, slightly dissatisfied...empty of any obvious answers. "Well, the only remaining clue we have available is the odd dreams from my wife combined with the recognized blistering on the snake hide that Father Merced noticed. It looks like Stonehenge is all we have left to go on....so?"

Chapter 13- The Voice

The descendant of Jesus sat admiring the Spanish country-side as the train pushed its way back to Barcelona. He wondered what might lie ahead for them at Stonehenge, realizing that at each stop of this vision quest they had collected another piece of some huge puzzle that none of them realized an ending just yet. He was generally surprised that they had been placed in as many dangerous and risky situations as they had been. On the surface this search was relatively tame, but it surprised him just how close to violence they had come those few times. His attention rotated to Dominic, as he skillfully bantered with someone on the other end of his cell phone, concerning the procurement of a proper private jet to fly them to Heathrow airport.

Looking to Jewell sitting directly in front of him, a single slim line of slobber dangling from the corner of his mouth, his head laid back with sporadic snoring sounds as his good friend slept. He couldn't help himself, he decided to get the feather and mess with his cocky longtime friend again. Capone sat beside Jewell, his eyes closed sitting straight up as the train pulsated. Rock leaned over and ran it over Jewell's inch wide scar, causing his friend to almost leap from the seat again. Jewell rubbed his face to discourage whatever made up pest was crawling on him. While Rock chuckled inside.

Rock's mischief was interrupted when Dominic handed him his
cellphone where the Apostle Paul's voice waited. "My young friend, I
trust your adventures have been productive?" Rock smiled and shared
the full volume of the events of the day, or at least those that occurred
since the two-thousand-year-old man had departed. "So, am I correct
in assuming that you are headed back to the U.S. now?" Rock
interrupted for clarification. "We are making plans to go to
Stonehenge." Paul became silent on the other end of the call for an
awkward amount of time. "Are you there?" Rock asked, confused by
the silence. "Rock, allow me to send you something." Paul could be
heard, tinkering with something while trying to maintain phone
contact, obviously attempting to have others assist him.
"Yes...yes...no... I need you to send the file from the Geologic scanner.
Yes...that one. Rock...I am sending you a picture of a geologic survey
provided to us just moments ago."

Paul waited back in Fort Knox, while Dominic retrieved a lap top from a
large burlap sack left for him by Titus. It took Dominic a few moments
of searching until he retrieved the email message sent by Paul and
opened, downloaded it, then rose and placed the laptop in front of
Rock, where he viewed a muted picture that seemed to match the
diagram on the back of the snake skin. Rock recognized it. "Yeah...that
is what is on the back of the snake-hide. Father Merced told us he had
done a study a while back and that the diagram in your layout is a
depiction of old-world Stonehenge. It is also the reason we are headed

that way." Paul cleared his throat. "Rock, we received this picture within the last hour from our Geological satellite people here at Ft. Knox." Rock wrinkled his brow. "Yes...and..." The communication went silent until Rock realized the point Paul was attempting to make. "Oh gosh...this picture is not of Stonehenge, is it?" Rock busily used his smart phone to view images of the Druid'ish relic not far from London. "Stonehenge has decayed to something else. But...if that is true where did you get this picture from?" Paul allowed his brilliant protege to circle around to a point of understanding. "This picture was taken of the North End of Sapelo Island, the same island our friends have managed to disappear from. There is some sort of visual distortion that hinders our normal viewing and for any radio communication occurring on that end of the island, as a matter of fact we have lost communication with our folks there completely. The last communication we have received is to inform us that your friends have penetrated the area to search for various types of unusual behavior including a sighting of your good friend Harry Moorer. Re-enforcements who were dispatched, experienced a near catastrophe when their helicopter crashed and subsequently, have also gone missing."

"I understand." Rock looked over at Capone and Dominic with a serious appearance. "Change of plans, we are headed to the U.S." Rock placed his ear back to the cell-phone as Paul wasn't finished speaking with him. "If you would be so kind, please ask Dominic to support this mission with us. Capone's men may not be enough. Once you have your flight, contact us here at Ft. Knox. We will meet you at the Savannah/Hilton Head International Airport?" Rock disconnected and informed his cohorts about the change of plans.

****

Signs of distress appeared on Clark's face as he marched around the inside of the shell ring prison searching for an exit, knowing there had to be one. Thinking, how did the dwarves enter to provide them with water and bread. He re-traced his steps where he had already walked, utterly confused by the situation. He gathered a few of the Knights Protego around him. "I think the best thing we can do is form a human tower. One of us should be able to get a look to the other side of the wall." Cruz wandered over to the wall, examining the twelve-foot barrier surrounding them. Scooter doing research on his own, was baffled by the disappearance of Harry and the dwarves. "How in the world did they get out of here? They can't have just vanished." The pilot, the only non-member of the Knights Protego, was the first to get down on his hands and knees, prompting the others to do likewise as they carefully built a human tower. Cruz coached them as they slowly stacked themselves, pyramid style until it was his turn to climb up to the top. He carefully crawled up the bodies of his men until he could just barely stretch his chin over the sharp craggy surface of the shell wall.

"That is just amazing!" Cruz exclaimed as he crawled down from the tower, allowing the others to untangle themselves before he spoke again. "What's our situation?" Clark asked, wishing he had been the one to look over the wall. Cruz shook his head, wiping sweat from his hair. "The entirety of the exterior, at least the portion I was able to view, contains literally thousands, if not tens of thousands of rattlesnakes. They are everywhere outside the shell-ring. However, this enclosure we find ourselves trapped in, does appear to be outside of the black-tree-line wall and whatever that huge creature was is nowhere in sight." He looked over to the other side of the shell-ring. "I am not positive but...it appears that this side of this enclosure butts-up against the lagoon where that alligator orgy is happening and I didn't see anything else encouraging."

The helicopter pilot asked. "So, nothing prevents us from hopping over the wall?" Lt. Cruz cast a grim look his way. "Well...only if you consider certain slithering death or gaping jaws waiting to tear you to shreds, nothing. Oh and... I assume there are still moody odd-shaped bovine roaming the surroundings as well. I guess none of the rest of you has had any success in locating any type of exit? There has to be one!" Clark added. "I have no problem jumping that wall if you guys can position me to find a space clear enough to prevent a snake-bite."

Most of the men, wandered around searching for an exit, before congregating in the middle again. Cruz looked to Clark. "If we had our weapons, we could certainly clear you a path thru the snakes. I wonder what they did with them?" After a short silence, he spoke again. "If you want to try to jump the wall...it will be very risky but...it seems the only doable action right now. Unless you would rather, we try digging a hole underneath the wall." Clark thought for a second. "I would rather jump on top of a snake than have one drop into the hole with me."

Feeling that the decision had been made, Lt. Cruz took his turn starting the pyramid, ninety-degree's inside the shell ring from where they had done so moments earlier. Once built, Clark struggled to climb to the top, causing numerous yelps as he placed his elbow or knee in a sensitive spot on one of the men supporting him. Just as he got to the top, a voice behind him startled him, nearly causing him to fall to the forest floor. "Do you really think he is going to allow you to escape?" The pyramid of Knights turned their heads and saw Harry Moorer with his tattered cargo shorts, and bare feet standing, his hair un-kept, bushy mustache and beard, even his eyebrows were disheveled and unruly. Clark jumped down from the pyramid as the men once again untangled themselves to listen to what he had to say.

Cruz challenged the wild-eyed man. "We were not aware we had to ask his or anyone's permission for that matter, to leave this place. Are we prisoners here for some reason?" Harry stood silent for a full moment. "Did it ever occur to any of you that he is protecting you by keeping you in here?" Scooter, irritated by the entire notion, squawked. "He who? Who are you talking about...and what the hell is all of this ...this...place."? Harry looked to his friend with a confused non-friendly look. "I don't know...I am not sure...umm...I only know that you are safe while you are in here." Clark was just as frustrated as the rest. "Well, can you at least tell us how you are entering and exiting this shell-ring?" Harry looked around the huge circular jail cell. "Honestly, I can't tell you. He has some method of opening a portal for me to get inside. I don't know how it works." Trace took his turn. "You haven't really given us much of any information. What is he doing out there? Who are the two short dudes? " Harry just stood there with a confused look on his face, as if the man spoke an entirely different language?

Scooter sighed hugely before asking. "Well, can you tell us what exactly you are doing here? We have been looking for you for a very long time. You just disappeared on us." Harry scrunched his face. "I don't know...or at least...I don't remember. I just know that I have to be here and that the reason I am here is important." Scooter looked to Clark with a scowl. "What do you mean you don't remember? How can you not remember how you got here or what you are doing here?" Harry answered through his befuddlement. "I apologize...I can only tell you what I know...and I was sent in here to tell you...he will not allow you to leave."

Clark was incensed. "We will see about that. Guys, build that pyramid again." The KP got back on hands and knees and once again began to stack man over man, until all that was left was Clark and Scooter. Scooter climbed the others and got into position for Clark to use him as a launching pad over the wall. Clark strained his way to the top of Scooters back, placed one foot then the other on his haunches, then peered over the other side. Beneath him were numerous snakes and a couple of alligators, not exactly the thousands Cruz had seen on the other side of the shell ring. He tossed himself over the side, careful not to cut himself up on the sharp oyster shells protruding from the top of the wall. He landed directly in front of the two huge alligators, each immediately opening their dangerous maws toward him, while dozens of rattlesnakes shook their tails to alert him of their intentions. He slowly stood, then remained completely frozen. "Scooter, this was not...a very well thought out plan!" He muttered. Scooter yelled down after him. "Are you okay?" Clark slowly rolled his eyes up to look at Scooter. "Well...other that standing directly in front of two dinosaurs and a whole bunch of slithering death, I think I" He checked himself."...no I am certain that I just pee'd a little bit. Couldn't be better. Remind me again, what was my plan once I got outside?"

Scooter looked down at Clark's situation. "I would jump down with you but...I don't want to cause them to attack you." Clark's eyes flew wide open. "Honestly, I could use a distraction right about now...come on down." The taller of the two friends carefully climbed up and tumbled over the top of the wall head first, landing awkwardly on his shoulder, but rolled with the fall and lay on his back, awaiting any resultant attack. But...the snakes and alligators remained firmly affixed on Clark, who exclaimed. "What the hell? They didn't even flinch when you landed." Scooter, after a brief opportunity to gather his composure, slowly got to his feet and found an eight-foot-long stick. He was currently in a position between the wall and two huge diamondbacks, the gators were on the other side of where Clark stood frozen. Scooter searched to ensure there were no other unseen critters around him, the closest appearing to be ten-yards away. He took the stick and flipped one of the rattle snakes near his friend as far from them as he could. He then, slowly did the same to the other.

The gators however, never moved, lying with their massive jaws agape waiting for Clark to make a mistake. "How fast do you think these gators can run?" Clark trembled as he asked. "Scooter calmed his friend. "I believe I read where they can run about 11 miles per hour. But I have also read articles that say 15-18 MPH." Clark hesitated. "And how fast can I run?" Scooter looked at the gators. "I would say it depends." Clark barked back. "Depends on what?" Scooter grinned with dry nervous wit. "Depends on if you are being chased by an alligator. How fast do you think you can run?" Clark was done asking questions, so he immediately bolted toward Scooter screaming as he ran, then bumped into his friend and hugged him for stability. "Well..." He looked up at Scooter. "Now...all I have to be is faster than you!" He made a right angle turn and started running through the forest, Scooter right behind him. As he ran, he noticed the Brahma bulls gathered up ahead of them, adjusting the friend's direction by funneling them toward the pond but the bulls were not fast enough.

The two friends out-maneuvered them and scampered out away from the shell ring and the circle of black trees just to the left of them. "When we get out of here..." Clark questioned. "I assume we are going to find some type of help?" Scooter running and almost out of breath, gasped. "That would be a heck of an idea, wouldn't it?"

Gaining distance from the bulls and knowing that the snakes and alligators were behind them, allowed them to slow down slightly from their full-out sprint. In front of them, a sudden loud thud and the appearance of a pair of massive blue-tinted legs necessitated them to slide to a halt, forest floor debris flung into the air from their sudden stop. They looked up to see the creature, who other than being enormous and tinted blue with ridiculous sized wings and a massive ugly face, looked almost completely human. They stood frozen with indecision, panting heavily. The huge man-thing stood completely erect, looking down on them indignantly as he snorted from his nose and opened his mouth once again, issuing his loud three voices that beat down on Clark and Scooter...and they both immediately fell unconscious.

Chapter 14- Search

Capone was the first to step off the ferry, during a miserable grueling rainstorm that had met him and his group when they had flown into the Savannah airport to meet Titus and Paul. He motioned to four of his agents to feather out to provide a safe corridor for Rock. The big man was the second off the boat, followed closely by the remaining members of their party. Paul, discussing logistics with the gregarious Dominic, lagged slightly behind, while Capone jogged ahead to talk to their impromptu host, Montel Barkley, who stood at the end of the landing in his khaki jacket and wide brimmed hat to deflect the rain.

The host led the group to a sixty's era military style personnel carrier with canvas cover on the rear. "My colleagues and I would be most appreciative and very interested in any information you might could share concerning our team mates here on the Island. I believe our friend Clark Korn has been communicating with you?" Capone inquired.

Montel shook his head. "Yessir...I warned them guys not to venture to North end of the island, just as I warn you to avoid that area as well. There is nothing for you there but misfortune." Paul walked up to the two men, a large hood covering his face to protect him from the weather. He interrupted them. "I understand...but still...If you will speak with your people, perhaps they can shed some light that might be helpful in this situation. We would appreciate their cooperation." The holy man smiled warmly at Montel, who appeared slightly annoyed by being interrupted. He turned to face Paul, blank faced, his smile faded. "As I have explained to your friend, they have been seen traveling to the wrong end of the island and much like I tried to warn them, I will do the same for you. It is best if you not visit the North end." Jewell, overhearing the meeting blurted. "What is there to fear on the north end of the island?" Montel was done with the conversation, turned away and did not reply as he walked to his own old truck.

Fumbling with his smart phone despite the downpour, Capone located a mapping program to share information with the others. Titus volunteered to crawl up into the large truck driver seat, while the others piled into the rear of the canvassed personnel carrier. With all the rain, Nonie and Jewell struggled to climb into the back of the vehicle. As they did, a huge bolt of lightning with an immediate boom of thunder gave notice that they were indeed in the south. It also caused them both to fall backwards into a drainage ditch, all the items inside Nonie's pouch spilling out onto the islands sandy soil. The two quickly collected the vial of blood, snake skin and wooden dowel of the cross but neither noticed the three-pronged tool the old man had given to Rock back in Naples, which had spilled several feet away and was covered by the water in the small ditch. Another significant lightning strike caused them to scurry for the truck bed, while others assisted by pulling each of the shorter men to the back. Dominic joined Titus up in the cab of the huge military-style vehicle. In the back, Rock sat next to Capone and Paul.

"So...what's the plan?" Capone looked to Paul, water dripping down his hood. "The north end of the island is key, there is no doubt. It is there that the island is cloaked, not only in mystery but with some unknown type of communication jamming technology. Lt. Cruz last reported that his men and another crew, were headed to the north end specifically to search for our friend Randall, who has disappeared. On a more positive but even more slightly bizarre note, your friends claim to have sighted Harry Moorer on the adjacent island." Rock and Jewell stared back with a perplexed look, the Puerto Rican spouted. "What in the world would Harry be doing here?" Capone answered. "At this time, we have yet to develop a credible explanation."

Paul reasoned with them. "It would be wise if perhaps our actions revolve around re-creating their steps if that is possible. Montel can lead us to his campground where they originated and, we can start from there. I would be surprised if the locals were overly interested in assisting us." Paul looked to the other Knights Protego. "Gentlemen, it would be best if we are discreet with your weaponry until we are out of sight. It may alarm those who live on this island." He received agreeable head nods from around the truck.

Once at the campground, the group searched thoroughly, noticing there were no weapons left behind inside the disheveled camp. Their tents had been left open and rain was inundating the interiors. They found nothing noteworthy at the camp, so Paul recommended they proceeded to the next known area where the other teams had spent time, Cabretta Beach. There they didn't expect to find clues, but certainly there were no footprints in the sand with all the rain and wind, Nonie did however notice and point out the abandoned Helicopter being pounded by the Atlantic Ocean as the waves crashed against it, half tearing off the fuselage. Dominic sent four of his men to investigate the crash. They returned with nothing appreciable to report.

Capone petitioned Paul's experience to develop a strategy for moving forward, then called the entire group together and drew out his two-pronged strategy for exploring the north end of the island. Of course, it contained an initiative to protect Rock in parallel. He used a stick to draw lines of responsibility in the sand, suggesting to Dominic that he take a path closer to the Blackbeard Island side of Sapelo and to investigate Blackbeard Creek and proceed as far to the northeast end as the situation demanded. Capone would take Rock, Paul and the remaining Knights on a wider path around the western inland side of the Island along the Mud River portion to get to the same destination.

With the rain continuing to pound them, they all piled back into the truck. Titus took Dominic and his eight men as far into the forest as he deemed safe then dropped them off for their mission. The Levite then continued west to the other side of the island before parking the vehicle. Rock's group spread out onto the dirt road to begin their trek north. For the next hour they trudged north despite the deluge forcing them to search with their head down through the saw palmetto, sable palm, and drippy Spanish moss filled live-oak tree's. The KP were instructed to withdraw their weapons, before fanning out to provide as much protection as possible

****

On the east side of the island, Dominic found himself completely out of his comfort zone, considering that the fauna he trudged through was unlike anything he had ever experienced, compared to his normal stomping grounds in and around the Mediterranean. He had directed his men to locate Blackbeard Creek where once found, enabled them to plod ahead north. His only concern was the sheer lack of visibility with the rain and heavy forestation. As he made his way with his men, weapon's tucked comfortably in the pocket between their arms and chest, Dominic and his men marveled at a few alligators lying on the bank of the creek, along with the heavy population of deer toward the center of the island. Wildlife seemed to be everywhere and completely unafraid of his men.

One of his men, Vincenzo peeled back from the front line. "Dominic, there is a freshwater spring in the middle of the forest. It appears to be newly formed." With the rain lashing at his face, the Italian leader hurried over to investigate. He stood looking down at the crystal-clear water bubbling up two-feet from the ground. "I am by no means a geological aficionado, but it strikes me as odd that a flat coastal piece of land has a pressurized freshwater spring gurgling up from nowhere. How does this happen? This island is surrounded by salt water." He called his men back and re-directed them, giving them new commands to follow the ambling fresh-water creek which weaved a consistent path toward the north.

Vincenzo straightforwardly announced. "There is movement ahead of us." The entire group instinctively dropped into a crouch, making themselves invisible as they separated and pushed their bodies down into the lush fauna. Dominic attempted to crawl ahead and peer towards the front of them. "What type of movement?" He whispered back to Vincenzo. "There appear to be two humanoid creatures, thick, stocky but very compact and shorter than a normal man. There are also dozens of enormous bulls wandering randomly around them." Dominic flicked a tick away as he caught it crawling on his forehead, before whispering. "Fan out further, I intend to make my way ahead of you to take a closer look. Again, prudence is necessary for using our weapons. Ensure it is a dire situation." His men scurried off at different angles toward the movement ahead.

Dominic crawled on his belly, elbow digging in the mud to propel him, until he was close enough to gather information. He peaked his head around a massive spindly live oak, where he saw two rounded creatures the size of a modern-day washing machine, their clothing covered in mud with waist long beards. He watched as one of them collected palm fronds, stacking them somewhat organized over his massive forearm. Glancing over to his left, he saw the huge dark shapes of the dozen or so, Brahma bulls he had been warned about. The more he studied the bulls muddling thru the surface vegetation, he realized that their numbers were more in the range of fifty than the dozen reported. At least from what he could visibly verify, back deeper in the woods. He rose to one knee, reached down to his belt and removed his combat knife, using it to cut away a slimy leech attached to his calf as he watched the dwarves retreat toward the north, away from his men. Up ahead in the tops of the trees, he noticed a large unusual dark area in one of the larger live-oaks just under where the dwarves were retreating. Ignoring the oddity above, he felt it wise to keep the stocky creatures in his view, so he rose above the forest floor, using his silent hand communications to direct his men to follow the dwarves, certain that he didn't have to warn them to stay hidden.

****

Capone's band of Knights darted fluidly through the forested area, their eyes peeled for any threat in the peripheral of their leaders, Rock and Paul. The men effortlessly matched their leaders meandering stride. The rain began to slack off and was nearly stopped. Paul and Rock paused every so often to get a closer look at the different palms and odd fauna as if they were strolling through a magnificent garden. "Ya know...despite the soggy conditions, this place is kind of gorgeous." Rock analyzed. Paul looked over to him, allowing the last drops of rain to splatter his face. "That it is, young man." Up ahead they noticed an opening in a line of live-oak tree's, where a roadbed wandered out onto a land bridge between two gray and unimpressive lagoons. Not far out onto the land bridge, Nonie stopped to investigate a set of odd markings down a bank. It appeared to him to be a set of rear tires from some sort of motor vehicle that had slid down the land bridge into the lagoon. He couldn't imagine the lagoon being deep enough to swallow the vehicle, a notion that was confirmed when twenty feet further up the path, he realized from another set of markings, that a different vehicle had tugged the unfortunate one back up onto the land bridge.

He decided to teach Jewell a lesson in tracking. "Something happened here recently. These are not weeks old." Jewell nodded, unable to provide any additional insight. Nonie, however, used his skills to point out a different variety of tracks another forty feet up the land bridge. "It appears there has been a considerable amount of very unusual animal behavior!" He walked over and looked down at a worn curvature in the road that looked like a smooth ditch cutting across from one lagoon to the other. "It appears a great number of alligators from this one body of water decided to take up space in the other." He directed Jewell's attention to the massive population of the amphibians moiling about in the lagoon to his right. The entire alligator situation weirded out the Bronx native.

Rock was perplexed by the amount of activity in the other lagoon, not understanding why Paul didn't seem to think anything about the alligators. "That cannot be normal behavior, can it Paul?" Paul rubbed his chin. "You are not going to believe this...despite my two-thousand years of life, I cannot really make the claim that I am an expert in alligator behavior. However, I cannot imagine this reptilian mosh pit we are witnessing is something natural." Paul watched the thousands of alligators pulsating for position in the lagoon. "Something unusual is indeed happening here. Perhaps we should proceed and distance ourselves from this pond." Capone ushered Rock away from the thin strip of land between the lagoons, circumstantially pushing the others to the far side as well.

Chapter 15- Rescue

Once he realized he had caught up with the dwarves again, Dominic stooped behind a saw palmetto bush not more than one-hundred-fifty feet from them. He observed closely as they meticulously laid out individual blades from the palm bushes in front of them on the ground. To the left of the dwarves, he could see a long concrete looking wall that rounded off for sixty or seventy feet and behind the compact men. Back behind the dwarves' right side was a longer wall of black trees, tightly formed and like the concrete wall in that they appeared to form a circular configuration. Stiffly rising to a half crouch from ancient injuries during his active Knight Templar days, he was thankful the Dwarves hadn't noticed him. His peripheral vision caught movement high up in the canopy of trees where he again noticed the large black mass in a huge live-oak. Peering harder he was able to make out thousands of buzzards lined up, filling each limb and almost every foot of the tree. They weren't flying around the tree...they just sat...waiting, triggering Dominic's discomfort with unknown circumstance. *Why would they just sit there?* He was simply baffled at the buzzard behavior.

When he turned his attention around to refocus on the dwarves, they had disappeared and had taken the saw palmetto straps they were arranging. Dominic stood fully erect attempting to locate their exit path. *How can they have simply vanished?* Unable to develop any logical explanation, he hand-signaled his men to approach each of the walls to investigate and determine the whereabouts of the unusual men. He took a quick glance back up at the massive population of buzzards before he advanced, shaking his head, again incapable of finding a feasible explanation.

Carefully weaving his way to the location where the dwarves were last seen, he noticed that what he thought was a concrete wall was plaster and oyster shells. A slight turn of the head and he realized the black tree wall was exactly that...a stand of tightly fitted black barked trees. Dominic hand-signaled half of his men to navigate around the shell ring to the left and the other half around the black tree wall to the right, in hopes of discovering an unseen entrance to the inside of the odd barriers.

The baffled leader stooped down to examine a cluttering of large thick humanoid footprints that tracked toward the black wall of trees then simply stopped. Out of the corner of his eye, he noticed a disturbance in the canopy as the buzzards took flight from the massive tree. This distraction prevented the seasoned warrior from noticing movement directly above him. Seconds later he was violently smashed into the ground face first, from a massive force applied to his upper back, driving his entire body two inches into the loamy soil. It crushed the air from his lungs and prevented him from moving even the slightest amount. Slowly, the leader of the Knight's Protego Italian branch, faded into oxygen deprived unconsciousness.

****

The Knights being directed by Capone, continued providing a loose umbrella of protection around Rock, primarily toward the front of the group, with Capone himself being the lone protector for anything from the rear. Nonie, using his unique tracking skills, led the group through the marshy area.

Stopping abruptly, he crouched to examine another set of unusual footprints. Looking up from the mud, he noticed a huge tree that contained...darkness. The entire sprawling tree was just black with buzzards or vultures. He motioned for the group to halt their forward movement as Capone had taught him. While Nonie stood evaluating the large birds as they just sat in the tree, Jewell strode over to stand beside him. "What's up bro?" Nonie pointed to the tree and the vulture silhouettes, prompting Rock and Paul to join them.

"My people, as well as other indigenous tribes, have a phrase for this...we call it *Nact'ii ben Tilla*, loosely interpreted as 'The Rotten Tree'. He pointed toward the massive collection of birds. "Around the campfire as a boy, I heard many stories of Uncle Buzzard. He is famous among Apache boys as a devious trickster, but I have never seen a gathering of so many in one place." He looked to the leaders. "Uncle Buzzard is not necessarily a sign of a bad thing, many times his appearance is misunderstood...and sometimes the stories indicate Uncle Buzzard is the harbinger of something good that others cannot understand. Still, I would recommend we proceed with caution. Things here may not be as they appear. It is almost always the case when Uncle Buzzard is nearby." Rock listened but could only shrug at Paul, unable to respond positively or negatively to Nonie's story.

Unsurprisingly, having listened to Nonie describe the legend of the buzzard, Capone stood next to Rock displaying a look of utter paranoia. "I do not like this situation." He fell into duty mode and directed his men out in a feathering pattern to continue their approach. Nonie continued ahead but after another half-dozen steps raised his hand to halt the entire group once again. The trained tracker pointed to a loan figure standing in front of a tightly formed wall of solid black tree trunks.

"It's Dominic!" Noticed Paul. They watched as the Italian leader positioned his men around to each side of him, half around a curved concrete wall and the other half around an obsidian wall. At that moment, confusion ensued as their eyesight was drawn to the scene of an enormous blue glowing creature that dropped down from the canopy and pinned Dominic to the ground with a grand sensatory thud.

The Knights Protego acted out of instinct, pushing strongly toward the scene. Rock struggled to interpret what he was seeing. What he thought he saw, was a human-like creature more than twice the size of a man, with huge blue glowing wings that stretched out ten feet to each side of his body. The creature's face was huge compared to a normal human being. It appeared oblivious to the group of protectors, spreading out and approaching toward him. Suddenly, the creature removed its foot from Dominic's back and snatched him up like a ragdoll, its giant hand grabbing the back of the KP leaders clothing. It held Dominic directly in front of his face as if studying him. Capone promptly reacted. "Protect him, use your weapons!" He yelled.

With that command, Capone's group of Knights opened fire on the creature, about the same time Dominic's men, having heard the thud, arrived to join in the fray, trained well enough to ensure they did not strike Dominic.

With bullets bouncing harmlessly off his wings, the blue-glowing creature interrupted his intense stare into Dominic's face to notice the many men scattered around the forest floor spraying ineffective gunfire at him. The skin of his blue tinted forehead wrinkled above the brow while bullets ricocheted off his head harmlessly. The creature's massive wings extended, rotating to its front where it gracefully tucked Dominic inside as if protecting him. Glancing about the forest floor, the creature slowly opened his mouth to scream at the men.

The sound it omitted was disturbing. It sounded to Rock as if it came from a multitude of men, all yelling at the same time. Rock only heard one word from the mouth of the behemoth..."STOP". It was as loud...and as forceful as any word Rock could remember ever hearing. Glancing around he watched as every member of the Knights Protego immediately collapsed to the ground like a Jewish mother presented with unwanted news. The gunfire ceased.

Rock turned to view what all had occurred, noticing Paul, Capone, Nonie and Jewell had all passed out around him. He stood alone.

As Rock stared at the massive blueish creature in front of him. he watched as it produced Dominic like a prized possession from under his wings, holding the leader directly in front of his face again. It appeared he was studying what next to do with him. *STOP HIM!* The loud voice inside Rock's head voiced a warning as if the creature was going to harm the Italian. *STOP HIM!* The voice repeated, inciting a sense of urgency to wash over Rock and without further hesitation, he launched himself toward the creature that was more than twice the size of any human being alive.

****

Randall crouched timidly inside a hollowed-out tree trunk, reluctant to give away his hiding place from the two dwarves. The ex-cop shook his head, marveling at his activities since he had run from the mosquito swarm that attacked him and his friends the day before. Since that attack, he had jumped into Blackbeard Creek to evade the mosquitoes, had been in near panic mode while in the water up underneath the protection of the upside down wooden canoe, he was chased from that position by two large uncaring alligators, which eventually forced him to swim deep under the surface of the channel to Blackbeard Island, coming up only once for air. His swim was fueled by pure adrenalin, having had to poke a smaller alligator in the eye to prevent it from making a meal out of him. Once he pulled his taxed body up onto the banks of Blackbeard Island, he was too terrified with any notion of swimming back over to check on Clark and Scooter and how they had handled the mosquito swarm.

He also was terrified to swim the channel back to Sapelo at Cabretta Island due to his fear of the hammerhead sharks lurking nearby. Both of those fears relegated him to spending the night in the red brick bird crematorium, he and his friends had seen Harry Moorer flee from earlier in that day. The next day, once he awoke, he convinced himself it might be safe to swim the Cabretta Island channel. He then walked all the way back to the campsite, snatched a bite to eat from the leftover food and when he saw no sign of the others, walked back to the North End of Sapelo to find his two friends.

That's when he stumbled upon the dwarves, and worse yet, they stumbled upon him, forcing him to flee and hide inside the hollowed-out tree where he now crouched. He planned to stay put until dark, then exit the stump. However, it was his misfortune that the hollowed-out trunk he was currently inside, happened to be directly next to another hollow tree, and this one housed an enormous bee hive. The incessant buzzing of the honey bees made him nervous as all get out. So much so, that he was forced to pack his ears with mud during the rain storm to shut out the noise of the bees to prevent him from going insane.

Once he was comfortable that the dwarves were nowhere in sight, he slowly made his way out of the tree. He was able to locate the dwarves again but made sure they didn't see him as he monitored their activities, hoping to glean some indication as to where his friends, Scooter and Clark, were located. Standing behind a man-sized sable palm, a loud voice or noise nearly made his knees buckle and he passed out, slinking to the ground beside the palm.

Once he regained consciousness, he figured he could use his sense of smell and vision to locate the smelly dwarves so he made the decision to leave the mud in his ears. Peeking up over the hollow stump, he was surprised when he saw his lost friend Harry assisting the dwarves in performing some function associated with a shell ring wall. Then the three simply vanished before his eyes.

He didn't know what to do next, so he stood up and got out of the stump, before another turn of events began. Just in front of him a tall sophisticated looking man appeared to be signaling to another group of hunters or soldiers of sorts. At that time a massive blue body smashed the man to the ground with a heavy thud. The impact caused Randall to fall backward, stunned by the enormous size of the muscled humanoid creature. He banged his head solidly on the stump as he fell back. As he lay there, he watched a giant set of wings on the creature as they spread, He slowly rose to take his place back into the protective confines of the stump, when a bullet ricocheted near his head, then another struck the exterior of the stump. He quickly ducked into the hollow tree. He rose his head up from the stump to sneak a peek and noticed that the bullets were simply bouncing off the huge creature, who had drawn its wings completely around itself. Suddenly, another sickening noise caused Randall to drop to his knees with disorientation.

Once he recovered some composure, he looked back up at the big blue humanoid and was shocked when inexplicably, he saw his friend Rock some distance on the other side of where he stood behind the creatures back. "What in the world is he doing here?" As he studied the scene further, he saw other men lying slumped on the ground on either side of Rock. "*Something bad is happening!*"

 A lump appeared in his throat at the thought of one, if not his best friend in the world, being dominated by the blue winged giant. Randall was at a loss for what to do...so he crouched and did nothing.

****

The creature leaned down to sniff Dominic's attire, as if his sense of smell could help him determine why the man was visiting the island. He caught sight of another human out of the corner of his eye, charging at him full human speed. Surprised but unconcerned, he looked back down at Dominic before tossing the unconscious leader to his rear twenty-feet toward the black-tree wall. It was almost as if he were trying to protect the man. Then the creature turned his attention to the bigger human running directly at him, reaching out with one freakishly long arm to grab Rock by his throat, lifting him effortlessly to his face, before slamming him down into the loamy soil, pinning both of Rock's arms up above his head. Bending over to drop to its hands and knees, it hunkered menacingly over Rocks face, slowly studying ever crevice, blemish and pore. Then simply, with no emotion, the creature sat up...and flexed its massive set of wings.

****

As he cowered behind a low growing palm tree, Randall was afraid to do anything with the huge creature hovering over the top of his friend. He was torn between fear of the beast...and his duty to a good friend. Something deep inside of him surfaced, causing him to stand and shriek like a mad man suddenly overcome by emotion. He jumped up from his spot and sprinted toward the melee with all the 'to hell with my fears' that he could muster. Leaping as high as he possibly could, he landed directly onto the back between the glowing creatures wings. With his heroic effort he managed to wrap his arms around its neck and squeeze tightly, struggling to hold on for a frightening ride.

****

As Rock watched the creatures face glide from top to bottom of his own, a set of hands clasped in front of its bluish neck. The huge set of wings along its back seemed to flex and calmly squeezed together behind its head. It was not until then, that Rock suddenly caught glance of Randall's determined face, grimacing with mighty effort as he attempted to force the giant to remove itself from the top of his friend. Randall rasped instructions toward Rock. "Rock...Run...Run!"

The creature calmly raised his long arms, reaching behind him to grasp Randall by the top of the head, dislodging and pulling the man from between his massive wings to toss him toward the black wall of trees, not far from where Dominic lay unconscious. Rock's friend slammed into the wall of trees with a sickening smack, sliding to the ground, causing Randall's face to contort weirdly giving a clue that he was trying desperately to regain his breath.

The creature immediately returned his attention back to maintaining his dominance of the big man lying docile beneath him. Again, he brought his huge blue face inches from Rock, staring him directly in the eyes. The beast slowly opened his mouth, which allowed a lone sliver of drool to make its way in slow motion from the corner, prompting the big man to violently resist the enormous weight of the beast on top of him.

Deep inside, that voice began to creep into Rock's conscious mind. It raised his bodies overall energy level, but the only thing he could focus on was that lone grotesque ribbon of saliva.

Rock suddenly became aware of an odd aroma...of black pepper and perhaps some other exotic spice, which caused the big man to shift his attention to the creatures all too human eyes and the fact that despite every bit of panic he felt...he was still able to see something familiar in the creature's gaze. With that realization the voice inside pounded its way to his consciousness...where it was heard loudly..."STOP...JEREMIAH!" Rock blasted these words from his own throat. The voice that came from inside him was not simply one voice...but three, and none of those resembled his own. The creature's eyes flew wide open as it quickly sat up straight on top of him, expanding its wings to their fullest extent, flapped once to rise above Rock's body and hovered as he studied the big man intensely. Recognition seemingly washed over the larger than human face, allowing Rock the opportunity to quickly scamper to his feet and start backpedaling as fast as he could away from the hovering oddity.

****

Randall managed to regain his breath along with a small measure of composure. He lolled his head toward his friend who appeared to be shouting something that he couldn't understand due to the mud in his ears, but the tone of Rocks' voice made him queasy. Managing to shake off the sick feeling somewhat, he returned his attention to the vision of the huge blue winged creature floating menacingly above Rock studying him. He then saw Rock jump to his feet and begin backpedaling as fast as he could, toward a line of at least twenty alligators. Randall's heart leapt to his throat, realizing that his friend was fleeing from one menace literally into another. He watched as the largest alligator in the line, opened his massive gaping maw to expose the cotton like interior inside, and Rock was quickly approaching unbeknownst. The ex-cop knew he didn't have time to warn Rock. Without fear, he jumped to his feet and sprinted as fast as he could.

While Rock scrambled backwards, he lost his balance and fell but managed continue his escape, scampering backwards like a crab. The hair on the back of the big man's neck began to stand erect, providing him with all the warning he should have needed about an unseen peril behind him, prompting him to skid to a sudden halt just feet from the massive fourteen-foot-alligator's fully agape mouth. It lunged forward to attack Rock's midsection. The blue tinted flying creature noticing the turn of events, bellowed a humanistic "NOOOOO!"

Rock was suddenly knocked sideways clear of the lunging gator as Randall's body took the place of the descendant of Jesus. The alligator crushed Randall's ribs before it ever had an opportunity to heed the command of the blue-tinted humanoid. Blood immediately bubbled from Randall's lips as the alligator opened its massive jaws and gently deposited his mangled and crushed body onto the forest floor. Then, slowly, the entire line of amphibians rotated around and began to retreat toward the pond from where they had originated.

When Rock picked himself up from the ground and was able to see what had happened, he rushed to his friend's side. "Oh my God!" He immediately went to his knees to hold Randall's hand, his midsection crushed by the massive jaws. Randall weakly looked up to him...coughing blood, he croaked out, "You owe me." Rock looked over his mangled body, his ribs looking like a car wreck. He turned to look toward the blue tinted creature who slowly drifted to the ground and stood stoically forty-feet away watching the scene unfold.

Paul, Jewell, Nonie and Capone could be seen slowly regaining consciousness over toward the lagoon. The blue creature surprised Rock when he spoke. "You speak the language of Yahweh?" He asked concisely and with solid civility. Rock turned his attention back to his dying friend, ignoring the question as the remaining Knights Protego all began to stir.

Paul sat up, dithering. He attempted to stab through his confusion. Capone staggered to his feet, accessing the situation. His duty filled eyes immediately locking upon Rock kneeling next to a bloodied body, prompting him to jog to the scene. The creature turned and spoke in the direction of the black wall, an apparent call to the dwarves as he motioned toward them while they stood near the shell ring. His nod prompted them into action as they followed the massive blue creature to stand solidly over Rock. "Again, I ask you, how is it that you come to speak the language of God?" Rock looked at the beast confused by his ability to communicate and secondly by the sheer nature of the question itself. He looked up at him, while he brushed the dirt and debris from Randall's tattered bloody clothing and wiped the blood slithering its way out of his mouth. Paul awkwardly staggered his way to Randall, kneeling to take his other hand as he whispered words of encouragement into one of the Knights Protego most recent initiates. Paul began to pray for the man, while Rock blubbered, tears streaming down his face. "He saved me...twice in two minutes." He motioned back to the blue beast. "Once from him...then he protected me from a monster gator."

Jewell ran to his friends, shocked by the condition it had left Randall, amazed that he was even conscious. He didn't know what to say to the dying man. Rock, through the fog of despair, finally interpreted the creature's question and responded. "I don't know what you mean by 'speaking God's' language. I just spoke...that is all."

The blue glowing beast seemed to relax, even smiled slightly as he looked over all the knights, Paul and Capone. "GOD's language is that which I spoke. It mentally overwhelmed your friends causing them to lose consciousness, but it had no effect on you. It is also the language that you shouted back at me while I attempted to cause you to forget." He paused. "If you speak GOD's language, then you are blessed with the capability of helping this man." He nodded his gigantic head toward Randall. Rock looked back to his friend, his eyes dimming. The big man wiped his own tear-filled eyes before speaking. "You saved my life Randall. You saved me...but..." He sobbed. "You shouldn't have...it should be me lying here." Randall looked up, pain numbed by shock. He sputtered and coughed up more blood. With pain...and tenderness in his eyes, he struggled but managed to get words out. "I think... it is what I was supposed to do. I believe...it was what I was born to do...protect you." He gurgled out a large amount of blood with the last words and with that, Randall slowly closed his eyes...and breathed his last breath.

Scooter, Clark and Cruz suddenly appeared at once from the oyster shell enclosure, rushing to their big friend's side, seeing Randall. Rock looked to them and with bubbling lips attempted to explain what had happened. His friends nervously eyed the massive strange winged creature behind them.

Jewell pleaded with Rock. "You have got to bring him back...just like you did with Paul." He pointed up at the blue creature. "This...this thing says you have that skill. Help him Rock, bring Randall back." Rock's eyes filled with tears, bent his head, defeated. "I don't know how to do that, Jewell. I know I can access the ineffable name...but I don't believe this is the situation. "

He looked up to the winged man. "My name is Rock Razie, I am a descendant of Jesus and I need for you to show me how to save my friend." The winged man solemnly asked. "You are the interceder?" Rock looked back to Paul with confusion. "I have no idea what that means." Paul chimed in. "Perhaps you mean...the INNER SEED. He is the INNER SEED...yes!" The winged man seemed pleased with the response. "The meaning is one and the same. If you are as you claim, then you have the capability to raise this man...if it is the right thing to do and should you so desire. But I must warn you...there are always consequences for actions. If you are to help your friend, you must tap back into the GOD language. There you will find the ability to raise him. I recognize this term INNER SEED. I have been expecting you. I require the use of your skills."

The creature stretched out as tall as he could, tucked his blue glowing wings neatly behind him as his demeanor changed and he bowed down to Rock. "My apologies to you and your friends...Rock Razie. I go by the name Metatron. I am an Arch Angel in GODs army."

The entire population of Knights Protego murmured with his admission. Rock's friends looked at each other, totally confused by the other Knights response.

"Rock, you may not remember, but you and I have history together. Many years ago, in your youth, you were my friend. As I was placed upon earth in human form. My earthly name at that time was Jeremiah and by the grace of God., you showed me much kindness and love."

"God allowed me to roam this earth as human for a brief period, to re-introduce myself to these things...love...kindness...hate...compassion." Rock looked to Paul, who helped him understand. "While we were protecting you in Florida, when you were young, you befriended a young man with Multiple Sclerosis. His name was Jeremiah. You played with him nearly every day. If what I am piecing together here is true, it appears Jeremiah or...should I say Metatron has much more he would like to explain to us. There are few coincidences of this magnitude."

The distinguished Angel stood and watch as the entire crowd of humans gathered about tightly around Rock. "Before I became an Arch Angel, I was born a human; my name was Enoch. I followed the laws of God always and I was transmuted into the form I now take. I was assigned the duties that I perform even to this day." He looked softly to those in his presence. "In the performance of my duties, it becomes easy to forget what it is like to be human, to make decisions that have consequence. I appreciated my time in Florida and I remember much. Obviously, his plan was to ensure we were familiar with each other on this day...today." Through his sorrow, Rock smiled, despite being totally flabbergasted. "I thought you gave me *Retardism*!" Paul and Capone couldn't help but laugh, remembering that day.

Nonie, of all people, asked the obvious question. "I believe these things that the Apostle Paul says, there are no coincidences. So, why are we here. There is surely a reason that GREAT FATHER has brought us all together."

Metatron eyed the Native American with whimsy, then looked to Paul to ask a question. "This is the INNER SEED?" Paul nodded with confidence. "Then there is indeed a reason we are all here." He looked down to Randall. "I am sorry for the loss of your friend, and I promise we will return to this matter, but right now we have very important business to perform. I have prepared and waited for what follows for centuries of your time."

Rock resisted, sighing as he looked emotionally at Randall's resting face. "I think I need to bring him back." He closed his eyes, attempting to tap into the inner voice he had used earlier. But, nothing happened...he struggled mentally and with no positive result. Shortly, he felt a hand touch him on his forearm. He opened his eyes to see Nonie standing next to him. "I did not know this man...but I believe you should think deeper before you attempt this thing." Rock was confused by the Apache's words. "What?" Jewell, of all people jumped to Nonie's defense. "Rock...you need to listen to him. Do you remember when you were angered by the clown in Atlanta? So angry that you smacked him in the face with the coconut pie? Your reasoning for taking that action? I mean...don't get me wrong...it hurts like hell to let Randall go. But do you remember?" Rock stared at Jewell with sadness in his eyes.

"He wasn't being what he was supposed to be. He wasn't being a clown." Jewell nodded. "Exactly, if you raise Randall, you would be preventing him from being what he has always wanted to be." Recognition flashed in Rock's eyes as he responded. "He always wanted to be a Hero!" Jewell expounded. "His last act while he was alive was being exactly what he had always wanted to be. He was in those moments no longer the husband of seven failed marriages, he wasn't an ex-cop and sure as hell was no longer that paranoid wanna-be. He was...and is... exactly what he has always wanted to be." As Jewell finished, Rock burst into tears. "It's so hard to let him go! But..." He wiped snot from his nose and drew in a long breath. "It is truly the one thing that we can do to show him that we love him. Let's just let him be." The entire group of friends stood tears leaking from each eye, not wanting to show their pain, but unable to hold back their emotions.

Suddenly from behind Metatron, the two dwarves appeared, followed by Harry Moorer. Rock could smell them long before he saw them as they proceeded directly to Randall's damaged body. Metatron strode to stand above Randal, waving his hand over the hero from head to toe. "This man has served you well...he is now in a place where the torture of life is over." Rock looked utterly tormented, because while the Arch Angel tried to console him...his heart was ripped at losing his longtime friend. He looked to Metatron. "I loved this man but he did live a tortured life. I... no... we loved him with all we had. Perhaps there are plans for him elsewhere...much like that of a man once named Enoch!" He looked in the blustery faces of each of his friends and they nodded their understanding.

"Okay, let's allow him to rest." He looked back up to Metatron, who responded by giving the slightest nod of his head, signaling to the Dwarves, who collected Randall's body and carried him over to the shell ring, before simply disappearing.

When the dwarves returned, Metatron gathered the entire group of human beings around him. He stood looking directly down upon Rock. "You are alone in having responsibility here. No other on earth can perform the duty you must now perform. For many years, the TREE OF LIFE...and the TREE OF KNOWLEDGE have been absent from the earth. It is time for them to be re-established. This is the place that will occur. It has been thousands of years since they both existed. It was in a place that you humans know as Stonehenge." He waved his hands toward the black wooded wall behind him. "Here is where they will reside. I have been charged to ensure the tree's establishment and protection until they are used in a final battle to come."

Scooter could not contain his question. "So, the Tree of Life and the Tree of Knowledge are inside those walls?" Metatron looked down toward him, emotionless. "They are not, at least not at this time. It is incumbent on your friend as the bearer of the INNER SEED to plant these trees."

Paul and Capone gave each other surprised glances. Rock looked to Paul, blindsided by the Angels claim. "What is he talking about?" Paul stood shaking his head. "I am just an old man. I have not been privy to the plans for this event."

A movement in the thick forested area behind the group, prompted Capone to direct his men, quickly into a defensive posture. Slowly, from the darker portion of the island foliage, a large group of the ancestral inhabitants of the island marched directly but slowly toward them. Montel and his mother, the island Matriarch, appeared to be carrying an item. Further behind them, the entire Hog Hammock community followed, softly singing an old Gullah culture hymn. They marched up to the umbrella formation created by the Knights. "Master Capone...one of our children discovered this item earlier today and at church this evening...it began to glow. Ms. Dorothy here was visited in spirit by her ex-husband who told her of the need to come to the North end of the island to return this to someone called the *SEED*. Our hopes are that you know what this means." Montel stepped to allow Capone to view the item. In his hands was dirty canvas that as he slowly removed the cloth, exposed the dullishly glowing three-pronged digging tool, the same tool given to Rock by the old man back in Naples.

Darkness seemed to suddenly creep in amongst the trees, as Capone thanked Montel, then turned to walk the tool over and hand it to Rock. The Hog Hammock residents, especially the children, gawked at the massive Arch Angel.

Paul noticing their stares decided to introduce the huge oddity. "Excuse our rudeness, sweet people of Hog Hammock, allow me to introduce the Arch Angel...Metatron." The locals gasped, backing away to give Rock and his crowd the privacy they thought the situation warranted.

With his usual booming voice, Metatron spoke in human as softly as he could. "The people of this island deserve to bear witness to this event. I ask that you all stay and participate." Montel looked to his people, knowing that while they were unsettled with the presence of a creature like Metatron, none of them would miss out on whatever event ensued on their home island. They gathered around closely behind the Knights Protego, as if using them for protection.

Rock gave each of his friends a large appreciative hug, even Harry. Clark hugged Jewell...and then turned to hug Nonie...stopping when he noticed the resemblance. "What in the world?" Jewell provided a clue. "He is a brother from another mother." Nonie then nodded and introduced himself to the set of friends.

Rock looked to Metatron, then at the dwarves, who had returned from depositing Randall's body inside the shell ring. "And these two are?" The angel understood the question. "I would introduce you to them but their names can only be spoken in GOD's language and I have already demonstrated the consequences of my doing so with your friends." Rock rubbed his head. "Can we improvise?" Metatron looked without any expression to him. "Rock Razie, perhaps you misinterpret the duties of an Arch Angel. I do not improvise. I do as I am commanded. You are more than welcome to provide them names of your own and perhaps they will adopt them." Clark spoke up. "Tweedle-Dee and Tweedle-Dum?" Jewell rolled his eyes. "Oh, my GAWD!" Clark look at his friends, searching for a better idea. None of them provided one so Rock called it. "Okay then, Tweedledee and Tweedledum it is." The two dwarves without expression knelt before the entire crowd. Metatron waited patiently through a moment of awkward silence before asking. "If you are prepared, we have duties inside the wall." He pointed to the two dwarves, who produced freshly lit torches that illuminated a hidden opening through the wall of black wooded trees.

Chapter 16-The Trees

Once inside, Rock was struck by the oddness of the enclosure's interior, with its light absorbing black walls and dull blue glow that emanated from the massive granite blocks located toward the center. His friends naturally congregated around him to protect him. Jewell directly to his left, Clark to his right with Nonie tagging to the Bronx natives left. Scooter drifted along to the side of Clark with Capone and Paul to the rear. The KP created a protective semi-circle behind Paul and Capone with the Hog Hammock community following directly behind them.

Harry, on the contrary, didn't fall in with his friends, appearing to have had a personality changed in his time spent on the island. He elected to walk with the two dwarves who had positioned themselves near the middle of the interior holding primitive torches, longer than their bodies. The oddness of the environment was enhanced by the optics of Metatron and his blue glow while he hovered over the wall of trees, fluttering neatly until he touched down in the center of the area slightly in front of Tweedle-Dee and Dum.

There is power in the blood. The faint voice whispered in the back of Rock's head.

He stared closely at the Arch Angel, as if to seek guidance, while Metatron looked down upon him as if he were expecting some sort of action.

After an awkward few minutes, the Angel finally spoke, his voice resonating boldly around inside the enclosure. "You are to plant the seeds!" Rock wrinkled his brow as he turned completely around, looking for who Metatron might be talking to. The entire group murmured with questions and uncertainty about what was expected and from whom. The big man turned back to the Angel with an exasperated look.

Metatron inhaled a huge audible breath thru his massive bluish nose, before advancing toward the group, until he was standing directly in front of Nonie. He looked down the bridge of his gigantic nose and stared at the Apache. Nonie, now uncomfortable, unexpectedly felt the pouch on his hip warm slightly. Recognition washed over his face as he reached inside his pouch to retrieve the seed pods collected in Montserrat. He stepped up to hand the pods wrapped in the dirty cloth to Metatron, who refused to touch them. He then turned and offered them to Rock, who opened the cloth to find the three seed pods.

One of the seeds looked like a peach pit and was a brownish-khaki colored. The second pit lying in the cloth was scarlet in color and was perfectly round. The third pod had a green hue and was elongated like a swollen green bean but seemed to be as hard as a stone.

Clark and Scooter peeked over Rock's shoulder, marveling. "What are those? Where the heck did they come from?" Rock reached into the cloth to touch each pod with his index finger. Nonie provided a reply to the two newest Knights Protego. "We found these during our spirit journey in a secret compartment in a monastery in Spain." Jewell nodded his head to affirm.

Rock held the entire package of pods up to Metatron.

"What am I supposed to do with these?" The Angel answered with a question of his own. "What would most human beings do with a seed?" Rock knew nothing about gardening, nor did any of his friends, save the earthy native American. "Where should I plant them?" The Archangel pointed to the arrangement of blue glowing stones laid out in three different areas. "Which one goes where?" Metatron answered without the slightest hint of sarcasm. "As I have alluded before. I am an Arch Angel. I specifically perform task directed by God but what you ask of me now is the responsibility of the INNER SEED. He alone makes the decision for where each of the three trees are to be planted, I am not equipped nor capable of assisting you in making that determination."

Rock turned to Paul for assistance. "Historically, angels have been very vocal about their limitations with respect to making decisions. There is a reason. Obviously if you have been paying attention to your religion, in the past when angels have exercised the capacity to make their own decisions, did so very unwisely and have fallen from grace in every instance...Lucifer for instance. I would not expect a great deal of help from our friend here. This is your destiny, embrace it and decide where you want the trees to grow."

The Gullah inhabitants began to softly sing another hymn, while Rock looked around the enormous stone arrangement.
He walked to the smallest of the rock formations centered inside the semi-circle of the huge Stonehenge shaped rocks. Looking down at the seeds in his hand, he became slightly aware of a sensation that one of them had moved. He dropped that seed pod next to the granite marker in front of him, half because he was surprised and partly because it was where he wanted to drop it in the first place. He and his friends stared at it like they expected it to magically burst into a plant, instead the seed just lie where it fell.

Nonie walked up beside him and whispered. "Generally, my people have found it very beneficial to bury the seed if one were wanting it to grow." Clark, Scooter and Jewell dropped to their knees digging like mad to create a hole for the seed. Unexpectedly, with each handful of black soil the friends scooped out, the black soil just seemed to refill the hole they had dug and the seed never became covered. Nonie handed Rock the three-pronged digging tool and joined the trio but with little additional success. He looked back up from his knees to Rock. "May I?" Pointing for the big man to hand him the digging tool. Rock did so and

Nonie began digging...successfully this time, he created a hole big enough that the seed sat in the bottom.

There is power in the blood!" The voice resonated inside Rock's mind once again, this time slightly more pronounced than the time before. Nonie attempted to cover the seed, but the dirt would not cooperate, simply falling to the side of the pod as if magnetically being forced to keep it from filling in around it. Rock scratched his head. Then an idea flashed in his mind. "Nonie, do you still have the remaining vial of blood from San Genaro in your pouch?" Nonie fumbled around to find the small bottle and handed it to Rock, who dropped to his knees and sprinkled a small amount of the blood on the seed pod, confidant he had solved the puzzle. "Jewell, you cover this seed. Scooter come with me." He ran to the small blue glowing stone to the left of the center of the rock formation, while Jewell attempted to cover the seed. The others rotated over to where Rock moved. He halted momentarily to see if the next seed pod would pick a planting spot of its own, and sure enough the next seed seemed to vibrate prompting him to drop it.

Nonie, using the tool, dug the hole into which Rock inserted the next seed, then sprinkled it with the blood from the Genaro bottle after which they proceeded to the final rock formation and did the same with the remaining seed. Jewell caught back up to the group to inform them that the seeds continued to resist the soil from covering them.

Paul watching the flurry of activity used his logic to give a suggestion. "Perhaps the blood of San Genaro is not what the voice is calling for, my young protege'. By chance are you listening to the song the wonderful people of Hog Hammock are singing at this moment!" In the background, murmured and unclear, he heard the words *nothing but the blood of Jesus ...the blood of Christ*. Paul added. "Again, I would insist...there are no coincidences." Rock mouthed the words with wide opened eyes. "The blood of Jesus?" He then knew what needed to be done. He looked to Nonie. "Can I borrow your knife?" Nonie nodded and retrieved it from the pouch on his leg.

Rock bent over the last seed he had dropped onto the black soil, placed the knife blade in the palm of his hand...then hesitated...uncomfortable with the thought about what he was about to do. Clark dropped to his knees beside his buddy and looked up to him. "Are you about to do what I think?" Rock looked at him nervously. Clark nodded his head. "It's the right thing to try." Rock took two deep cleansing breaths before bringing the ridiculously sharp blade across his palm, tightened his fist around the pain. A thin line of blood leaked out of his fist, down on to the seed, coating it. Nonie rushed over to use the garden tool to quickly cover the seed.

Before any of the friends could get back to their feet, the ground began to shake, and a green stalk immediately protruded from the soil. Within seconds, everyone located inside the wall of black trees, witnessed as an enormous forty-foot tree exploded from the ground, tossing Nonie, Jewell, Clark and Rock from their current spots. The leaves of the tree popped out from the branches as a deep garnet, the bark of the tree trunk the same color. It was perfect in shape and symmetry. Rock stepped back from the tree to notice one lone piece of garnet colored fruit, unlike any Rock had ever seen before, dangling almost from the very top.

The big man grabbed Nonie by the arm and sprinted to the next seed as quickly as possible to prevent his hand from clotting up. Kneeling next to the seed hole, he allowed the blood from his fist to coat it. Nonie and Jewell quickly covered it, pre-emptively jumping away, expecting the same growth explosion to occur...and it did. This seed pod created a tree that grew massively horizontal but was only twenty feet tall. The tree itself was also as odd as any Rock had ever seen, in that it appeared to be twelve different trees in one. It had an odd array of different sized and shaped fruit, some looked like oranges, others huge strawberries, pomegranate, lychee, kiwi...and other wide varieties of fruits of differing shapes and colors.

Scooter knelt next to the final seed pod, waving for Rock to repeat the bloodletting on the final nut, which exploded into a magnificent apple looking tree. This tree only contained a few fruits located at the top much like the first. The apples appeared to be pristine in nature, perfectly uniformed in shape with the most inviting red color. However, the fruit was unreachable without some type of machine to gather it.

Metatron strode over to the tree with the twelve differing fruits. "Pay attention to my voice. This is the TREE OF LIFE, those who would eat from the fruit of this tree, shall experience life spans beyond those of normal human beings. Some of you will have opportunity to taste the fruits on this day." He took one huge step to stand before the gorgeous apple tree. "This is the TREE OF KNOWLEDGE!" The angel provided no further information about the tree. He then walked to the tree that was scarlet in color with the single piece of garnet fruit hanging way up top. "The knowledge of the purpose of this tree is forbidden for discussion. No human will ever touch this tree, nor eat from the fruit. " He finished the forceful warning.

The blue angel then strode to the exit passage, sliding a man-sized granite block over the opening to prevent any human that might want to leave the area, from doing so. Standing tall, he inhaled deeply, then opened his mouth to bellow in his three-voiced GOD speak. Rock alone heard him say the word...SLEEP. The big man watched as every individual inside the Stonehenge shaped fortress, lost consciousness...save the dwarves and Harry Moorer. The angel then removed the granite stone from the exit portal. Rock stood confused by the turn of events, so he turned to the angel. "What is happening?" Metatron strode to a lone four foot alter shaped stone positioned in the middle between the three freshly grown trees. The dwarves carried one of the members from the Hog Hammock community to the stone alter, laying the person carefully face up with arms and legs spread. They made a point of opening the individual's mouth to ensure there was no blockage.

Rock recognized the person splayed out before him, as the man who had presented the three-pronged digging tool. Metatron then positioned himself over the top of the inhabitant. Slowly, a thin line of drool began to dangle from the angel's mouth, before making its way to the island dwellers tongue. Once complete, the dwarves closed the man's mouth, collected him, handing him to Harry Moorer, who tossed the man over his shoulder and carried him outside of the black-tree wall. "What are you doing?" Rock asked the angel, confused as to the purpose. Metatron stood up straight waiting for the next member of the community. "I am forcing them to forget!"

Every member of Hog Hammock was subsequently brought to the altar and drooled upon before being removed to somewhere outside the tree sanctuary, Rock assumed to the odd concrete Shell-ring enclosure adjacent to the tree-ring. Once they had all been relocated, the giant angel simply stood and waited as each of the Knights Protego, Paul, Capone regained consciousness.

Once they regained their senses, Metatron addressed them with instructions. "Each of you, with the exception of the INNER SEED, must now select a fruit from the TREE OF LIFE. Individually, you come from differing tribes of Israel, thus, your choice will be predicated upon from which tribe you originate. Pick the fruit that you desire, but only pick of one fruit."

Paul was the first to make any sort of movement toward the tree...following some inner inane familiarity with the situation. He could not locate a reason for his choice. Still, he made a choice, picked a fruit and ate it. A barely perceptible light flashed over his face, then faded, before a huge satisfied smile washed over him. Jewell, Clark and Scooter followed his lead, joined by Nonie, Capone and Cruz.

Metatron sniffed the air as if something unusual had been detected...he motioned toward Tweedle-Dee and Dum, directing them to take control of the pilot, Trace. They escorted him to the altar stone, sprawling him out over the rock. The Arch Angel gave him an explanation. "I am sorry friend, but you are not allowed to eat from the TREE OF LIFE!" The dwarves held the man down as Metatron forced his mouth open and made him forget as well. Once complete, Harry Moorer removed him from the tree-ring.

Rock watched as each of his friends and every member of the Knights Protego partook from the fruit of the TREE of LIFE. Each one of them, experienced the same strange glow wash over their faces before they appeared extremely invigorated after even the first bite.

Metatron looked out over the crowd of humans. "Have you all finished?" The men looked up at the Arch Angel like school kids finishing an ice cream cone, extremely pleased. Metatron nodded his head to signal for the dwarves and Harry Moorer to select fruit. The three retrieved and ingested their fruit, fulfilling their own experience.

The Arch Angel then gathered the crowd together beneath his towering presence. "I apologize for what is destined to follow, but knowledge of the location of these sacred trees is not permitted." The crowd looked nervously around as Metatron spoke in GOD's language yet again, *SLEEP*, forcing them into an unconscious state. Rock watched them all fall to the ground. The dwarves worked feverishly to retrieve each member of the Knights Protego for their individual opportunity on the stone altar and its associated private sampling of the Arch Angel drool ceremony.

Rock watch them all be forced to forget, as the dwarves cleared the tree-ring of everyone but himself and the Giant Angel. He had to ask. "I suppose it's now my turn for the big mind erase?" The Angel looked down at him with no emotion at all. "It is time for you to make a decision, yes. Something for which I envy you greatly. You must decide if you would like to eat from the TREE OF KNOWLEDGE." Metatron pointed to the gorgeous tree and the fruit high above that looked like an apple. "Why would I have this opportunity and none of the others?" The Angel smiled, having expected the question. "You are the only human being alive that is capable of handling the effects of eating this fruit. "Rock nodded his acknowledgement for the acceptable answer. He looked back up at the Angel. "What will happen to me if I eat from the tree?" Metatron replied. "I cannot say, but...I assume based upon the name of the TREE...that you will gain knowledge."

Rock nodded to him. "Okay, how do I get to the fruit? Climb the tree?" Metatron placed his large hands under Rock's arm pits, rotating him around as he left the ground, flexing his muscular wings to elevate, slowly rising to the top of the tree where Rock reached out and plucked an apple from the top. Metatron drifted down to the black soil, while the two dwarves and Harry Moorer gathered near. The Arch Angel released the big human.

Rock stared at the fruit, rotating it around in his big hands before placing it between his teeth to chomp off a big bite. He immediately began to tremble, dropped to the ground, shaking in resemblance to an epileptic episode. The dwarves moved to restrain him to prevent him from injuring himself while Harry positioned himself so that he could place the shirt tail of his ragged oxford into his mouth, to prevent the big man from biting his tongue off. Moments later Rock stilled, opened his eyes and sat up. He struggled to stand but with assistance eventually made it to his feet.

He looked squarely at Metatron. "Thank you for your servitude. It would appear, that I have many things to prepare for." He nodded to Harry Moorer, convinced that Harry had made the choice long ago to never return to humanity. Harry confirmed what Rock already knew. "Rock, I cannot go back. While I understand I have the DNA of one of the Levites. I have decided to serve my god here as a guardian of the TREES."

Rock smiled at him and while he didn't understand Harry's choice, he was convinced he knew what his motivations were. He looked to the dwarves, speaking to them in GOD's language to thank them for their part of the day. His attention then shifted back to Metatron. "I appreciate you. My knowledge of all things has drastically evolved today after eating the fruit from the TREE. It is obvious that there is one lone secret unavailable to me. He looked at the SCARLET TREE...and the lone garnet piece of fruit. "What is the name of that TREE? What is its purpose?" Metatron hesitated before speaking. "Now that you have taken from the TREE OF KNOWLEDGE, you are keenly aware that a massive war is inevitable. This is as it should be, but the knowledge of this TREE...is no concern of yours. Nor will you know the purpose of this tree until the time comes where that specific knowledge is necessary."

Rock sighed. "Does this mean it is now time for you to drool into my mouth?" The ARCH ANGEL looked directly into Rock's eyes. "What purpose would it accomplish. You have eaten from the TREE OF KNOWLEDGE and are more than capable of uncovering any secret. The knowledge you have just gained ensures that you realize why the world cannot know the whereabouts or even the existence of the THREE TREES." Rock nodded his head, as if to confirm. "That it does."

He then turned, making his way toward the exit of the tree wall to collect his friends, confident that his life path had changed permanently.

The end- of this adventure.